**Praise for the *New York Times*
bestseller *Donnie Brasco***

"A daring double life . . . reveals the full extent
of his dangerous voyage into the underworld."
—*Time*

"So entertaining, you have to remind yourself it's
deadly serious." —*The Boston Globe*

"Thoroughly absorbing true-life adventure."
—*Newsday*

"The tension builds with mach

More praise for *Donnie Brasco*

continued . . .

Also by Joseph D. Pistone

NONFICTION

Donnie Brasco: My Undercover Life in the Mafia

NOVELS

Deep Cover

Mobbed Up

SNAKE EYES

A Donnie Brasco Novel

Joseph D. Pistone

AN ONYX BOOK

ONYX
Published by New American Library, a division of
Penguin Putnam Inc., 375 Hudson Street,
New York, New York 10014, U.S.A.
Penguin Books Ltd, 80 Strand,
London WC2R ORL, England
Penguin Books Australia Ltd, Ringwood,
Victoria, Australia
Penguin Books Canada Ltd, 10 Alcorn Avenue,
Toronto, Ontario, Canada M4V 3B2
Penguin Books (N.Z.) Ltd, 182–190 Wairau Road,
Auckland 10, New Zealand

Penguin Books Ltd, Registered Offices:
Harmondsworth, Middlesex, England

First published by Onyx, an imprint of New American Library,
a division of Penguin Putnam Inc.

First Printing, November 2001
10 9 8 7 6 5 4 3 2 1

Copyright © Joseph D. Pistone and John Lutz, 2001
All rights reserved

 REGISTERED TRADEMARK—MARCA REGISTRADA

Printed in the United States of America

PUBLISHER'S NOTE
This is a work of fiction. Names, characters, places, and incidents either
are the product of the author's imagination or are used fictitiously,
and any resemblance to actual persons, living or dead, business
establishments, events, or locales is entirely coincidental.

BOOKS ARE AVAILABLE AT QUANTITY DISCOUNTS WHEN USED TO PROMOTE
PRODUCTS OR SERVICES. FOR INFORMATION PLEASE WRITE TO PREMIUM
MARKETING DIVISION, PENGUIN PUTNAM INC., 375 HUDSON STREET, NEW YORK,
NEW YORK 10014.

I wish to thank all the people at New American Library, and my editor, Joe Pittman: Best of luck in your new position.

Also my agent, Carmen LaVia, and all at the Fifi Oscard Agency, without whom none of this could have happened.

1

"I thought you were fired," Adam Kinard said to Donnie, looking up from whatever he'd been reading on his desk.

Kinard was an impeccably groomed, pudgy man with pale, smooth skin and a lean, hawklike nose that didn't fit the rest of him. He carefully put on his rimless round spectacles, the better to give Donnie an inquiring look, and went from hawk to owl.

Kinard did register mild surprise when he saw how Donnie was dressed. He'd known him only as Donald Billings, the uniformed security guard who'd been hired with the highest references. And who'd been caught just before the bank opened in an unauthorized strict-security area.

Billings had been fired immediately.

That had been three days ago, and here was Billings today, standing coolly in front of Kinard's desk and wearing a neat blue suit instead of his gray guard's uniform. And wearing . . . well, an alert but unconcerned attitude as well. It was just the sort of attitude Kinard expected to see in a man who'd just been unceremoniously shit-canned and was now in

1

the presence of the Global Allied BancGroup vice president, who had personally dismissed him. With a uniformed New York cop to ensure there would be no trouble, Kinard had walked Donald Billings to the door and politely wished him good day and good luck. With a smile.

Donnie Brasco, who had played Billings flawlessly in his latest undercover role, stared across the desk now and noticed the subtle change of expression on Kinard's face. He knew it was soon going to change some more.

Behind Donnie, a handsome black man in his forties, muscular beneath a gray double-breasted suit, stood up from the soft leather chair where he'd ostensibly been waiting to talk to a loan officer. The man moved with an easy, fluid stride, unhurried, his dark eyes taking in everything around him, and stood beside Donnie.

This was one of those rare moments when Donnie would use his real name; the rest of the time he thought of himself as Donnie Brasco, the alias he'd used when living undercover for six years as a member of the Mafia. He was the FBI agent who'd almost single-handedly reduced the East Coast Mafia to a crippled and ineffectual shadow of what it had been. Then had come the bestseller about his exploits, then the movie with Al Pacino and Johnny Depp. Then the TV series *Falcone* based on Donnie Brasco. By now he didn't have to be deliberate; it was automatic to think of himself as Donnie Brasco.

It sounded strange, almost as if he were pretending to be his real self, when he flashed his FBI identification at Kinard and said, "Adam Kinard, I'm FBI Special Agent Joseph Pistone. This is FBI agent C. J. Logan. You're under arrest for bank fraud, illicit transfer of funds, stock fraud, and interstate transportation in aid of racketeering."

"You can just call it money laundering and then some," C. J. said with a smile.

Williams from the Bureau's New York field office had entered the bank, accompanied by two more agents and several NYPD uniforms. All of them were wearing alert yet somber expressions, as if somebody had just died.

Or was about to.

The bank's customers and other employees realized something unusual was happening and stopped what they were doing and stared. It was suddenly very quiet in the bank, not even the hushed sound of money being made.

A stunned Kinard reached tentatively for his desk phone.

"I wouldn't call Beltram," Donnie said. "It's a conversation that might cost you another ten years in prison."

Kinard went pale and withdrew his hand.

Donnie nodded to him, as if to convey that Kinard had made the right choice. Then he and C. J. walked across the carpeted lobby toward the door to the office of Global Allied's president and CEO Albert Beltram.

Behind them Williams was reading Kinard his rights, legal step one on the road to conviction.

Beltram's personal assistant, a precise, gray-haired

woman named Margaret, stood up when they entered the anteroom. She recognized Donnie as the dismissed guard almost immediately. Her eyes didn't change but her lips tightened and her face took on an expression of wariness.

"Don't bother to announce us," Donnie said.

She moved out from behind her desk. "You can't—"

"We are," C. J. interrupted.

Leaving the puzzled Margaret standing in shocked silence, they barged into Beltram's office without knocking.

Beltram looked up from where he was seated behind his desk and appeared even more stunned than Kinard. This simply wasn't done, this serious breach of etiquette, this rash act of disrespect.

The bank CEO was a handsome, sixtyish man with lean features and a still-athletic body. His eyes were bright and wise. His straight dark hair was gray only at the temples. He didn't look his age, more like a young actor the makeup department had prepared to play someone's father. He'd removed his suit coat and was wearing a starched white shirt, a gold-and-blue-striped tie, and black leather suspenders that he no doubt called braces. Frozen in motion, he was holding the receiver of his multibuttoned desk phone about six inches from his ear.

As his shock at being interrupted faded, he replaced the receiver in its cradle and narrowed his eyes at Donnie. "Aren't you—"

"He is," C. J. interrupted.

"Not exactly," Donnie said.

He and C. J. displayed their Bureau identifications,

and Donnie explained the charges he'd enumerated for Kinard, and that they also applied to Beltram.

Beltram sat back in his desk chair, his jaw slack with astonishment.

His intercom buzzed, and he leaned forward and pressed a button.

"Mr. Beltram? Is everything all right?"

Margaret's voice. Worried. She would be more worried shortly, when the New York agents and the tide of blue invaded the outer office.

"Everything is fine, Margaret," Beltram said, and sat back in his soft leather chair that looked more as if it belonged in a library than behind a desk. Even a desk like Beltram's, with a Sotheby's pedigree. To Donnie and C. J. he said, "I've done nothing wrong, nothing illegal. . . ."

"Except for getting in bed with the Russian Mafia," Donnie said. "And using the recently created Global Allied Holding Company to illegally transfer funds between Russia, the U.S., the bank, and Prudent Rock Insurance Company, also recently acquired by the holding company."

"A complex dance," C. J. said, "but we managed to follow the steps."

As C. J. read him his rights, Beltram sat silently staring at his desk, barely listening. Now and then he would shake his head in disbelief. "This is all absurd. You can't have any proof of this outrageous accusation."

"We have proof," Donnie said. "That's why I spent the last six months as your employee, gathering evidence. That's why your phones and offices have been bugged and Kinard's meetings with the Russians videotaped."

Beltram raised his eyebrows in amazement. "Adam Kinard? You're telling me *he's* in league with the Russians in some kind of bizarre money scheme?" He gave an incredulous little laugh. "Is this for real?"

"It's time to put away the act and come along with us, Mr. Beltram," Donnie told him.

"I would vouch for Adam Kinard."

"And he would vouch for you."

"This is a misunderstanding that will soon be straightened out. You'll see."

"We'll see."

"I don't want handcuffs," Beltram said.

"They'll be necessary, sir," Donnie said. "It really won't seem so embarrassing, being seen and photographed in handcuffs, considering you're going to prison."

Beltram slowly stood up, his shoulders sagging. "Let me put on my suit coat before you apply the handcuffs." He stepped over to where his tailored dark coat was draped on a hanger. It was a thick wooden hanger as wide as Beltram's shoulders and was hooked over a brass ring set in a shallow alcove in the paneled wall.

He hadn't mentioned his attorney. Not once. Donnie thought later that he should have noticed that.

Beneath the buttoned coat on the hanger was a leather strap, and on the strap was a leather holster, and in the holster was a small, pearl-handled .25

semiautomatic handgun that Beltram drew swiftly and smoothly.

"Donnie!" C. J. yelled.

But Donnie was already reaching around behind his back. His hand found the butt of his Heckler and Koch Bureau-issue 9mm tucked in his belt.

He shot once, and hit Albert Beltram on the bridge of his nose. The soft-point bullet entered Beltram's brain and spread and tumbled and broke into pieces that spread and tumbled.

Beltram dropped straight down. Somehow he landed on his back with an arm twisted beneath him, the handgun he'd drawn lying on the floor beneath the heel of one of his glossy black shoes.

Donnie stood numbly, smelling burned gunpowder, staring down at Beltram.

C. J.'s shouted warning, the sound of the shot, Beltram falling, none of it had seemed to make much noise in the plushly carpeted, heavily draped office that was probably soundproofed.

But some of the noise had made its way outside the office. Margaret's voice came over the intercom. "Mr. Beltram? Is everything all right?"

Donnie wished he could tell her that it was.

2

Killing someone isn't an easy thing.

C. J. assured Donnie that if he hadn't shot Beltram, both of them might have been killed. Maybe that was true, but not in the dreams that disturbed Donnie's sleep for the next several nights.

He couldn't get it out of his mind that Beltram had intended to shoot himself. He kept seeing over and over again Beltram's arm, his hand gripping the gun coming out from inside the hangered suit coat. Something about the angle of the arm. Had Beltram intended to raise it so the gun was aimed at his own temple? Or was the arm going to extend forward, toward Donnie and C. J.?

Not an easy thing. Another question that would never be answered. Another memory to carry.

The teakettle clock near the register in the Victory Coffee Shop near Second and East Fifty-fourth said it was eleven a.m. The sun was shining, but layers of dark clouds were moving in from New Jersey, casting shifting shadows on the faces of the buildings across the street.

"We got a situation in Louisiana," Jules Donavon said, then blew on his coffee to cool it.

Jules was Donnie's supervisor and contact for his undercover work. It was a comfortable arrangement. Jules's superior in the Bureau, Victor Whitten, gave Jules considerable leeway and protection from the bureaucrats, and Jules passed the favor down the line to Donnie. Whitten often referred to Donnie as a very special special agent, recognizing not only what Donnie had accomplished, but that the rest of his life had been permanently changed.

There was no going back for Donnie. Not with an open-ended Mafia contract on his life that would pay his assassin half a million dollars. And as a result of a pact made between the Italian and Russian Mafias, the legendary Russian assassin Yesar Marishov had been given the task of finding and killing Donnie. It was said of Marishov that he might take longer and not travel in a straight line, but that he was as true and sure as a perfectly aimed bullet. Under these circumstances, Donnie lived not so much his own life, but assumed one identity after another as he continued his work for the Bureau.

There was little else for him, and he knew it. His marriage with Elana was destroyed, and he missed his daughters. Even spending time with them might make them targets or bait to lure him into the open. He moved now from city to city, role to role, not knowing who or what he would be next, only that he would be lonely.

Donnie was surprised by what Jules had said. Usually after a case was wound up, Donnie had to stay around to give depositions, then to testify in court. The physical evidence had to be backed up by demonstrable human expertise. And the testimony of what had become a celebrity FBI agent contributed to the prosecution in ways that were intangible but persuasive, even if he was speaking from behind a curtain so he could retain his anonymity.

Donnie looked out the window at people passing by on Second Avenue. He and Jules were sitting in the glassed-in area of the restaurant that extended onto the wide sidewalk. It was too early for the lunch trade, so the place was almost empty and they could talk without being overheard. Donnie sipped his own coffee and said, "This situation in Louisiana mean I'm not going to get my usual time between cases?"

" 'Fraid so, Donnie. You might have to return here once or twice to testify in the Global Allied case, but I think we can get most of your testimony in the record through depositions. And when I tell you about this new situation, I think you'll be eager to get involved."

Donnie wasn't so sure. More and more, he needed his downtime before going undercover again, becoming someone else. It was tough, being reborn on short notice. "The last time you sent me to Louisiana," he said, "what the mosquitoes left of me was almost eaten by alligators."

Jules smiled. He was about Donnie's age—mid-forties—and had risen in the Bureau along with him. Shorter and stockier than Donnie, Jules was still in excellent shape, with a lean waist and flat stomach that were the result of a daily exercise regimen. He liked to dress smart, and with his broad, symmetrical features and thick salt-and-pepper hair, he could look distinguished enough to have had Beltram's job at Global Allied. "This assignment won't take you anywhere near that part of the swamp," he assured Donnie. "Closer to New Orleans."

That sounded better. Donnie had spent time there, knew the city and liked it. In his situation it was always safer if the terrain was familiar.

"Actually just outside New Orleans," Jules continued. "Little town called Julep."

"In the swamp?" Donnie asked, not liking this angle of the conversation.

"Sort of. Interesting place, Julep," Jules went on before Donnie could reply. "Population's only about sixty thousand, and lots of those drive into New Orleans to their jobs. Not much industry in Julep, except the one I'm going to tell you about, and that's illegal."

"Drugs?" Donnie had learned the value of the swamp in illicit narcotic smuggling.

"Gambling," Jules said.

"There's gambling right in New Orleans," Donnie said. "On a riverboat that cruises the Mississippi regularly. Not to mention a Harrah's Casino the size of a small city right on the edge of the French Quarter."

"Plenty good enough for tourists and amateurs, but not for the high rollers," Jules said. "They play a larger game, and they don't like paying taxes on their winnings. So there's this place in nearby Julep, the Circe Country Club, one of those exclusive clubs just about anyone can be a member of. Only this country club's got a room behind the restaurant, bigger than seems possible from the outside because it's built partly into a hill. You gotta belong to the *real* club to gamble there. Quite a few people around Julep are members, but it's also for some big-money men from New Orleans."

"So far it sounds like something for Louisiana law," Donnie said.

"Except that the Russian Mafia owns and operates Circe."

"They're probably skimming off what they save their members in taxes."

"Oddly enough, that's not the case. I suspect that's because they want to keep them coming to the casino. And because there's something else going on at Circe."

"More money laundering," Donnie said, knowing the traditional underworld use of casinos. Las Vegas existed largely because the Mafia needed a money-laundering operation.

"Could be."

"Too much of that green stuff's a problem."

"Wouldn't know about that," Jules told him. "And maybe the Russians do run Circe so they can do laundry there. If that's the case, we need to know how and whose money's being washed, and where they got it. And whether the Russians are also up to something more important."

"The usual questions," Donnie said.

"There's another question," Jules told him. "Who killed the undercover agent we sent there before you?"

Donnie watched but saw only vaguely a figure walking half a dozen different-sized dogs go past outside on the sidewalk, a small woman leaning back against the pull of the bunched leashes gripped in both hands.

He said, "You've got my full attention, Jules."

"Agent managed to get inside the club as a blackjack dealer, started to send us a flow of information. Then something went wrong."

"Sounds like," Donnie said. The dog walker was crossing the street. One of the small dogs, maybe a poodle, nipped at the man in the crosswalk. He made an obscene gesture and shouted at the woman as he hurried on. All of the dogs seemed to be barking, but Donnie couldn't hear them in the Victory.

Jules said, "We would never have found the body except that it lodged in the fork of a tree."

Donnie looked away from the street scene, directly at Jules. "Not a smart place to hide a body."

"Wasn't meant that way. Her arms were bound behind her with duct tape. Ankles and mouth were taped, too. She was dropped into the swamp at night from a small plane or a helicopter, meant to hit hard, sink, and disappear in the muck. Area's mostly grass and reeds, but somehow her body landed in one of the few trees there. Fisherman found her. She'd been tortured, worked on mostly with a knife, but hadn't been fatally stabbed or shot. She was alive when they threw her out into the night sky."

A female agent, Donnie thought. What must have been going through her mind?

"Christ!" he said.

"Lily Maloney," Jules told him.

Donnie felt all the air rush out of his lungs.

3

Donnie took a late flight into New Orleans, then cabbed to the Robespierre Hotel on Chartres in the French Quarter. It was an old but well-kept redbrick building with a small parking lot on its east side. In the cozy, walnut-paneled lobby he registered as Donald Wells, with a home address in Elmira, New York. The clerk ran his Bureau-supplied secured Visa card in that name, welcomed him to the Robespierre, then handed him his old-fashioned room key attached to a large red plastic tag numbered 214.

"Donald Wells" was traveling with only a scuffed leather suitcase that looked as if it had been bought at a garage sale. It didn't take him long to unpack.

He was tired, so he took off his shirt and shoes, lay back on the soft bed, and read the *Times Picayune* he'd picked up at the airport. Absorbing a newspaper was something Donnie always did as soon as possible after arriving in a city. It gave him an overview, and sometimes nuggets of information that might help to keep him alive. Once in Los Angeles the name of a Mafia soldier he'd known five years ago in New York, and who would recognize him, appeared in the L.A. *Times* as a witness in a local homicide. The murder had nothing to do with why Donnie was in the city, but crime could be a small world. A phone call to Jules Donavon, and the man went from witness to suspect and was detained and off the streets for the week Donnie was in Los Angeles.

Tonight Donnie was scanning the paper for names he'd recently memorized. Former confederates of the late Donald Wells, a bank robber who'd died recently in prison. It wasn't likely any would appear, as Wells spent most of his life and criminal career in the northwest. But travel was easy, and there were northeast hoods who liked jazz and jambalaya.

Wells had served most of a ten-year sentence and would have been released in less than three years, only he attained even earlier freedom by dying of pneumonia in the prison hospital. State and federal records of him were voluminous, but the fact of his death had been expunged. He'd been released as scheduled, and was now in New Orleans at the Robespierre Hotel. Or so records and his trail of activities since his release would lead someone to believe if they were curious enough to check.

There was another exclusion in Wells's records. Aside from not mentioning that Donald Wells was dead, the records also didn't mention that Donnie Brasco was now Donald Wells.

Donnie let the newspaper slip to the floor and switched off the light.

Before going to sleep he thought about Lily Maloney. Red-haired, green-eyed, and freckled Lily, who in the last case they'd worked together had helped to save his daughter Daisy's life. When the Italian Mafia had held Daisy captive to force Donnie to cooperate and feed inaccurate information to the FBI, it was Lily who had been most responsible for Daisy's rescue. Lily who had taken a bullet.

She'd been a member of the Extraordinary Operations, or EO, team, which was at Donnie's disposal in extreme and dangerous circumstances. Team members were drawn from a pool of agents with specialized skills and character traits. One of the most important of those traits was loyalty. And that was Lily Maloney, selfless and fierce in combat, with her square-jawed, reckless smile that took over when it was crunch time. Only she wasn't really reckless at all. Unless it was necessary. Maybe it had been necessary at the Circe Club in Julep. And that time Lily had lost the gamble.

Donnie knew it would eventually be like that for him. The longer you played the game, the longer the odds that you would survive.

He missed Lily. They had been friends in ways that were closer than the bonds of lovers. They'd trusted their lives to each other. Loyal Lily.

Time to repay that loyalty, Donnie thought, closing his eyes to the dark. Jules didn't use the word *revenge* when they'd discussed this case. And when Donnie had mentioned revenge, Jules corrected him and told him to think of it more as professional motivation for his assignment than as balancing the scales in memory of Lily.

But Donnie knew it was revenge that made this

case something special to him. He did understand what Jules was trying to tell him. Understood it before Jules had redefined the emotion with bureaucratic bullshit. However anyone chose to describe it, it was revenge, all right. But revenge wasn't necessarily hot rage that would burn out fast. It could be a cold thing that lived long and got stronger.

Donnie no longer existed in a world where he could afford to blunt truth by coming at it from an angle. Self-deception might lead to death.

He was here for revenge, all right.

He accepted that. Even embraced it for what it was.

It might even be sweet.

Donnie awoke to the phone chirping like an insane cricket on the nightstand alongside the bed. He raised his head from the pillow and squinted at the red digital numerals of the clock radio: 8:06.

Rolling onto his side, he dragged the phone over to him and mumbled a sleep-thickened hello.

"Welcome to another day in the life," said a voice Donnie recognized as Jules Donavon's. Jules sounded as awake and new as the beignets down the street at Cafe du Monde. All full of freshness and with powdered sugar that would dust you in the slightest breeze like dandelion pollen. He always ruined his diet by eating there when he was in New Orleans, and he'd told Donnie he'd call him for breakfast. "Hey, Donnie Wells, you awake?"

"Not by choice."

"C'mon down to Cafe du Monde and I'll buy you breakfast. We need to talk."

"Gimme twenty minutes, Jules."

"Okay. I'll be sitting toward the back, wearing a black beret."

"A what?"

But Donavon hung up.

One thing Donnie had learned was how to shower, shave, and dress in a hurry. He longed to stay in the shower and let the hot needles of water bite into his neck, relax his muscles, and bring him all the way awake, but he knew there wasn't time.

It was 8:30 when he crossed Decatur toward the Cafe du Monde. Dining there was mostly outside, and mostly beneath a roof that shielded patrons from the sun. About half the tables were occupied, and it took him a while to spot Jules seated by himself toward the back of the outdoor eating area, well away from the street.

Damned if he wasn't actually wearing a beret, a black one with one of those little tabs on top that look like a snipped noodle. Jules could bring it off. Somehow it looked natural with his gray slacks and black sport jacket. He might have been a prosperous Parisian shopkeeper seated at a sidewalk café.

Donnie sat down opposite him and smiled. "I'm not making fun," he said, "but you look like you might own this place."

"I wish I did."

A plate of beignets coated with powdered sugar was in the center of the table. A half-eaten beignet lay on a white paper napkin beside a coffee cup in front of Jules. Donnie noticed that beneath the plate was another plate. Jules was on his second helping of beignets. Jules loved food. The diet was going to hell, as usual. He still managed to keep his trim figure, but it was an effort. Jules was setting himself up for a lot of exercises and diet-drink lunches.

A waiter came and Donnie ordered coffee. He picked up one of the beignets and took a bite. Wonderful. The warm little confections tasted just as good as they had during Donnie's last visit to New Orleans. He was glad Jules had chosen this place to meet.

After Donnie's coffee had arrived, Jules brushed powdered sugar from the lapels of his black jacket and said, "Facts you need to know." From a bag alongside his chair he drew out a large brown envelope with a clasped flap. "More background material on Donald Wells, Donnie. Being Donald Wells, you can't know too much about yourself."

Donnie nodded, sipping the strong, aromatic coffee made rich with canned cream.

"Many of the employees at the Circe Country Club aren't Russian Mafia," Jules said. "Aren't any kind of criminal, other than that they know illegal gambling's available there and they're not reporting it. The place creates jobs and brings in a lot of money, so citizens of the law-abiding and orderly town of Julep take a lenient view."

"But they know what's going on at the club."

"Sure. Most of them, anyway. Right along with the ones who work or gamble there. But the bettors and employees keep quiet about it. And the others don't want to know, so if they do, they pretend to themselves that they don't. It's kind of like a prosperous high-class whorehouse that few people want to disturb for fear that lots of relatively innocent folks will get hurt in some way."

"And what's the harm, as long as everyone involved is of consenting age?"

"That's the attitude. Very laissez-faire."

Donnie liked that last part. It was just what a guy wearing a beret would say.

Jules chewed another bite of beignet, then swallowed and dabbed sugar from his mouth with a folded paper napkin. "Now here's the thing, Donnie. One of the rich-out-of-state investors in the clubs senses that something's wrong. He's rich because he keeps a close eye on his investment, and he can't figure out what the Russians are up to there. He doesn't want his ass in a sling because he's involved in money laundering or moving narcotics. Being a major investor, he's got some pull. That's how you got a job at the place. On his recommendation."

"Can we trust this investor to stay silent?"

"I think so. He knows his cooperation with us is the one thing that might make a hero out of him, as opposed to his being a goat behind the walls when the bad guys at Circe take the fall."

"People that rich don't go to prison."

"They do as examples. Ask Charles Keating."

Donnie couldn't argue with that one. Keating had been the sacrificial goat; plenty of savings and loans' board members who got just as rich just as illegally as Keating never saw the inside of a courtroom.

"Ought we be meeting publicly like this?" he asked Jules. "Or is the beret supposed to make you blend in with the bourgeois?"

"I'll be in and around New Orleans," Jules said, "and we won't often be meeting so publicly. You'll check in with me by phone as usual. Sometime tomorrow the word will get to the Circe Country Club about giving ex-con Don Wells a job. That's when the game will begin."

"Will you be wearing the beret when we talk on the phone?" Donnie asked.

"Don't ever lose your sense of humor," Jules said without smiling.

"Okay. I'll be imagining the beret." Donnie couldn't let it alone.

"Also in this envelope," Jules said, ignoring the remark and tapping said envelope, "is an address and keys to your flash pad." A flash pad was the temporary living quarters arranged by the Bureau for an undercover agent. "There are also keys to a car parked in the lot next to your hotel, a maroon 1984 Honda Accord."

"I had a Honda on my last assignment."

"They're the most often stolen car in the country, so the Bureau finds itself owning and rebuilding them when they're confiscated in chop shops."

"A 1984 Honda? Does it run?"

"Better than you can imagine. It's been outfitted with a lot of engine. Not a looker, though. Donnie Wells can't afford a sexy set of wheels. And by the way, he actually is—was—sometimes called Donnie."

"Good. That'll make things easier." Jules would

know what Donnie meant. An undercover agent usually at least used a pseudonym with his own initials, or one that rhymed with his real name. If it could be his genuine given name, or one he was intimately familiar with, all the better. Any hesitation or absence of that flicker of familiarity in the eyes when a real name was used would attract suspicion and could prove fatal. Often the people UC agents were dealing with would notice such things. That kind of observation and alertness was what kept them alive or out of prison.

"Circe's manager, Ewing Bolt, is going to get a phone call about you," Jules said. "That should clear the way for you to be hired to work at the club."

"As what?"

"Something menial. Wells wasn't qualified for much other than bank robbery, and considering the time he spent in prison, he wasn't very good at that."

"It might be difficult to glean information from that far down in the company hierarchy."

"Not so much in this case. Some of the hired help who do the groundskeeping and park cars also serve as the enforcement brigade."

"That could cause problems in other ways. I can't be part of robbing or killing someone."

"They won't trust you to be in on that kind of thing at first."

"Sure they won't. Not until they trust me enough that I might learn something. This is going to be a hell of a balancing act."

"Timing is everything," Jules said, biting into a large beignet and deftly avoiding a puff of powdered sugar. "That's why the agent before you has to get out."

"Whoa!" Donnie said. "I thought the agent before me was Lily."

"She was about to be pulled herself, when she was killed," Jules said. "We have another undercover agent inside, works in the casino. He thinks they might be suspicious of him. Since we'll be pulling him off the job shortly after you get there, he's not going to know about you. But you need to know about him so you don't waste your time going down the wrong street. Name's Frank Allan, but his name at the club is Felix Anders."

"How long's he been there?"

"About three months."

"It didn't take them long to get suspicious of him. What makes him think they are?"

"An accumulation of things."

Donnie understood. That was how it usually ended, rather than a single, colossal blunder that allowed the bad guys to suddenly see the light.

"What Frank Allan's learned, which isn't a great deal, is also in the envelope. Scant as it is, pay attention to it, Donnie. It might give you some insight. Especially into a guy named Iver Mitki, head goon of the enforcers. He's not as dumb as he seems, and more vicious than a riled gator." Jules the chameleon, taking on the color of his environment.

Donnie studied Jules across the beignets and dusting of sugar on the table. "The Bureau must have been curious about the Circe Country Club for a long time."

"We've been trying to crack the place for over a year. Management there is good at keeping secrets, being ready to kill people as they are. That sort of commitment tends to discourage loose talk."

"And not all the hired help are Russian Mafia?"

"No. Some of them don't know about what's going on. You'll be one of those for a while. But if the club management sees possibilities in a man, the proper combination of toughness and viciousness, they bring him into the organization. We hope you become one of those."

"Vicious Donnie Wells."

"It'll fit. He shotgunned a bank guard to death when it wasn't necessary."

"Great! I'm feeling better about being him already."

"When we're finished with breakfast," Jules said, "check out of your hotel, drive your hot-rod Honda to Julep, and move into your flash pad. Then you wait."

"I do a lot of waiting. It might be the worst part of my life."

"You shouldn't have to wait very long this time. Someone from the Circe Country Club will contact you. When they do, I hope you won't wish you were still waiting."

"That's another bad part of my life," Donnie said, "dashed hopes."

"This one is worth doing, Donnie," Jules said. "Think of Lily."

"I am about every ten seconds," Donnie said.

Jules pointed to the plate in the center of the table. "You want that last beignet?"

Donnie did, but Jules had already picked it up and bitten into it.

Dashed hopes. It was starting already.

Donnie didn't know the half of it.

4

Checkout time at the Robespierre was eleven o'clock, so Donnie had time to do a few things before leaving. He wanted to go into this operation as prepared as possible, but he knew he was going undercover too soon after his last assignment to be at a hundred percent efficiency. Gloom and apprehension still clung to him, and guilt still lived in a dark part of his mind. Having to kill Beltram, then learning about Lily's death, had added to his uneasiness. His life's work now had to be done with everything he had and required a period of rest and regeneration after each immersion into danger and a different identity. So soon after Global Allied, would he have enough of what he needed for the Circe Country Club?

In his room, he checked the mechanism of the blue-steel Walther PPK .32-caliber handgun he'd brought with him, and the smaller .25 semiautomatic he could conceal taped to his ankle. Both were the sort of guns a career criminal like Donnie Wells, with connections, might buy on the street after getting out of prison. And Wells would probably arm himself immediately. The Donnie Wellses of the world weren't much interested in rehabilitation.

The last thing Donnie did before leaving the room was to stretch out on the bed with his head propped on the pillow and read the contents of the envelope Jules had given him.

There was more detailed information on Wells, even his favorite meals in prison, his preferred drink when he was on the street. His speech patterns were included—not much of a problem, as Wells and Donnie were both raised in the Northeast. Donnie wouldn't even have to modify the remnants of his New Jersey accent. There was information on Wells that probably even he had forgotten. Donnie devoured all of it; he couldn't learn enough about himself.

As Jules had said, Frank Allan/Felix Anders hadn't discovered much in his time undercover, but he strongly suspected that Circe might be a major money-laundering operation. An increasing amount of cash was moving through the club. There was no hard information on the source of the illicit money. Allan hadn't seemed to believe it was drugs.

Allan did express a healthy respect for the thug Iver Mitki, who was the overseer of waiters, valets, and groundskeepers at the club. And something else lived between the lines of Allan's report on Mitki: stark fear of the big Russian. That worried Donnie.

After checking out at 10:30, he drove Highway 10 out of the city, then headed north for a while, mostly on two-lane state highway, then on winding county roads. He was dismayed at seeing more and more swampy areas on either side of the car, planes of dark water and wild foliage, stands of black cedar trees shrouded in Spanish moss.

When traffic was light, he tested the old Honda, braking it hard, running it through the gears manually as he accelerated, pushing it through corners. The nose dived a bit in heavy cornering, but any slight fishtailing was easily converted to a controlled skid. Jules was right: the car had more than enough engine, and the suspension had obviously been beefed up for emergency maneuvering.

Feeling more confident, Donnie set the cruise control and relaxed behind the steering wheel.

Then there was Julep.

Though it was a surprisingly large town for where it was located, it still didn't look as if the population of sixty thousand boasted about on its welcome sign could be accurate. Much of that population must live far from the center of town, well into the swamp. There was virtually no limit on how much swamp country a town might acquire, considering that alligators didn't vote against annexation.

Donnie drove around town a while before going to his flash pad. There was a small downtown area of office buildings and shops. The rest of Julep seemed to be made up of medium-priced houses radiating out mostly to the east in neat subdivisions. Soon the houses were smaller, in disrepair, and Donnie was in a poorer section of town.

He drove back through downtown and headed west. There the houses were more expensive. He passed a fair-sized high school and some small strip shopping malls. The usual fast-food franchises lined the road; McDonald's, KFC, Wendy's. There was also something called Chicken Vittles that was doing a curb-service business. The waitresses were attractive young women wearing yellow blouses and black shorts. Chicken Vittles looked so much like a sixties restaurant that Donnie was a little disappointed the waitresses weren't on roller skates.

After heading back toward the center of town, he drove north to a neighborhood of old frame houses that had fallen victim to time and disrepair and been subdivided into apartments. The address of his apartment was on Barrack Street and belonged to a gray three-story Victorian with a gallery porch. It needed paint, and some of its green shutters were hanging crooked. The gutter of the porch roof sagged, and a leak had left a rusty stiletto stain down one of the supporting posts.

Donnie parked the Honda at the curb and carried his suitcase up to the porch. As he clomped up the wooden steps he saw that the yews on either side of them were turning brown from plant disease or lack of water.

The front door was tall and ornate, stained wood with a small leaded-glass window. It was the sort of door you knocked on before opening, except that the stenciled red letters on the wood sign tacked to it spelled *Enter.*

Donnie did.

The old house's foyer looked as if it might be preserved almost intact from Victorian times. You had to look closely to see that the gas fixtures on the walls had been converted to electricity, as had the large brass-and-crystal chandelier dangling from a long chain. Threadbare Oriental throw rugs lay on a polished hardwood floor, and the walls were covered with maroon-and-green flower-print wallpaper. A stained-glass window softened the light that gleamed on wooden lamp tables. On the wall at the base of a curved staircase with a thick wooden banister was a sign indicating the numbers of apartments on the second and third floors. Another sign had an arrow pointing to a door leading to the ground-floor apartments. There were a surprising number of apartments in the ancient house.

"Would you be Mr. Wells?" asked a woman's voice in a soft syrupy Louisiana accent.

Donnie turned and saw that a door with lace curtains had opened and a woman in her seventies stood smiling at him. She was wearing a pink-and-white dress with stains down the front, was slightly bent over, and had a round, cheerful face with guileless blue eyes.

"I would be," Donnie said.

"I am"—she pronounced it "ah aa-um"—"your neighbor Mrs. LaValierre, and I do wish to welcome you. Usually I show prospective tenants the apartments and amenities and get to know them, but since the realty company rented to you direct and long distance, so to speak, we are absolute total strangers. I thought I should make you feel welcome."

"You have," Donnie said, unable to resist returning the warm smile. "How did you know I rented the apartment?"

"The realty company told me, as I am the unofficial what you might call *concierge*, so to speak. Would you like me to show you to your unit?"

He didn't want to see her take the stairs. "That won't be necessary. I was given all the information by the real estate agency."

"It is unusual for them to rent in such a manner." She was looking expectantly at him, her blue eyes wide, as if awaiting an explanation.

"Maybe they've changed their policy, or made an exception."

Her smile held. "Exception? Would you be an exceptional man, Mr. Wells? You do look as if you might fall into that category."

"Now, Mrs. LaValierre," he said, "doesn't any man think he's exceptional in the presence of a woman like yourself?" Donnie was turning on his own southern charm, even if it had a slight New Jersey flatness if you listened closely.

Mrs. LaValierre might like flattery, but she also knew it when she heard it and could wade through the goo. "Please don't think it's my old-woman's nature to pry."

"I don't think that. Not at all. Someone at the real estate agency is a friend of a friend, and that's how I got the apartment."

"Then you *are* new in town?"

"You mean you couldn't tell?"

"Now why would you ask a thing like that?"

She had him. "I've, uh, been away quite a while and thought maybe it showed."

She studied him from behind her impenetrable smile. "But you choose not to say where."

"Where?"

"You have come from."

"It's not important."

"Most generally," she said, "I know at least some facts about my neighbors. Such as their place of employment and its phone number. It's good to know these things in case of emergency."

"I can't tell you that yet," Donnie said. Before she could comment, he added, "A job for me has been arranged."

She waved a hand in front of her face as if shooing away a pesky insect. "I do prattle on. Certainly none of this is any of my business."

Donnie figured it didn't matter if she knew—or thought she knew—he'd been in prison. It might even be convenient and add a layer to his cover. Donnie Wells revealing himself. A little.

"I hope you're not uncomfortable to have an ex— to have me here," he said. "I mean, I believe in being honest with people, having things out in the open."

She looked surprised. "Why, I'm not at all uncomfortable." She stared openly at him. "I can tell about people, see inside them, and you'll be just fine."

Donnie nodded gratefully, a penitent glad for shelter and understanding.

"I have a son, Mr. Wells, who spent time in a state institution, so to speak. He was unnecessarily ashamed of that. Every person deserves a second chance. Sometimes even a third. I do not want you to tell me if you are recently released from a penitentiary."

"Well, then," he said, smiling, "I won't."

She nodded. "It's always good to come to an understanding with new neighbors, is one of my rules. I expect you'll want your privacy, Mr. Wells. You do seem that sort."

"I am, Mrs. LaValierre."

"But if you need anything . . ."

He thanked her as she withdrew behind the lace-curtained door, leaving behind a scent of lilac.

Donnie fetched his suitcase and trudged up the staircase to the second floor, thinking he was probably the only tenant who was glad the steps squeaked like an amateur playing a violin. Everyone in the building would know when someone entered or left.

His apartment, 2D, was at the end of a hall. He pushed open the old six-paneled door and went inside.

Looked around.

Old was the word that came to mind. Old four-poster bed with a well-worn comforter on it. Antique dresser with a hazy wood-framed mirror mounted on the wall. Half of the adjoining room had been converted to an efficiency kitchen with a yellowed stove and a narrow refrigerator about the size of a cheap casket. The closet had been converted to a tiny bathroom. Tenants hung their clothes in tall mahogany wardrobes with double doors and a single large drawer in the base.

Donnie set his suitcase on the bed, then walked to the heavily draped window. It had old wooden venetian blinds that when parted afforded a view of the street. Through the branches of an elm tree he could see his Honda parked below.

He opened the wardrobe doors and found that the right half of the interior was made up of shelves. The left half had an extendable rod for hanging clothes. On a middle shelf was a small TV, qualifying the wardrobe as an entertainment center. The inside of the wardrobe was probably lined with cedar; a faint acrid scent still emanated from the darkened wood. On the inside of the left door was a small, oval mirror at eye level, probably for shaving with a straight razor, then making sure your hair was greased and slicked back and your cardboard collar buttoned.

"Where are my spats?" Donnie asked aloud, and began to unpack.

When he was finished he used the remote to switch on the TV and ran through the channels. The gang was all there, old movie stars, the CNN crew, talk show idiots ranting and waving their arms, soap opera sincerity, incredibly sexy women talking about equities and price earnings ratios on the financial channel. None of them seemed to belong in a nineteenth-century mahogany wardrobe, but there they were, and in color.

Donnie switched off the TV and closed the wardrobe door. Then he went into the cramped green-and-white-tiled bathroom and rinsed off his face, combed his hair. He studied his reflection in the medicine cabinet mirror for a moment, saw a man an inch over six feet, lean face, strong jaw, keen blue eyes, broad shoulders, dark chest hair showing where the top two buttons of his gray pullover shirt were undone. His was a face that asked no compromise and gave away nothing. Like an ex-con's face. He said hello to Donnie Wells.

Walking from the bathroom, he looked around again at the four walls. On one of them hung a framed photograph of General Sherman in his Civil War uniform, the shot where he needs a shave and looks a little insane.

Donnie's instructions were to wait. Simply wait. But he knew that if he didn't get out of the apartment soon he'd begin to look like Sherman.

He decided to take a walk and look over the neighborhood, see if there was someplace nearby where he could eat lunch, then maybe buy a few groceries. A guy who'd spent the last ten years in prison would want to get out and walk around, enjoy some space.

Whoever from the Circe Country Club wanted to talk to him would manage to get in touch.

He was right about that. When he approached his car he saw that a gleaming black Buick had parked behind it.

Two men were leaning back against the Buick with their arms crossed, watching him and smiling. They were both wearing dark slacks and white short-sleeved shirts. The one nearest Donnie was about five-foot-five but wide and powerfully built. The other was a much larger version of the first, maybe six-foot-three and over three hundred pounds.

Donnie knew from the description the Bureau had provided that the larger of the men was Iver Mitki. He felt adrenaline kick in, and the core of icy calm that controlled it and kept him alive.

The two men became very still, yet seemed somehow more alert.

This was trouble.

His job was to walk into it.

5

"You Wells?" Mitki asked.

Donnie, staring straight ahead and putting on the minding-my-own-business act, was walking past the two men toward his car.

He stopped and faced them, studying them without apparent alarm or animosity. Taking his time. This was important, this first dance.

"Do we know each other from someplace? You guys don't look familiar."

Mitki smiled. He had a wide face with prominent cheekbones and a bulbous forehead beneath a crew cut that was merely coarse black bristles. A hairline like a gorilla's. Intense dark eyes like a gorilla's, too, only with a bright, sadistic gleam of intelligence. Donnie remembered Frank Allan's notes: this was a smart ape.

"I'm Iver Mitki," he said. He thumbed the air in the direction of the man next to him. "This fireplug with muscles is Vic Ratinsky, goes by the name of Rat. We're from Circe."

Donnie hesitated, getting into the act. "The country club?"

"Only Circe in town," Ratinsky said. He had a voice like a nail on a blackboard.

"He mighta meant the siren," Mitki said.

"What . . . like a cop car?"

"Shut up, Rat." Mitki crossed thick forearms coated with dark hair and corded with muscle. "We came to talk to you about a job," he told Donnie. "I'd be your boss, and I'm also a sort of personnel manager for people that want positions under me."

Donnie put on a pasted grin and offered his hand. Neither man moved to shake it.

"How about you come with us?" Mitki said.

"To the country club?"

"Naw, just take a little stroll here in town."

He and Rat flanked Donnie, and the three of them walked toward the corner. A few cars passed them, their drivers glancing over and doing a double take at the size of Mitki. The afternoon sun seemed suddenly warmer.

"So how do you like Julep?" Mitki asked.

"Haven't had much chance to look it over," Donnie said.

"Place is a shit hole," Rat said. "They'd roll up the sidewalks at sunset, only everybody's already sleepin'. Women all look like they're in the middle of a sex change. Somethin' in the air maybe makes 'em that way."

Mitki laughed. "Rat's with the chamber of commerce."

Near the corner, they turned right and made their way along a cinder-block wall. They were behind a 7-Eleven, in an alley. A sweet, decayed smell wafted from a nearby Dumpster stuffed too full of trash for the lid to close all the way. Donnie looked around. Unless somebody happened to look out a window in the next block, no one would see them here.

"He don't seem scared," Rat said.

"Why should I be?" Donnie asked. "I came to Julep for a job. Isn't this a kind of interview?"

"Kind of," Mitki said, and punched Donnie hard in the chest with a straight right.

Donnie was sitting on the ground before he knew it, gulping for air, his chest aching. He wondered if the blow had been hard enough to crack his sternum. It had certainly been powerful and accurate enough to cause his heart to skip a few beats, causing a momentary blackout and putting him on the ground.

He caught his breath but didn't try to get up; instead he scooted backward and sat on the hard concrete until his shoulders were against the heated steel of the Dumpster. The garbage smell from inside it was nauseating.

"What was that for?" he asked.

"We do the asking," Mitki said, "not you. Opening question: Are you tough enough to get up?"

Donnie looked from one man to the other. They were both smiling, amused and curious. If he got up and ran away, they'd probably find a dog or cat to torture.

"Getting up would be more dumb than tough," Donnie said.

"Right answer," Mitki told him. "You're definitely a candidate for our company." He leaned down, clutched Donnie with hands like grappling hooks, and yanked him to his feet. Donnie's instinct was to grab Mitki's testicles on the way up, wring out his balls like a dishrag while butting him in the face with his head.

Donnie restrained himself.

"He don't seem scared," Rat said again.

"Then he's a dandy actor," Mitki said. "I like that."

"Hell of a job interview," Donnie said.

Mitki released him and shrugged. "Hell of a job, if you pass muster."

"We know about you," Rat said to Donnie.

"All about you," Mitki said. "S'posed to be a hard case, robbed banks, shot a guard. Now you wanna go straight and be an upright vanilla citizen."

"Something wrong with that?"

Mitki slapped him hard in the face. Apparently there was indeed something wrong with it.

Donnie backed up a step. The lower left side of his face was burning, his left ear ringing. He swallowed his anger. He had the training and expertise to defend himself, maybe cripple both these creeps. But he thought of Lily. Anger was a luxury he couldn't afford. And actually he wasn't so sure of the result if he did try to get physical. Mitki he might be able to take alone, but Rat was an unknown.

He could barely hear Mitki's voice. "We don't give a healthy shit about straight, so long as you play it that way with your employer."

"There's people in this world get fucked, and there's the people who fuck them," Rat said. "You're one of the latter."

"Former," Mitki corrected him, looking annoyed.

Then to Donnie: "But you follow orders and every once in a while you might get to fuck somebody for a change instead of taking it."

Rat was frowning fiercely, trying to figure out *former* from *latter* and what exactly had been said.

Donnie winced, shook his head, and stared at the two men. "Let's put a stop to this bullshit. All I know is I was told to come to Julep and there might be work for me at the Circe Country Club. Beyond that I'm in the dark. And let me tell you something—I don't much give a damn what kind of job it is. There's not many jobs I won't do. Tell me about this one, and if I don't like it or you don't like me, we split."

"Maybe you split," Rat said, "right down the middle." He'd drawn a long-bladed folding knife from his pocket.

"I don't goddamn understand this!" Donnie said.

"Rat will do things even I won't do," Mitki told him. "He's got the strongest stomach I ever saw on a man. Things'd make you upchuck all over yourself, Rat'd stick his finger in 'em and taste 'em."

Donnie rubbed a finger of his own around in his left ear, trying to regain full hearing. "You guys ever been reported to the Office of Equal Employment Opportunity?"

Mitki threw back his head and laughed. Rat's laugh was a nasty, squealy sound that grated on the nerves. Rat was probably following Mitki's lead, but Mitki apparently had a sense of humor. Dangerous quality in a thug.

When they'd stopped laughing, Mitki said, "You

ever hear of the Office of Knives and Slices of Internal Organs? Well, it's standing right next to you."

Rat squealed again. The screechy laugh sure sounded weird coming from a guy who looked like he should be a pro football lineman in some kind of short league.

"How the fuck," Donnie said, "do you guys ever hire anyone?"

"We don't, unless they pass the initial job interview," Mitki said. "You passed."

He extended his hand. Donnie shook it, not wincing at the deliberately finger-crushing grip. Rat didn't offer to shake, but he did fold his knife and put it back in his pocket. Obviously he wanted to be pals.

"What now?" Donnie asked. "Do I have to kill someone?"

"That comes later," Mitki said. "If the manager approves you and you get the job, what you'll mostly be doing is parking cars." He puffed out his chest, hitched his thumbs in his belt, and glanced around. Then he spat off to the side. "C'mon."

He led the way back to the street.

"That your car?" he asked as they approached the Honda parked in front of the black Buick.

"That's it," Donnie said.

"Piece of shit," Rat said.

"They don't give you a Hertz coupon when they let you outta prison," Donnie said.

"It hot?" Mitki asked.

"No. I bought it off a guy."

"How about the gun?"

Donnie was surprised. His Walther PPK was

tucked in his belt at the small of his back. Mitki had known it was there and not bothered to disarm him. Thinking back on the time behind the 7-Eleven store, Donnie realized Mitki had always been close enough or in position so Donnie couldn't have gotten the gun out. The object had been to see if he'd lose his cool and try.

"The gun is one I hid in a safe place before I went behind the walls," Donnie said.

Mitki nodded. "I like a man who thinks ahead. Not like Rat, here, who only thinks as far as is he gonna be able to use his knife."

"Hobbies can take over your life that way," Donnie said.

"Beats sittin' around doin' nothin'," Rat said.

Mitki grunted agreement. "Idle hands are the devil's workshop."

They'd reached the two parked cars.

"We'll drive out to Circe," Mitki said. "You follow in your car."

"Junk pile with wheels won't keep up," Rat said, motioning with his head toward the old Honda.

"We'll take it easy," Mitki said, "and if it starts falling behind, he can put out a foot and push."

The unsmiling Rat looked remotely puzzled. He didn't completely share Mitki's sense of humor.

"Let's go," Mitki said to Donnie. "Don't worry; you can get back before you turn into a pumpkin."

"I like carvin' pumpkins," Rat said with an edge of sadism.

Both men from Circe laughed.

Some jokes they shared.

6

Circe was less than half an hour outside of Julep. Donnie played with the Honda, pretending to fall back now and then on curves and when passing, so the Buick ahead would slow slightly and permit him to catch up. He wondered if his car would outrun the Buick if it ever became necessary. The anonymous-looking little Honda had quite a bit of pedal left beneath his right foot.

Both cars slowed, then made a right turn onto a long private road. Donnie drove behind the Buick through an ornate wrought-iron archway painted stark white. There was no sign announcing where the grand entrance might lead. Half a mile ahead was what looked like a sprawling mansion that had been built onto over the years. It was beige with dark beams and a steeply pitched tile roof, as if it might snow a lot in Louisiana. And lots of gables. Whoever designed it loved angles. Directly behind it was a low hill that was probably artificial. Donnie remembered Jules saying the casino off the restaurant was larger than it appeared from outside because it was built partly into a hill.

Aside from that low hill, and an even lower one off to the left, the surrounding countryside was flat. Cypress and banyan trees were clustered off in the distance in three directions, indicating swamp country. There were no other buildings in sight beneath a deep blue sky that seemed to arch low over the lush landscape and Circe's many pitched gables. To the left of the building, parked cars stretched away in neat, sunlit rows.

The Buick parked in the shade of a large portico. Its doors were opening as Donnie braked the Honda to a halt an inch off its rear bumper. He watched a parking valet in a neat tan uniform hand a guy who'd just climbed out of a red Cadillac a ticket stub, then drive the car toward the lot while the man walked inside.

Mitki was standing beside the Honda. He opened the door, and Donnie climbed out, looking around.

The building was even larger than it had appeared from a distance, and meticulously maintained. It might have been built and painted last month. Even the concrete of its foundation, walks, and drive had an unmarked, bleached look to it, as if recently poured.

"Impressive place," Donnie said. "Keeps up with the Joneses."

"We are the Joneses." Mitki led the way up some wide, shallow steps that were sheathed in maroon-and-green outdoor carpet, then inside. Rat stayed behind, taking up position at the side of the entrance like a chunky little sentry.

The club's interior was hushed, cool, and comfortable. Plush red carpet ran through the waiting area and beneath an archway that led to a bar and the restaurant. Donnie noticed that the bas-relief design on the archway was the same as that of the white iron arch over the driveway entrance, an ornate and elegant arrangement of nude women casting dice and touching fingertips. The sort of thing Michelangelo might have done if he'd been a crapshooter.

Straight ahead was the entrance to the restaurant. Donnie could see several diners seated at round tables with white tablecloths. There was no buzz of conversation, but the clinking of eating utensils and china and the occasional ding of crystal were in the air.

No one was seated in any of the overstuffed chairs and settees in the waiting area. Behind what looked like a carved wooden pulpit stood a maitre d' in a tailored black tux. He was a tall, slender guy with a long, long nose and no chin. There was a look about him as if he snubbed the queen of England whenever he wanted. When he said twenty minutes, he meant twenty minutes.

Mitki nodded to the guy, then led Donnie up a wide flight of stairs. On the landing, Donnie glanced at the maitre d', who glanced back and seemed to be looking down on him, even though Donnie was eight feet above him.

Down a hall illuminated by sconces that looked as if they might have come out of an Egyptian tomb was the office of Circe's manager, Ewing Bolt.

Mitki stepped out ahead of Donnie, knocked twice,

then pushed the door open. He went in with Donnie close behind.

"Mr. Bolt, Don Wells," Mitki said by way of introduction.

Ewing Bolt was a man in his late fifties who immediately brought to mind the word *smooth*. He had flawless tanned skin, catlike blue eyes, and perfectly groomed graying hair that was long above the ears and combed straight back so it had a silken look to it. He was wearing a tailored tan suit, a pale blue shirt, and a tan-and-blue tie with a subdued swirling pattern that looked like melted fudge mixed with antifreeze in a blender on slow. He put on the busy act and finished writing on a sheet of notepaper; then he smiled at Donnie and stood up behind the desk. Six feet tall. Couldn't have been built better for the suit. Donnie wasn't surprised when Bolt's voice was modulated and cultured.

"You come recommended, Mr. Wells." He extended his hand.

Donnie stepped forward and shook the cool, dry hand, feeling rather than seeing Mitki fade off to the side.

"Have you become thoroughly reacquainted with the outside world?" Bolt asked Donnie.

The oblique reference to prison wasn't accidental. "To tell you the truth, not yet. But I will. It just takes a while."

"I can imagine." Letting Donnie know he'd never been inside the walls himself. Too smart for that. Establishing distance between them.

Donnie figured it was time to be quiet and let Bolt continue steering the conversation.

"Our employees begin at what might be called entry-level jobs," Bolt said.

"Makes sense," Donnie said. "People who start at the top usually don't stay there long."

"Ah, you didn't tell me Mr. Wells was a philosopher," Bolt said to Mitki.

"I see him more as wiseass," Mitki said.

Bolt shrugged and almost but didn't quite wink at Donnie, as if they shared the knowledge that Mitki had no soul. "In your case, entry level would be parking valet. Can you drive adequately?"

"Sure."

Bolt quoted a reasonable hourly wage. "Will that be sufficient for you?"

"More than," Donnie said. Off to the side, he heard Mitki snicker.

Bolt didn't seem to notice. "If Mr. Mitki didn't approve of you, you wouldn't be here, Mr. Wells. Mr. Mitki will be your supervisor."

Donnie thought he'd better show a little gratitude, even though he knew one of the investors was sponsoring him and Mitki would probably just as soon have left him beaten up in the alley behind the 7-Eleven. "Thanks. That is, if I've got the job." The ex-con showing a touch of bewilderment and disbelief at his good fortune.

"You have it. Your timing is good, Mr. Wells. One of our employees seems to have disappeared three days ago, doesn't answer his phone or his doorbell. It's reached the point where we can assume he's left

Julep. And if he hasn't, he'll be fired. Someone will move up to take his place, and others beneath him will advance a slot. All of which leaves a low slot open for you."

"Right now, any slot anywhere is fine with me."

Bolt fixed him with a level look. "Here at Circe we're not concerned about your previous . . . er, place of employment. That's all in the past. Here you'll have a fresh start."

"And maybe a chance to use some old skills," Mitki said.

Bolt shot him a look. "Mr. Mitki, take Don—or is it Donald?"

"Donnie, usually."

"Take Donnie to the conference room and give him the standard forms to fill out." To Donnie: "We need to make your employment official and be sure we have the proper information for tax authorities. In our business, we have to be positive we're in strict adherence with the law."

Donnie knew he didn't mean the restaurant business. He was reasonably sure Bolt knew he'd been told about the casino, but he decided to say nothing. People generally got into more trouble by talking than by being silent.

Bolt smiled. Test passed?

"When do I start?" Donnie asked.

"Tomorrow, if it's convenient."

"It is."

"Today we'll measure you for a valet uniform. Our help is always neat and well groomed. It's vital we keep up a respectable appearance."

Front, you mean, Donnie thought. But he said, "Sure, I understand."

"Aside from parking cars, part of your job will be to drive a limo into New Orleans occasionally to provide transportation for Circe's special clientele. You'll be expected to drive carefully within the speed limit and be polite at all times."

"I'm known for my driving," Donnie said, remembering reading in the Donald Wells information that Wells had been an excellent wheel man during his earlier days robbing banks.

Bolt smiled. "Then all you need to do is brush up on your manners."

He nodded toward the door, which Mitki had opened. Mitki was waiting for Donnie to leave first.

Donnie thanked Bolt and would have offered to shake hands, but Bolt was already concentrating again on paperwork, the lowly new employee dismissed from his mind as well as from his office. Donnie got the message.

He walked from the office.

Mitki led him to a room with a wall of tinted windows and an oval mahogany table surrounded with wooden chairs with black leather upholstery on their arms and backs. Out the tinted window the land swept away green and level to the distant trees. The room smelled as if someone had been smoking a cheap cigar in it.

The only papers Donnie had to fill out were for tax and medical insurance purposes. Apparently Circe didn't have on file résumés of its low-level employees. One penitentiary was pretty much like another. But it made sense, Donnie had to admit, for a professional thug to have a medical plan.

A round little guy named Jack took Donnie's measurements with a tailor's detachment and expertise.

"You're an easy fit," he told Donnie, stuffing his cloth tape measure back in his pocket.

"That's my talent," Donnie told him. They were alone in the room. Donnie said, "I hear one of the employees failed to come in to work and can't be found."

Jack the tailor shrugged. "It happens. Maybe he got a better job offer someplace else, had to take it right away."

"A valet?"

"Nope. One of the dealers. Guy name of Felix Anders. Nice fella. I hope he's in a better place."

"Me, too," Donnie said.

7

Organized crime in and around Julep had already shown the capacity to move fast. Donnie couldn't trust his apartment phone not to be tapped. He walked back to the convenience store on the corner, then crossed the street and went another block until he saw a Dairy Queen.

Donnie casually scanned it before entering. A woman and small child were seated up front near the window, making messes of chocolate-coated ice-cream cones. A woman behind the counter was showing a teenage boy how to use a blender. Other than them and a man waiting at the order counter, the place looked empty. Donnie went inside.

Luck. It was cool, and there was a pay phone toward the back near the drinking fountain, where he couldn't be overheard if he kept his voice down.

He waited his turn behind the man at the counter, a scraggly haired skinny guy in work clothes who looked as if he'd never in his life eaten ice cream or anything else even remotely fattening.

The man carried a large chocolate Blizzard outside and climbed into a work van. Donnie was hooked.

"I'll have what he had," he said to the pimple-faced teenage boy behind the counter. The kid had *Roger* sewn on his uniform and shirt.

Roger gave him a superior smile, knowing the power of the Blizzard.

Donnie paid him, carried his chocolate Blizzard back to the pay phone, and called his contact number.

When Jules answered, Donnie identified himself, then said, "Be proud of me, Dad; I got a job."

"Good. When do you start?"

"Tomorrow." Donnie filled Jules in on the events of the day, beginning with his lively job interview in the alley with Mitki and Rat.

"The word on Mitki," Jules said, "is that he could be more than an enforcer, only he enjoys his work too much. He's plenty smart. Don't underestimate his intelligence just because he likes rough stuff and looks like a pro wrestler."

"Some of them are smart, too," Donnie said.

"Most of them. Grow up to be governor, even. That's my point. So what are your duties out at Circe?"

"I'll be parking cars. Sometimes driving a limo into New Orleans to shuttle high rollers."

"That's fine. Just do your job and don't dent any fenders for a while; gain their trust out there while you keep your eyes open and make your judgments. What's your assessment of Ewing Bolt?"

"Educated and merciless, tea-party manners and a shark's appetite."

"That's pretty much how Frank Allan saw him."

"Speaking of Allan, I don't think I should reveal my identity as another agent to him when he does show up. He's being pulled off the job anyway. It won't hurt if I know who he is, but it'll serve no purpose if he knows who I am."

"You don't have to worry about any of that," Jules said. "Allan's disappeared on this end, too. He was supposed to meet his contact agent three days ago and never showed up. Every effort to get in touch with him has failed."

Donnie was silent for a while, then said, "What do you think?"

"Same as you," Jules said.

There was little doubt in the mind of either man that Allan was dead. Like Lily. Bolt and his minions had tumbled to both of them. Or maybe Lily had been made to talk before being dumped over the swamp, and had given Allan away. Donnie knew that anyone could be made to talk. Even Lily.

He felt the cold rage that came over him whenever he heard of a fellow agent's death. First Lily, now Frank Allan. The Bureau hadn't pulled Allan fast enough. Donnie had never met him. Hadn't had the chance. The man's death—this man who might have been him—didn't get to him quite the way Lily's had. But it got to him. It added to the fire in his gut that would burn until both deaths were avenged.

Vengeance again. It was part of this assignment and no doubt about it, whatever Jules thought or however he described it. Motivation or obsession— or maybe affliction—there it was, heat without smoke. But it was a fire that had to be banked or it could consume everything and everyone around it.

"Donnie?"

"I'm still here." Donnie remembered the tailor at Circe telling him Felix Anders/Frank Allan hadn't called in or reported for work in three days. That provided the slot that was passed down the chart so Donnie could be hired. Bolt hadn't known that Allan was going to quit soon, and probably it wouldn't have made any difference if he had known. Allan would still have been killed. His body was already in its grave when his replacement at Circe arrived and was fitted with a parking valet's uniform. Maybe even Allan's old uniform. Dead man's clothes. Donnie felt an icy insect crawl up his spine.

Jules said, "Allan rented a room in Julep under his UC name. The place is cleaned out, as if he'd moved in a hurry. Left owing two weeks' rent. Landlord thinks he skipped out to avoid paying. Undercover agents don't do that. Also, we found traces of blood in his room. More than he might have shed from cutting himself shaving."

"You sure it was his blood?"

"Absolutely. DNA match."

"Throwing a body from a chopper didn't work with Lily," Donnie said. "The killers would have been more careful next time. We'll probably never find Allan." The blood meant Allan had been injured when they'd taken him. Maybe seriously. Which meant he might have died having being made to talk under torture. "Do you think Lily talked?" he asked, knowing Jules would have seen her wounds.

"In her place, I would have talked," Jules said. "But even if she talked, she didn't know enough to satisfy them. That's probably why they took Allan. He knew Lily had been killed and his cover was slipping. He'd have at least suspected what was going to happen and put up a fight if he had the chance. He wouldn't let himself be taken alive. Not after what happened to Lily."

Donnie's mind shied away from thinking of what must have happened to her. "Didn't you say Mitki enjoyed his work too much?"

"Yeah, the word is he absolutely relishes it. But don't let your imagination run wild with Mitki, with Lily or with Allan. The images you conjure up stay with you."

Donnie felt like reminding him of their conversation about motivation but decided against it. He knew Jule's advice was wise. And he was glad now that Allan hadn't been told of his impending arrival at Circe.

"We'll know more soon," Jules said. "There's a lounge outside town called Other Rooms. I want you to be there about ten tonight and meet Allan's contact agent. She was a liaison between him and his supervisor in the New Orleans field office. She'll drive down from New Orleans to fill you in on what we've learned about Allan."

"How'll I recognize her?" Donnie asked.

"Tell me what you'll be wearing and she'll recognize you. She'll signal you, and you and she can find someplace private enough so you can talk."

Donnie didn't like the idea of someone else already

knowing his true identity. The more people who knew a secret, the sooner it wouldn't be a secret at all. Part of his job lay in pushing that inevitable day of revelation as far into the future as possible.

"Don't worry about this agent," Jules said, guessing what Donnie was thinking. "She plays it close."

"I'll be at the meet tonight," Donnie said. "Tell her I'll be wearing gray slacks, black pullover shirt."

"Will do. Donnie, this agent's a comer in the bureau. Not because she's got connections, but because she's good at her work. Our work."

"She must have *some* connections, Jules." Donnie was letting him know he understood what Jules was really saying. The bureau higher-ups were observing the woman and possibly grooming her for bigger things. She had an angel somewhere. A mentor. Maybe one Jules didn't want to anger. That way lay bureaucratic purgatory.

"Yeah, we're all connected in some way," Jules said noncommittally.

"Family of man," Donnie said. He could hear the relentless whirring of the milk shake mixer up front.

"Uh-huh. And an occasional monster that provides work for us. Check with me again when you get a chance. Let me know how the job's going."

Donnie said that he would, and was about to hang up.

Jule's voice stopped him: "Bureau politics is always in it in some way, Donnie. We both know that. It's a pile of crap, but there it is, and it won't go away. We deal with it.

"I know," Donnie said. "And Jules?"

"What?"

"You wearing your beret?"

For an answer there was a click and a buzz in Donnie's ear.

Donnie hung up on the broken connection and carried his Blizzard to one of the red plastic booths, where he could sit down and wield spoon and straw.

He still wasn't wild about the idea of meeting this woman tonight. She might be talented and gutsy with a big future in the Bureau. She might understand what being undercover was all about and play it close for Donnie's sake. But would it be close enough?

Frank Allan, the previous agent she'd met with from time to time, had disappeared.

And probably died hard.

8

Other Rooms looked as if it had been dropped along-side the highway by a mother ship.

Isolated on a flat plane, it was a sharply angled dark gray building without apparent doors or windows, a simple dusky rectangle of mysterious purpose. Donnie thought that if it were an aircraft, it would be a stealth bomber.

He steered the old Honda into the parking lot and drove around the corner of the building. There was a red neon sign that could be seen by vehicles coming the other way on the highway. A dozen cars and pickup trucks were parked in the lot, half of them nosed toward the gray building. There were a few small horizontal windows in the building, and a flat black door with the letters *OR* stenciled on it in red.

The Honda's tires crunched on gravel as Donnie drove to the end of a line of cars and parked. Other Rooms was about fifteen miles outside of Julep, and it seemed that the only other business he'd passed in the last three miles was a small hotel, the Lazy Bones Inn. It was a desolate location for a motel. He wondered if there might be a convenient arrangement between the Lazy Bones Inn and Other Rooms. Cynical Donnie.

But assuming the worst in people had helped to keep him alive.

The lounge's interior was dim. Lighted liquor advertisements behind the long bar and on two of the walls provided some illumination. In select areas, track lighting created pools of brightness that seemed to bleach the color out of everything.

Half a dozen men sat hunched over drinks at the bar, except for two down at the end who were swiveled toward each other on their high stools and engaged in earnest conversation. A man in jeans and a Saints T-shirt sat with a redheaded woman at one of the several small round tables. They seemed interested only in their drinks and each other. Body language suggested that maybe the Lazy Bones Inn was part of their near future. Another man and woman were talking softly in one of the booths. The woman suddenly laughed with her mouth open wide, and a small silver ring in her tongue glittered.

The lounge absorbed sound well. None of the conversation was audible to Donnie. The only intelligible voice in the place was Peggy Lee's wafting from speakers up near the ceiling, singing "Don't Smoke in Bed." Donnie found himself feeling at home in Other Rooms.

A third woman was standing toward the back of the lounge. She was blond like the woman at the table, only much more attractive, in her late thirties. About five-foot-eight, Donnie judged. A tight, athletic body that bordered on sensational. Wearing Levi's and a white blouse without a collar. She didn't seem to notice Donnie and was throwing darts at one of those boards that opened up like a cabinet to reveal the cork target. Throwing them in a way that made Donnie glad he wasn't a dartboard.

Though the woman hadn't glanced his way, there was something about her movements and the expressionless cast to her features that suggested she'd known he was there from the time he'd walked through the door.

Donnie leaped to no conclusions. He got a Heineken at the bar and carried it back toward the woman with the darts, noticing a glass and a bottle of Bass ale near her on a table.

She added another dart to the ones clustered around the bull's-eye on the cork board, then glanced over at Donnie with calm blue eyes. "You here to pick me up?"

"Not unless you fall down."

She smiled, but only slightly. "You look like your description." Then she turned, offered the hand not holding a dart, and they shook and introduced each other. She said her name was Susan Bristol. Sue. Didn't say if it was her real name. Donnie didn't ask.

After another near bull's-eye with the final dart, they went to the table with the Bass ale on it and sat down.

"You're not bad at darts," Donnie said.

"Yeah. In the army I used to be responsible for firing Hawk missiles. Had to hit what I aimed at. This is just a smaller and less destructive version of that."

In a way, Donnie thought. "Jules told me you were Frank Allan's liaison."

"Sometimes," she said. "I'll be yours sometimes, too. Julep's a small enough city that some precautions are necessary. It'll be less obvious if your contact agents vary."

"And it give Jules more opportunity to take it easy and scarf down Cajun food in New Orleans."

She showed no reaction to this bit of blasphemy he'd thrown out to test her. "Also," she said, "it'll seem logical for other reasons, which I'll be modest and not mention, that you'd be spending time with me."

Ah, a bit of diversion. She hadn't joined him in bad-mouthing a superior in the Bureau. Donnie liked that. She didn't know his relationship with Jules. Didn't know enough to trust him that far.

"Any luck finding Frank Allan?" Donnie asked, knowing the answer but nonetheless hoping.

"Not good luck," Sue said.

They must have found Allan's body. Despite the fact that this was no surprise, he felt the same withering coldness he'd experienced on learning of Lily's death. "Where was he?" Donnie asked.

Sue appeared puzzled for a moment, then shook her head. "We still don't know where Allan is, but we can be more sure that he's dead."

Donnie took a sip of Heineken. "Explain."

"Yesterday some workmen were digging a grave in a cemetery near Julep. The side of the excavation suddenly caved in and they saw a human arm. At first they thought they'd dug too close to the nearby occupied grave. But as it turned out, there was a body buried alongside the casket in the other grave."

"But not Allan's?"

"The body of a woman," Sue said. "She'd gone missing from her job as a dentist's receptionist two days ago. Her boss worked on her teeth and had X rays. That made it all the easier for a positive ID through her dental records. Marla Grant, age thirty-four, single and a part-time real estate agent. She was about to go into real estate full time, and in a way she did. She has her own plot of ground."

"Full-time as it gets," Donnie said.

Sue matched the sadness in his voice. "Forever."

"So how does this tie in with Frank Allan or Circe?" Donnie asked.

"Marla had been tortured, small pieces of her cut away with a sharp knife, as if someone was trying to get her to talk." The line of Sue's jaw hardened. "Things had been done to her. . . ."

Like Lily, Donnie thought. He remembered Mitki and Rat behind the 7-Eleven, Rat with his long-bladed gravity knife. "That the only connection?" he asked.

"No," Sue said, "when the grave site was thoroughly examined a silver cigarette lighter was found. There was a thumbprint on it. Not Marla's. The computers matched it immediately. It was made by Frank Allan's thumb."

"The body was clothed?"

"Nude."

"Then the lighter might have been dropped accidentally by whoever killed her."

"Right. Frank Allan's lighter, kept by whoever killed *him*."

Donnie sat back and thought about that one. "So Allan and Marla Grant were probably murdered by the same person. Was there any kind of link between her and Allan? Were they acquaintances? Secret lovers?"

"Possible but not likely. Allan was happily married, had two kids. We showed Marla Grant's morgue photo to his wife, and she didn't recognize her."

"Lots of people aren't recognizable from their morgue photos," Donnie said, remembering countless photographs of damaged faces with dull, staring eyes.

"The widow—name's Ida—was sure she'd never seen the woman. She was also sure her husband was faithful."

"Doesn't eliminate that secret lover possibility," said Donnie the cynic.

"That might be what whoever tortured Marla Grant thought. Made her talk, then killed her. The thing is, so far we've made no connection between her and Frank Allan. Why would the killer or killers link the two?"

Donnie had no answer and could only speculate. "Marla Grant might have spent time at Circe, run into Frank Allan there."

"Nope. Everyone who knows her says no. She didn't believe in gambling."

"Allan happen to go to the dentist she worked for?"

"Never. The dentist doesn't gamble, either." Sue reached into her purse on the chair next to her and laid a five-by-eight photo in front of Donnie on the table. "Marla Grant. Know her?"

Donnie felt his stomach contract as he stared at Marla Grant's morgue photo. An ear had been severed, the tip of her nose cut off, and there were long knife slashes on her cheeks. Pathetically, her blond hair had been brushed aside to make her features more visible, as if she'd just rearranged it before going out. He thanked God her eyes were closed. It was the eyes that stayed with you forever.

"I never saw her," he said, and gave the photo back to Sue, who'd been studying him.

"It's pure shit, isn't it?" she said.

"It is that."

She sighed hoarsely, as if she smoked too much. But there were no butts or ashtrays around and she didn't smell like tobacco smoke. "Ready for more complication, Donnie?"

"Oh, sure. That's what my life is made of."

"Marla Grant had no police record. But she has a twin sister, Mona, in Chicago, who's had plenty of fun and games on the wrong side of the rules. Prostitution, assault, forgery, drug possession. Chicago law says she's on the street now, and heavily involved with drug dealers."

"We talking identical twins?" Donnie asked.

Sue nodded. " 'Fraid so. But other than their physical similarity, there are differences. Marla took the high road. Mona started young on the low, got pregnant, dropped out of high school, had an abortion, left town, started doing drugs, went from bad to worse to even worse. It can happen that way, and fast, like going over a cliff. She's been in and out of rehab several times during the last ten years, but it hasn't helped. Married twice and divorced, the last time five years ago. Sister Marla married right after college. No children. Her husband left her six years ago and moved to New York. The twins' father's dead; mother's still alive and lives in New Orleans. Marla saw her regularly. Mona's estranged and has been for years."

"From what you say, nobody would have reason to torture and murder Marla Grant. Maybe she was mistaken for her sister."

"Maybe. But Mona hasn't left Chicago in the last six months. More important, there's no apparent connection between her and Frank Allan or Circe. Neither sister seems to have gone near the guy or the gaming tables."

Donnie pondered that, staring into his beer.

"I hope you're out of information for me," he said after a while.

"I am for now," Sue told him. She smiled, becoming even more beautiful. Sweet-looking woman. Leading him on? "Want to play darts?"

Donnie declined.

Thinking, Hawk missiles.

9

Donnie wore his street clothes to work the next morning, arriving at Circe fifteen minutes early and changing into his valet uniform in the small locker room behind the kiosk near the club's portico. As the new man, he worked the early shift, parking the lunch crowd's cars. The tips weren't as plentiful; the magic of night and the slot machines hadn't yet taken hold.

It was eleven o'clock, so there was time before the socialites who lunched, businessmen and -women from Julep, and habitual gamblers began to arrive.

Mitki appeared on the wide, shallow steps to the club entrance and nodded to Donnie. He was wearing a navy blue and gray sweatsuit with gray silk trim, jogging shoes, a ton of gold chains around his thick neck. It was more a casual outfit than one you would actually want to sweat in, but Donnie nodded back and asked, "You been working out?"

"Sure," Mitki said. "Do every day. The kind of job I got, you never know when you're gonna take something apart, put forth a little effort." He pulled a half-smoked greenish cigar from his pocket and lit it with a great deal of puffing and lip smacking, using a match. Donnie wondered if he'd recently lost a lighter. Mitki grinned and placed the match, still burning, in his mouth, quickly smothering the flame before it could damage tissue. Tough guy, he was telling Donnie. Keep it in mind. Well, Donnie wouldn't want to try that match thing.

A medium-height man who looked to be in his early twenties emerged from the building to stand next to Mitki. He was darkly handsome, well built if a little on the thin side, with brown eyes and a head of wavy black hair. On his face was a pleasant, slightly puzzled and anticipatory smile, as if he liked everyone right off the bat and maybe they'd help him solve the riddle of his life. He had on a tan parking valet uniform exactly like Donnie's.

"This here's Nick Nordo," Mitki said. "He's gonna show you how things work here; then you and him can handle the lunch business. By tonight you should know enough to keep up with the high rollers and potential suicides when they drive outta here drunk."

Donnie took one of the shallow steps and shook Nordo's hand, which was cool and soft.

"I'll get you up to speed in no time, man," Nordo said, grinning. Donnie thought that in a war movie, Nordo would be cast as the handsome, cocky kid who gets killed.

Mitki rolled his eyes, flicked his smoked-down cigar away into the bushes, and sauntered back inside.

"That match thing's his favorite trick," Nordo said.

"He got any others?"

"Sure. You saw him walking upright."

Donnie thought he might learn to like Nordo. Or was Nordo feeling him out? Trying to get him bad-mouthing the boss first day on the job? Donnie shrugged. "However he walks, he's the head honcho."

"Not much doubt of that," Nordo said, still with his crooked, reckless grin.

"How long you been working here?" Donnie asked.

Nordo didn't have to think about it. "Seven and a half months."

"Like it?"

"Wouldn't say it sucks." He stretched, raising his arms high and taking a deep breath. Donnie thought he might remark what a wonderful morning it was, but instead Nordo said, "So let's start your training, man. There's not much to learn, but around here it pays to, like, get it right. Kinda place where everyone gets all uptight over nothing." He led the way beyond the shade of the portico roof and over to the kiosk.

The system was simple enough. When a customer arrived he was given the stub of a numbered ticket. After parking the car, the valet jotted down the lot's row-identifying letter, the car's make and color, and first three license plate numbers. The car keys, on a string attached to the ticket, were taken to the kiosk and hung on a board marked with parking lot row letters. When the customer requested his car, the valet took his stub, matched it with the letter on the board, and armed with the information scrawled on the ticket, found the car and drove it to the customer waiting in the portico.

Nordo showed Donnie how to open a car door for arriving customers, the door for the woman on the passenger side first, if there was a woman. He obviously enjoyed pantomiming the motions of everyone involved as he acted out the scene, smiling and bowing to the imaginary female passenger, looking amiable but efficient for the driver, assuming the driver was male. He got in his make-believe car, went through the motions of putting it in gear, then snapped back his head as if under sudden acceleration as he drove away to park.

"I guess that was a Cadillac," Donnie said.

"Rolls-Royce, man. Like, if I'm going to imagine a car, it might as well be a Rolls."

Donnie thought that made a kind of sense.

"Most of these people have got money coming out their ass," Nordo said. "At least when they arrive. Be extra polite to them. Most'll tip you after you pull up in their car. Some'll tip you coming and going. The parking valets put all the tip money in a jar and it's, like, divided up for them." He tried to look serious. "Do not fuck with that last part of it, Donnie."

"Not my style," Donnie said.

"I think you'll be happy with how much you pull down at the end of a busy night."

"What about daytime, the lunch crowd?"

"They don't tip jack shit, man. Some of them don't tip you at all. But you don't wanna get wiseass with them, 'cause they might be the same people show up that night and win a bundle in the casino. When that happens they tip you large."

"I don't wanna get wiseass with anybody," Donnie said.

"Sure you don't, man. I didn't mean it like that."

"No offense taken," Donnie said.

"Where'd you work before?" Nordo asked.

"I been away. How about you? You do this between going to college?"

"Naw. Got thrown out of Florida State last year. This female anthropology professor put the moves on me. I turned her down and she got pissed off, threatened to shout rape. Then she accused me of stealing a video recorder. You try and defend yourself against that these days, you're, like, pissing into the wind, man. I had to leave or get arrested."

Donnie wondered if any of that was true. "Why didn't you just fuck her and stay put?" he asked.

Nordo gave a mock shiver. "She looked a lot like Mitki, man."

The lunch clientele started to arrive. Most of them were driving expensive cars, Lexuses, BMWs, big Lincolns and Caddies.

At first Nordo parked most of the cars, Donnie watching. Then Donnie began doing his share. Some of the customers stood and watched, so you didn't want to lay rubber or test cornering ability.

Donnie sized up the customers. Most of them were well dressed, the men in suits or sport jackets, the women in dresses or expensive business suits. They looked like a normal bunch, only more polished and moneyed. The men were mostly chamber-of-commerce types. The women seemed the sort that got weekly pedicures and lent their names and time to charities. Honest citizens all.

But honest only up to a point. Donnie knew some of them would return to gamble that evening.

It didn't take Donnie long to advance to the evening shift. It happened the same day, in fact. Both Donnie and Nordo were asked if they'd stay on and cover for a manpower shortage, work a double shift. Nordo seemed hesitant, but he agreed. Donnie made a show of being eager to put in more hours. Starting tomorrow, they were both told, they could come in to work in the late afternoon and stay till the club closed. It was time for a shift change anyway, and if the usual evening shift valets didn't like it, fuck them.

Nordo was right; in the evenings the tips were better. Donnie stuffed plenty of bills in a big jar, which used to be a pickle jar, sitting on a table under the key board inside the kiosk.

About two a.m., when the flow of cars had slowed, an exhausted Nordo leaned against the back of the kiosk out of sight and lit a joint. "Wanna smoke?" he asked Donnie.

Donnie shook his head no. "I'm on my best behavior." That would translate to parole to Nordo, who nodded and took a deep drag.

"So whaddya think, man?" Nordo asked.

"It's a job," Donnie said.

"You did all right, for the first day."

Donnie said nothing.

A green Jaguar drove up fast and parked beneath the portico. Donnie waved for Nordo to stay smoking and jogged over to the car. The driver, a fat man in a cream-colored suit that made him look even fatter, had liquor on his breath. Donnie had to steady him as he climbed out of the low car. He accepted his claim ticket stub, tipped Donnie a five, and made it into the restaurant without falling down.

Donnie parked the Jag in Row C, then walked back toward the kiosk.

He heard voices coming from behind the kiosk, where he'd left Nordo doing dope.

". . . not to smoke that shit!" Rat's voice. "How many times I gotta say it?"

Donnie walked around to the rear of the kiosk and saw that Rat had Nordo backed against the wall. He was inches from him, and in his right hand was his long-bladed gravity knife. Rat looked like he was having a high time. Nordo looked terrified.

"An' last week I found you snoopin' around the office," Rat said. Then he caught Nordo's eye movement toward Donnie and shut up and turned, stepping away from Nordo.

"I wasn't snooping!" Nordo said.

Rat ignored him.

"And I wasn't smoking dope!"

That obvious lie got to Rat. He turned his attention back to Nordo. The knife point was suddenly at Nordo's throat. "Didn't I tell you not to fuckin' lie to me, you little prick? Didn't I fuckin' say them exact same words?" The little barrel of a man rose

73

on his toes so he was almost Nordo's height, looking him in the eye.

"I guess," Nordo croaked.

"I'm gonna slit you gullet to gut," Rat said.

A trickle of blood appeared at knifepoint and wormed its way down Nordo's throat.

That might have been what set Nordo off. Panicked him. He suddenly shoved Rat away and broke free. Tripped and fell. Tried to scramble to his feet but couldn't make it. He was lying on his side, supporting his upper body with one elbow.

Rat whirled and was on him, dropping toward him, knife drawn back for a lethal strike.

Donnie stepped forward and used the edge of his hand to hack Rat's wrist, numbing the arm so the knife slipped from his fingers. That slowed Rat down, and Nordo rolled away.

Rat got to his knees, retrieved his knife, and glared up at Donnie. "That's gonna cost you, my friend."

Donnie didn't like Rat's abrupt mood change, how cool he'd suddenly become. As though his mind had been made up for him.

"I couldn't let you kill him," Donnie said. "And that's where it was going. You oughta thank me for keeping your temper from getting you into big trouble."

"Exactly what I was thinking," a voice said.

Donnie glanced away from Rat and saw Ewing Bolt. Mitki was standing beside and a little behind him. Donnie wondered how long the two men had been there, watching. Judging.

Donnie picked up on it. "I wish to hell somebody'd stopped me."

"Meaning?" Mitki asked.

"Never mind," Donnie told him. "I didn't mean tonight." He appealed to Ewing Bolt. "I wasn't gonna stand here and let him kill the kid over something like smoking a joint."

"You did the right thing, Donnie," Bolt assured him. He glanced over his shoulder toward the portico. "We've got a business to keep going here. I think somebody needs his wheels."

Somebody did. The fat guy in the Jaguar had decided it was already time to leave. Either that or the bartender had turned him away. One of the lapels of his cream-colored suit was all wrinkled, as if someone had grabbed it and bunched it up in his fist.

Donnie got the Jag, delivered it to the guy for another five-dollar tip, then walked back behind the kiosk.

Only Nordo remained there. He was still leaning against the wall where he'd stumbled after rolling away from Rat and getting to his feet. He looked as if he'd been crying.

"You get fired?" Donnie asked.

"No. They forgot to do that, at least so far. Thanks for saving my ass, man."

Donnie gave a slight nod but didn't say anything.

"The bastards!" Nordo said. "There's something wrong at this place. I know it!"

"What do you mean? The casino? You knew about that when you hired on, didn't you?"

"I don't mean the casino. Like something else.

You're parking cars here awhile, you'll see. It doesn't feel like it should around here."

"You're shook up," Donnie said. "I don't blame you. Go home and get some sleep, start over tomorrow."

"That's what Mr. Bolt told me to do."

"I'd do it, then," Donnie said.

Nordo looked humiliated and furious. Then the air seemed to go out of his tense body. He managed his cocky grin. "I guess I better." He used both hands to shove his dark hair back from where it had flopped down on his forehead. "Ewing Bolt's the big boss."

"You're lucky he was tonight," Donnie said, watching Nordo push away from the wall then make his way unsteadily toward where his car was parked at the end of Row G. As he walked, he extended his right hand and touched every other trunk lid as if maintaining his balance.

"Thanks again, man!" Nordo called over his shoulder. "I'll pay you back someday."

"Maybe sooner than you think," Donnie said too softly to be heard, wondering about Nordo.

10

Donnie called Jules Donavon the next morning from a public phone outside the 7-Eleven. He shot a quick glance toward the back of the building, where he'd been "interviewed" by Mitki and Rat from the Circe Country Club's personnel department. The business world really was a jungle.

The day was still cool but the angled sun lay warm on his shoulders as he listened to the phone ring at the other end of the connection. Sparse traffic hummed past on Barrack Street. Donnie decided that he felt all right, considering. He thought that when he got through talking to Jules, he'd go into the store and see if he could buy a cup of coffee.

"Hold, Donnie," Jules said brusquely, when he'd answered the phone. He sounded as if he might be off to a bad start this morning.

"Sorry," he said when he came back on the line. "Lots of things happening today. And now you."

"Now me," Donnie said. He filled Jules in on the events of yesterday.

"Rat got on this kid for smoking pot on the job," Jules said when Donnie finished. "You think there might be a major narcotics operation of some kind going on there, and the gambling might be just what it seems?"

"Always possible," Donnie said. "Or more likely one operation would complement the other, the casino to launder money made in a drug operation. But that's a lot of speculation based on a guy like Nordo smoking a joint. Sorta kid who's seen too many sixties and seventies movies or something. It's hard to imagine him *not* smoking dope."

"Kinda thing you're there to sort out," Jules said, as if Donnie didn't know it.

"There's this about Rat losing his temper with Nordo," Donnie told him. "Rat would have stabbed him. There was nothing to stop him from bringing down the knife. He doesn't have the brakes that most of humanity has. I think if I hadn't been there he would have knifed Nordo to death."

"Which is genuinely scary," Jules said. Not in the wiseass way he and Donnie sometimes conversed in to ease stress, to stay sane.

Donnie knew what he meant. "They kill almost casually. They don't worry about consequences. That means they might be plugged in to people who can protect them."

"That's what Frank Allan and Lily ran into," Jules said sadly. Then in a more normal tone: "How'd the meet with Agent Bristol go?"

"Sue?"

"It's Sue, huh? I guess it went okay."

"Sure. Impressive woman. Good at darts."

"Used to fire Hawk missiles in the army," Jules said.

"She told me that. I figured she told it to all the boys."

"Went in as a second lieutenant, came out five years later a captain."

"I'm not surprised."

"Used to love jumping out of airplanes, worked some undercover, knows martial arts, has a pilot's license. And don't shoot pool with her."

"Why are you telling me this, Jules?"

"So you know that if the time comes when you have to count on her, you can."

"Noted," Donnie said. "Anything else on Marla Grant, the woman who was killed and will never have the chance to jump out of airplanes or fire Hawk missiles or shoot pool?"

"No. It seems logical to assume she was killed by whoever did Frank Allan, and probably Lily. But there doesn't seem to be any connection between her and either of them. Or between her and Circe or anybody connected to the club."

"Through the twin sister, maybe," Donnie said. "That one's got a police record for drug possession, runs with users and dealers."

"But in Chicago. And Marla Grant's mother says Mona, the evil twin, has been estranged from the family for years. The two sisters haven't even spoken since high school."

"I wouldn't be so sure," Donnie said. "Twins . . . They might've had contact the mother never knew about."

"Could be. But everybody from family, friends, employer, they all say Marla Grant was a straight arrow, hard worker, wanted to make a fortune selling houses instead of lining up dental appointments for Dr. White's patients."

"Dr. White?"

"Dentist she worked for as a receptionist."

"Good name for a dentist."

"He couldn't find enough superlatives to use for Marla Grant."

"Think there was anything going on between them?"

"No. None of the signs are there. And White's married to a woman who looks like a movie star and they have three kids. Of course, all I can give you is an opinion."

"You say she looks like a movie star, I believe you."

"You know what I'm talking about, Donnie."

Donnie did. And he valued Jules's opinion. Donavon had great instincts about people, and had in fact sniffed out secret relationships when Donnie had no idea they existed.

He said, "Jules, I need to know more about Nick Nordo. He seems uncomplicated enough, just a naive kid with a job parking cars. I don't think he's connected to the Russian Mafia or knows for sure anything illegal's going on at Circe other than the gambling. But he's suspicious. Something about the place is bothering him, and when Rat was really pissed off and careless with his words, he mentioned catching Nordo snooping around in an office."

"Most likely looking for something to steal or smoke," Jules said.

"Probably," Donnie agreed. "But I think Nordo's worth checking out. He's not crazy about his employer and might prove useful, but I need to know how far I can trust him."

"We'll get some info on him," Jules said, "pass it on to you. Frank Allan figured Ewing Bolt knew who his direct bosses were and followed orders, but that Bolt might not know the big picture. The thieves-in-law would see him as an underling and keep him pretty much in the dark." Thieves-in-law were the Russian equivalent of Italian Mafia dons, only even more vicious. Didn't dress as well, though.

"That would make sense," Donnie said. "Bolt would be a medium-large fish."

"We want the names of the big fish that might eat the medium-large fish."

"I'm working my way upstream," Donnie said. "Only the game fish . . ."

"Swims upstream," Donnie finished for him. "You don't know how much better that makes me feel."

"They do sell a lot of salmon," Jules told him before hanging up.

Donnie had been back in his apartment only a little over an hour when he wondered if he should try to get some sleep. Last night had wrung him out, and he'd be going back in to work at Circe that afternoon before he knew it.

But the phone rang.

Jules was calling him. Which meant his apartment

phone line had been checked and was clear and un-tapped. That was a circumstance that might change anytime. Which meant the call was important.

Jules was back to his hell-of-a-day tone. Calm, but with an underlying vibrato in his voice like electric current humming through a wire.

"There's something I need to show you, Donnie. You'd better drive into New Orleans."

"Now?" Whatever Jules had, it must be important.

"Soon as possible. Be sitting on one of the benches in Jackson Square at eleven-thirty, near where the street artists have their work displayed on an iron fence."

"I know the place," Donnie said.

"Play the pale tourist, just out of prison, won-drously all the way alive again and marveling at the big world. A rebirth in midlife."

"I'll be there," Donnie said, keeping the conversation short, getting off the line before it could be tapped or Jules broke into poetry.

He switched off the TV, a women's soccer match in Paraguay. A stocky player with a short, ragged haircut and the most muscular legs Donnie had ever seen was skillfully working the ball downfield when the screen went blank.

Donnie snatched his wallet and keys from the dresser top and made for the door.

He hadn't really been interested in who'd win, anyway. Better to concentrate on the game he was playing, where the score was calculated in lives and deaths.

11

It was a pleasant time to sit in Jackson Square.

Donnie found an unoccupied bench in the sun and settled into it. The square wasn't too crowded. Tourists were wandering past, pausing to examine the bright oils and watercolors hanging on or propped against the black iron fence Jules had mentioned. There was a guy near the corner selling fanciful creatures made from long balloons twisted together. When anyone stopped near him he'd make a round, red balloon shape with a crease in it, then insert the person's nose in the crease so they were standing there with a bulbous artificial nose. Donnie thought you had to be careful who you did that to. Half a block down, an elderly black man was artfully playing "Night Train" on a sax. Didn't seem like the right musical accompaniment for sticking artificial noses on people's faces, but there it was.

Just when Donnie was getting into really enjoying "Night Train" he saw Jules standing in a knot of people watching a caricaturist sketching the likeness of a pretty teenage girl. Jules saw him at about the same time and casually ambled toward him. He was wearing a pale blue T-shirt with MARDI GRAS in large red letters across the chest, baggy jeans, dark sunglasses with tiny round lenses, and his black beret. In his right hand he was carrying a cloth shopping bag by the strap. Such a tourist.

"Where's your disposable camera?" Donnie asked when Jules sat down about two feet away from him on the bench.

"It's somebody else's camera I want to guard against," Jules said, talking to but not looking at Donnie. The act was that these were just two strangers enjoying the day, carrying on an impromptu conversation. Donnie knew that even if such precautions seemed corny now and then, they worked. Jules might look like a tourist from 1957 Boise, but he sure didn't look like the guy Donnie'd been talking to a few days ago in the Cafe du Monde. Except for the stupid beret. Donnie was about to point that out when another guy dressed like a tourist wandered past wearing an identical beret.

"They sell 'em by the hundreds at the big flea market on Decatur," Jules said, guessing what Donnie was thinking. "They can change your appearance, make you anonymous."

"I'll remember," Donnie said. He watched the man sketching the teenage girl, listened to "Night Train," waited for Jules to get to the reason for this meeting.

Jules shifted his weight around on the hard bench, as if holding in words that made him uncomfortable. Donnie understood him well enough to know bad news was on the way.

"We found Frank Allan's body yesterday," Jules

said. "Helicopters using infrared scanners spotted a site where a body might have been buried. It turned out to be Allan's, three feet down in the mud. Not far from where Lily was found, in deep swamp country."

"Dropped from a chopper or plane like Lily was?"

"No," Jules said, "but tortured with a knife like Lily was, in some of the same ways, maybe even in the same order. Marla Grant was worked on the same way, too. Somebody's trained in torture, an expert in combining pain with psychological horror."

Donnie had a pretty good idea who that might be. He didn't want to hear what Rat had done to Lily or Frank Allan or Marla Grant, or in what order. He didn't want to think about Mitki watching the bloody proceedings, participating, asking the questions.

Jules held out a photo of Allan's body, like one tourist showing another a shot of the kids. Donnie didn't look at it for long. Jules was trying to make a point here. "We're going to keep the discovery of Allan's body a secret for now. As far as they'll know at the Circe Country Club, everyone thinks he's still a missing employee who ran off without notice to take someone up on a better job offer. No reason for anyone to tie him in with what happened to Lily."

Donnie took a deep breath and leaned back, tilting his head so his face was in direct warm sunlight. It was a bother that this business didn't compute even a little bit.

"Are we absolutely sure there was no connection between Frank Allan and Marla Grant?" he asked.

"Sure as we can be, given that there are no absolutes. Every avenue of investigation in that direction is a dead end. Same way with Lily. She and Marla Grant don't seem to have ever met."

"But all three were carved up by Rat."

"Allegedly."

"How long can you keep the discovery of Allan's body a secret?"

"Long time."

"What about his widow?"

"She'll know, but don't worry about her talking. She lives in Kansas City and will keep her silence. We haven't told her yet, but she already figures her husband's dead. She wanted whoever killed him arrested, tried, and executed."

"Just executed will do for me," Donnie said. He saw the expression on Jules's face. "Don't worry, I won't play outside the rules without unofficial permission."

"I didn't hear any of that," Jules said. "Wouldn't believe it if I did hear it." He frowned. "Doesn't that guy play anything other than 'Night Train'?"

"Do one thing and do it well," Donnie said.

"Over and over is what I object to." Jules placed his hands on his knees, about to get up off the bench. "Thing is, Donnie, all these people you're dealing with need is to be suspicious of you, and you'll join the list of victims. They'll torture you to find out what you learned and might have passed on; then they'll do you the favor of finally killing you."

"I knew that going in," Donnie said.

"Yeah, but here, right now, is your chance."

Donnie looked at him. "To do what"

"Back out. This one is getting particularly dangerous, and you're valuable to the Bureau."

"I'm valuable because I'm good at undercover
work," Donnie pointed out. "I can be somebody else.
Hell, I've got no choice but to be somebody else. If
I weren't Donald Wells, I still wouldn't be Joe
Pistone."

Jules looked at him, his eyes barely visible behind
the dark lenses of his sunglasses, showing no more
emotion than the rest of his features. "We don't want
to lose you. We've been friends a long time. *I* don't
want to lose you."

"Don't go soft, Jules."

"This'll be the last time you see it."

"Good. I don't need soft. Soft is dangerous. Soft'll
get me killed."

Jules studied him harder from beneath the ridicu-
lous black beret, through tiny tinted lenses. Now
there was something about what Donnie could see
of his face, the slight downward arc of his lips, the
set of his jaw.

He pitied Donnie, which made Donnie uneasy.

"It's a shame, but I guess you're right," Jules said
at last.

"We both know it," Donnie said.

"But you live it."

"That's the way things shook out," Donnie said.
"I made the choices that got me where I am. I'm not
complaining and I don't need anybody's goddamn
pity."

"Pity? Who's offering pity?"

"Nobody. And that's the way it has to be."

"You think pity's dangerous, too?"

"The most dangerous thing there is. The thing I hate most."

Jules nodded, then leaned forward and levered himself to his feet. "Walk carefully and watch your back," he said. It was what he often said on parting with Donnie. There wasn't much else that could be said, after a conversation like this one.

"Wear a different disguise next time we meet," Donnie told him.

"Sure. Maybe I'll dress as a woman."

"Nobody'd notice, here in the Quarter."

"I'll have to find out if I'm winter or summer," Jules said.

"What?"

"You know, for buying makeup, clothes. Do I have a winter or summer complexion, eye color? I'll have to find out."

Donnie wondered, just for an instant, My God, is he serious?

Then Jules grinned, touched a forefinger to his beret, and walked away across the square.

Donnie'd been had. A joke this time. Maybe next time a bullet.

Better than pity. Or so it seemed sometimes. Almost anything was better than pity.

He watched Jules, hoping he'd pause near the guy at the end of the block and get a balloon stuck on his nose. But it didn't happen.

Donnie rotated his wrist and glanced at his watch. There was plenty of time to drive back to Julep and make it to his job at Circe.

He sat for a while longer on the bench, soaking up the sun, listening to "Night Train."

Over and over.

Pitiful.

12

Donnie hadn't eaten lunch, so he stopped on Royale on his way out of the Quarter. Since he didn't want to take time to go in someplace and sit down, he bought a frankfurter with sauerkraut and a can of iced tea from a vendor pushing a cart that was shaped like a hot dog on a bun.

He ate and drank as he drove. It was on Highway 10, headed north out of New Orleans, that he glanced in his rearview mirror and noticed the black van with tinted windows gaining on him.

About three car lengths behind the Honda, the van's speed dropped off to the same as Donnie's.

Donnie took the Honda up to seventy-five and held it there. The van followed suit. The distance between the two vehicles didn't vary.

Donnie ducked slightly and adjusted the mirror to get a better look at the van as the highway curved. It was a jet-black Ford Windstar. An odd thing about it was that not only were the side windows tinted, the driver was also only an indistinct form visible when tall vehicles passing in the other direction momentarily cast shade on the van.

He held his speed while he thought. So he'd been followed into New Orleans. His phone line had been cleared, so someone had been watching his apartment. Upon entering New Orleans, Donnie had routinely gone through a series of maneuvers he was sure would have shaken anyone tailing him. Which meant the van's driver must have lost him, then picked him up again, most likely in the Quarter when he'd stopped and bought the hot dog on Royale. Probably he hadn't seen Donnie seated on the bench in Jackson Square and talking to Jules. And even if he had, the conversation wouldn't have seemed so unusual, two strangers passing the time of day. Donnie smiled slightly. He was glad now that Jules had worn the sunglasses and beret.

This business with the black van tailing him so obviously was most likely a show of strength, Donnie decided. Something to let him know that when he was working for Circe his off time wasn't really his. He was on a leash.

Donnie slowed the Honda, hoping the van driver would give up the game and pass him.

Didn't happen. The van slacked off speed and held its distance behind the Honda.

Donnie made a point of looking back over his shoulder, then took the car back up to seventy-five, then eighty miles per hour. The Honda's engine remained smooth and made a low snarling sound as if to let Donnie know it had plenty of power left if it was called on.

The van stuck with him as if he were towing it.

He didn't go any faster. It wouldn't do to reveal

the old car's real capabilities. They might be needed as a surprise someday.

He dropped back to the speed limit and pretended to ignore the persistent black van, still following him slightly too close to be safe.

When Donnie was off the federal highway and on the state road to Julep, the van suddenly began growing larger in his rearview mirror.

Donnie started to stomp on the accelerator to avoid being rammed, when the van put on a surprising burst of speed for such a large vehicle, swung hard to the left, and roared past the Honda.

It slowed then, forcing Donnie to brake the Honda to a corresponding speed. Time for a new kind of game, Donnie thought, with a tight grip on the steering wheel.

The speedometer needle didn't waver at fifty as Donnie tailed the van at about four car lengths. The vehicle's wide back window was tinted almost as black as the van's exterior. He could see nothing inside. The van might as well have been empty. He noticed the license plate, conveniently splattered with mud so the numbers were unreadable.

Both vehicles slowed a few miles an hour going into a curve. The van's dark bulk glided smoothly to Donnie's right as it began its gradual turn. Donnie nudged the steering wheel to the right to follow.

Then suddenly the van was no longer in front of him.

Neither was the road.

The graveled shoulder, a shallow embankment,

and green field and trees were his view out of the windshield.

He realized with a jump of his heart that the Honda's front wheels had turned but the car hadn't. It was still going straight. Off the road!

He kept his composure, pressured the brake pedal, and yanked the steering wheel harder right. Left, right, right again. Nothing he did mattered. He was traveling straight and at the same speed.

Even strapped in as he was, Donnie felt his buttocks rise from the seat, then slam back down. He was completely off the road, bouncing off the gravel shoulder, then over the green field of tall grass. More violent bouncing. Without his seat belt to hold him in, he would have been ricocheting all over the car.

He fought the steering wheel and felt a sluggish response this time. Branches scraped the car, and a tree trunk flashed past only inches from his side window.

More trees!

Donnie swallowed the lump in his throat and braked and steered with ever fiber of strength in him, concentrating with a cold core at the center of his terror.

A thick branch howled against steel on the passenger-side door. The car slid left, just missing a cluster of saplings, almost turned over, then righted itself so hard that despite being belted in, Donnie bounced off the seat and rammed his head on the inside of the roof. The cloth headliner didn't provide much in the way of padding.

Then the car nosed down like an airplane trying to go into a steep power drive.

The rear end rose.

Fell.

Bounced twice.

Donnie felt himself hurled forward against the constraining safety belt, his lower chest inches from the steering wheel. If the old car had been equipped with an air bag it would have exploded outward and knocked the wind from him.

He fell back hard, slamming into the seat on the rebound.

Sat there with his heart hammering, realizing the car had finally stopped.

Shaking, his head throbbing painfully from hitting the steel roof, Donnie climbed out of the car.

He was standing in knee-high grass and about six inches of mud. The car might have stopped, but the world seemed to have continued in motion around him. Nauseated as well as dizzy from his wild ride, he leaned with an elbow against the warm steel of the roof. Squinting in the bright sunlight, he peered down the road to see if the van might be coming back.

There was no sign of it. A truck passed without slowing, and he realized he'd driven far enough off the road that people in passing vehicles wouldn't notice him. It was an infrequently traveled road anyway at this time of day. Which meant he was stranded at least for a while. Even stopping a car and asking for its driver to phone for a tow truck, then waiting for the tow, would take a long time.

He slogged around to the back of the Honda and looked down at the rear wheels mired in the mud.

Then he opened the trunk and surveyed what there was in it that might help him.

Not much. The spare tire looked good in case he had a flat, and there was a jack and a lug wrench. The jack wouldn't help him to get the car free in this soft surface. It would simply sink to the level of the car.

He got back in the Honda, restarted the engine, and gently rocked the car between low gear and reverse.

About all he accomplished was making a lot of noise. The front drive wheel simply spun this way, then that, and settled deeper in the mud.

As Donnie sat back in frustration, he noticed his 9 mm lying on the floor on the passenger side. It must have come loose from where he had it tucked in his belt at the small of his back when he was jouncing all over the place in the car. As he picked it up and slid it back beneath his belt, concealed by his untucked shirttail, he knew what his next move should be if he was going to have any chance of getting the Honda back on the road sometime soon.

Leaning down and to the side, he lifted the faded red rubber floor mats and climbed out of the car with them. He wedged one beneath the drive wheel, then laid the second mat end-to-end with it. If he could baby the wheel up onto the dry rubber, he might be able to make it out of the mud. He knew he'd have only one chance; then the mats themselves would be coated with mud and too slippery to provide traction. The Honda didn't weigh much, so the trick would be to get it up in its tracks and moving. Then maybe he could gain some momentum and drive it back onto the road's gravel shoulder.

He'd just wedged the dry rubber mats in place when a loud crash startled him.

He straightened up and turned to see a blue Volvo crumpled against the large tree he'd barely missed when he went off the road.

Listening to the suction sound of his shoes sloshing through the mud, Donnie trudged laboriously toward the wrecked car.

As he got closer he could hear the hiss of escaping pressure. Steam was rising from beneath what was left of the hood. The car's interior was draped with deflated air bags. The windshield and side windows in front were shattered.

A small, balding man had the driver-side door open and was easing himself out from the cushions of limp, deflated air bags.

Free of the car, he stood bent over in the manner of someone trying to touch his toes, gingerly feeling his legs as if to reassure himself they were still there.

"You okay?" Donnie asked.

Surprised, the man looked sharply at him but didn't straighten up.

"I think so." His voice was shaky.

Donnie saw a burn on the man's thin wrist where the escaping gases of the air bag had seared his flesh. He didn't seem to notice the minor injury. Now he was feeling his face, and there was the brilliant red of blood in the sunlight.

Donnie stepped closer and looked. The facial injuries weren't serious, a number of cuts and scratches around the eyes and the bridge of the nose.

"I was wearing sunglasses," the man said. "Air bag shoved them into my face."

"It doesn't look bad," Donnie said, "but maybe you oughta sit down."

"No, no, I'm fine." The man leaned back against his totaled Volvo. "Don't know what happened. I just was driving along. Then the road curved and the car didn't."

"Wait here," Donnie said. "I wanna go check something out."

He slogged back to the road, then walked along the gravel shoulder to the curve where he'd lost control behind the black van.

It wasn't much of a curve, but on the pavement was a light film of liquid. Donnie crouched low, touched his finger to it, and knew immediately that it was oil. The van had been equipped to lay down a film of oil behind it and had deliberately transformed the gentle curve into a death trap.

Well, not quite.

Donnie was sure the play wasn't meant to kill him but to illustrate that he lived only at the whim of the people who controlled him. And if he *had* happened to collide with a tree and maybe hit his head just so and died, it would have been no great loss. . . . Maybe this was standard indoctrination for new Circe employees since the infiltration by Frank Allan and Lily.

He walked back to the Volvo to offer to drive its owner somewhere so he could get help, but the man had already retrieved a cell phone from his car and was talking on it.

As Donnie approached, he finished with the phone

and laid it on the Volvo's front seat. "I've got help coming," he said, then smiled. "Roadside service is a great thing to have in your warranty." He extended his right hand. "I'm Sam Rollins."

Donnie shook his hand. "Don Wells."

Rollins glanced toward the road, where Donnie had just come from, and said, "What the hell happened?"

"Oil on the road," Donnie told him. He didn't tell him how it had gotten there. "It makes steering through the curve almost impossible."

"Damned dangerous," Rollins said. "Somebody else is liable to go into a skid. I've got some warning flares in the trunk, if we can get it open."

The Volvo's trunk opened easily enough, and Donnie and Rollins walked back to the road and set three of the flares out to warn drivers away from the spilled oil.

Donnie thought about waiting with Rollins for the tow truck, but instead enlisted Rollins's help and tried to break the Honda loose from the mud by using the mats.

It might not have worked without Rollins pushing like crazy as the Honda made its way up out of its ruts, then through the grass and mud back to the road.

Donnie thanked the winded Rollins, told him the muddy rubber mats were his if he wanted them, then continued the drive to Julep.

The rest of the way to town, he kept an eye out for the black van but didn't see it.

There was no guarantee whoever was in it didn't see him.

13

"You're goddamn late," Mitki said, when Donnie arrived at Circe an hour past starting time.

The big Russian was dressed in another expensive tracksuit, this one maroon and white, same gold neck chains thick enough that maybe they should have anchors on them.

Nordo was climbing into a gray Lincoln to park it and winked at Donnie.

"I'm asking why you're late," Mitki said.

"Some asshole who didn't know how to drive ran me off the road," Donnie said, taking the steps past Mitki and continuing toward the locker room.

"See it don't happen again!" Mitki called after him. Maybe he was miffed. Donnie hoped so.

"It won't," Donnie called over his shoulder. "Guy as stupid as that can't have long to live."

Mitki was nowhere in sight when Donnie, clad now in his sharply pressed tan parking-valet uniform, returned to the portico.

The temperature had gone up to about ninety, and the fetid breeze that came off the swamp beyond the trees only made Donnie hotter. There wasn't much in the way of shade other than beneath the portico roof or close alongside the kiosk. Already Donnie could feel dampness building up around the back of his collar and beneath the arms of the valet uniform.

Nordo was walking back from having parked another car. He ducked into the kiosk to hang the key on the board, then wandered over to Donnie. The only cool thing in all that Louisiana heat, he was wearing his crooked, smart-ass-kid grin, as if he belonged in a movie about growing up in Brooklyn.

"That Mitki," he said, "dresses like a bad dream outta the seventies or something, don't he? Like, don't he know fat guys just don't look good in sweat suits?"

"Maybe he's training for a marathon," Donnie said. "Gonna work some of the lard off."

Nordo laughed. "Marathon ass-kicking's all he trains for. From what I can see, he does a lotta beating on people, and Bolt must know about it and approve."

"What is it you see?" Donnie asked, fishing.

"Huh?"

"You said, 'From what I can see.' "

"Bruises all over me," Nordo said through a grin.

A blue Caddy with gold trim and hubcaps, containing four gray-haired women, turned into the long drive and stopped under the portico roof. The car's engine was idling smoothly, sounding something like *money-money-money*, and the gleaming steel hood ticked in the heat.

"Somebody rich musta died, man," Nordo said softly to Donnie.

"Happens every day," Donnie told him. "Maybe someday it'll be you."

"If it is, my old lady'll be inheriting a red Ferrari convertible."

Donnie would have told him tastes change, but thought it was time to get to work.

He walked over and opened the Caddy's front then rear doors for the two on the car's right side. Then he walked around the car and handed the driver, who'd already gotten out with the third passenger, her parking ticket stub.

The four women paid little attention to him, talking animatedly and interrupting one another as they moved toward the club entrance. A couple of thousand dollars' worth of clothes on their backs, Donnie figured, watching them disappear into the dimness beyond the doors.

Not to mention the jewelry. They didn't look like criminals. Plenty of clean money as well as dirty must move through Circe.

He parked the Caddy toward the end of Row B, locked it, and turned to walk back to the kiosk. That was when he noticed the black Windstar van in the shade of a tree at the edge of the lot.

He glanced around, then walked over to the van. The license plate still had strategically placed mud on it to conceal the numbers, and the windshield was tinted almost as dark as the side glass. There was no doubt it was the same van.

With another look around, Donnie very gently tried to open a door.

The van was locked. Might have an alarm system. He'd better be cautious here.

Looking toward the club, he saw Nordo leaning with a hand against the kiosk, gazing the other way and smoking a cigarette. Donnie went around to the rear of the van, got close enough to shield light with his hand, and tried to peer in through the tinted back window.

Heat came off the glass at him. Dim inside. Probably nothing unusual to see, anyway.

He got down in push-up position, careful to stay on his hands and toes and not dirty his uniform, and lowered himself until he could peer beneath the van.

Nothing unusual to see there, either.

Squatting behind the van, he reached beneath it and ran his hand over dirt-coated steel. He felt a slight protuberance, withdrew his hand, and saw that his fingers were coated with oil.

Some additional exploring revealed four more such valves placed along the rear of the van's undercarriage, well back so no oil that sprayed out of them would get on its rear tires. So there was a container inside, probably concealed beneath the floor, with lines running to the valves. If that much trouble had been gone to in order to install the oil-spraying system, it was undoubtedly controlled by the driver, maybe a switch out of sight beneath the dashboard. Donnie guessed the container was filled from inside the van and was pressurized. Pressure would be maintained with a service-station air hose, the way you'd keep your spare tire properly inflated.

The setup was something to know about if there was ever a reason to give chase to the van.

Donnie was getting warm and his thighs were starting to ache from squatting. He wiped most of the oil from his fingers on the right rear tire, then straightened up and rubbed his hands together as he strode back toward the portico.

Mitki was standing there in the shade, facing the other way with his fists on his hips and talking to a man in a gray suit. Donnie was pretty sure he hadn't been seen snooping around the van, but there was no way to be certain. He guessed he was meant to see the vehicle anyway, or it wouldn't have been parked there. What good was a near-death-experience warning if you didn't know who'd almost killed you?

When Donnie came out of the kiosk after hanging the Caddy key on the board, the man in the gray suit had gone into the club and Mitki was alone. Nordo was off parking another car.

"Job for you," Mitki said, "if you think you can manage it without having another accident."

"Today was the first accident I had in years," Donnie said. "It'll probably be more years before I have another."

"Well, you haven't been doing a lot of driving these past years, unless you been going ten feet this way, eight feet that." Mitki raised the heels of his jogging shoes from the ground and bounced slightly on the balls of his feet, as if getting ready to take a run at a high-jump bar. Big guy feeling frisky on a sunny day; wouldn't it be great to find something alive to tear apart? The gold chains clanked and caught the sunlight. "The boss told me to have you drive into New Orleans and pick up some people, bring them here." He came down off the balls of his feet and handed Donnie a folded sheet of paper. "Here's the addresses, in the order you're supposed to follow picking them up. Street map and keys are in the limo. These are important people, Wells. Don't fuck this up."

Donnie nodded, accepted the paper, and tucked it into a back pocket.

"What's that all over your hands?" Mitki asked. He'd taken a cigar from a pocket and paused in stripping away its cellophane wrapper.

Donnie looked down at his stained hands as if in surprise. "Oh. That's dirt or grease. There was something all over the steering wheel of that last car I parked. I tried to get most of it off the wheel so the driver wouldn't figure it happened here."

"Our employees don't have grease under their fingernails, not ever."

"I told you—"

"Shit. You told me shit. It don't matter what you tell me, Wells. All that matters is what *I* tell *you*. Clean hands. That's the goddamn rule."

"I'll go wash it off before I leave," Donnie said.

Mitki grinned. "Fuckin'-a-right, you will."

He was still grinning as he walked away, concentrating again on unwrapping his cigar.

Cat and mouse, thought Donnie the mouse.

There were three addresses, all in the Garden District. Donnie used New Orleans's crisscross of downtown avenues and heavy traffic on Canal to pretend to be lost, peering around as if looking for street signs or anything familiar, actually driving through yellow lights and along one-way streets to make sure he'd shaken anyone who might be following him.

He'd learned all the tricks involved in shaking a possible tail when you were driving, and invented some of his own. It was a skill he'd known would be invaluable in keeping him alive, and he could be confident at times that he wasn't being observed. As confident as possible, anyway. Donnie knew exactly where the addresses were in the Garden District, and he could continue his "I got lost" act if necessary when he got back to Circe.

Which meant he'd manufactured a little spare time for himself. He goosed the limo out ahead of slower traffic and made a left turn.

Near one of the big hotels just outside the Quarter, where there were a lot of similar limos, he parked and went into the lobby of the hotel across the street. In an alcove around the corner from the registration desk, he found the public phones and used one to call Jules Donavon.

After filling in Jules on the day's activities and warning him about the oil-spewing black van, Donnie asked if there were any new developments.

"Nordo," Jules said. "His real name is Nicholas Dominick Nordano. One arrest and conviction three years ago for dealing drugs. Small-time. He sold a few joints to an undercover narc at a party and accepted money from him to cover his expenses. Didn't even make a profit."

"Jail time?"

"Naw. Probation for a year. First and only offense, and he was barely twenty-one. Kid stuff. Been a perfect angel ever since."

"Far as we know," Donnie said.

"Here's the interesting thing about him," Jules went on. "He's the nephew of Vito Cantanzano."

"Rings a bell."

"Should. Cantanzano was high in the New Orleans Mafia and was one of the few capos who managed to live a full and destructive life, then retire—inasmuch as they ever really retire."

Now Donnie remembered. "Numbers. Prostitution. Drugs. Protection. Murder."

"The whole menu," Jules said.

"My God, Jules, that was a long time ago. He must be a hundred years old."

"Maybe. We've got him down as eighty-six. Nick Nordano—Nordo—is the son of his younger sister Maria and her husband, Rico. Rico has a clean sheet and is half owner of a Ford dealership in Metairie. Far as we can tell, he's straight. Spoiled this kid Nordo, then sent him off to college. But sending Nordo to college is like sending a handball up against a wall. He gets in trouble and bounces right back where he came from. Usually it's because of his grades, but also he drives like he's on fire. One of those kids in love with fast, expensive cars. After four universities, Nordo worked for a while washing cars at the Ford dealership, then quit and bounced around a while at other odd jobs. Wound up at Circe parking fast, expensive cars."

"Sounds like an inevitable journey," Donnie said.

"Yeah. Maybe he's just what he seems."

"Nobody's that, Jules."

But Donnie had to admit Nordo sure seemed to be nothing more than a typical airheaded kid with a lot of growing up to do. Since he loved cars, there was every reason to figure he'd wind up parking them someplace where the best and fastest were to be found. And in and around Julep, that was at the Circe club.

"Gotta go, Jules," Donnie said. "Time to pick up my high rollers for the limo ride to Circe."

"After you get there, remember to be careful. Don't get taken for a limo ride yourself."

Jules hadn't said it as if he were joking. Donnie didn't think it was a joke, either.

14

Donnie jockeyed the long white limo through downtown New Orleans traffic to Magazine Street, then cut over to St. Charles, where wooden streetcars still clattered along carrying passengers to and from the French Quarter.

He easily found the addresses Mitki had given him. They were all in the Garden District. Two of them belonged to hundred-year-old mansions that were well kept and managed to turn the patina of age into an asset.

A handsome, fiftyish guy in a silky gray suit had gotten into the limo at the first stop. Harcourt Lineback, according to the itinerary Mitki had given Donnie.

The second stop was an antebellum, cream-colored clapboard structure almost totally concealed behind close groupings of magnolia trees. Donnie parked in the circular drive, and almost as soon as he tapped lightly on the horn, one Mrs. Wilhemina Jones emerged from the place and flounced down the porch steps. Despite her energy and motion, she was well into her sixties, with thinning gray hair and wearing a yellow-and-brown dress with a skirt that had lots of swishy folds. Pearls encircled her neck, bracelets jangled on both wrists, and she seemed to have more rings than fingers. Donnie thought she could have used some sequins. She said hello to Lineback as if she knew him. Dedicated gamblers were thick as thieves.

As he drove to his third and last stop, Donnie could hear his two passengers chatting in the back of the limo but couldn't understand what they were saying.

The last address was that of a house that had been grander than the others but was now in serious disrepair and apparently had been partitioned into apartments. It reminded Donnie of his own apartment in Julep.

His passenger was waiting in the foyer and came out the front door even before Donnie had a chance to tap the horn. George Stopps was this guy's name. He was about fifty, balding, and portly, and unmistakably smelled of bourbon.

"Three lemonsh tonight," he said to Donnie, as Donnie held one of the limo's rear doors open for him. Donnie almost asked him if he meant himself and the other two passengers. "The shlot machines are my friendsh tonight," Stopps slurred to his fellow travelers. "I'm Shtoppsh, I'm lucky, and I'm ready. Tonight there'll be no shtopping Shtoppsh."

"You're wobbly, stinking drunk, and I hope you lose the fillings in your teeth," Donnie heard Wilhemina Jones tell Stopps matter-of-factly, as he shut the door to walk around the car and get back in behind the steering wheel.

Nobody talked much the rest of the way out to Circe.

"How'd they tip?" Nordo asked, after Donnie had let his passengers out at the entrance, then walked back after parking the limo.

"They tipped large, like you said," Donnie told him, and stuffed four twenties and two fives into the tip jar in the kiosk.

"High rollers," Nordo said, eyeing the money. "Love 'em!"

Around midnight Lineback and Wilhemina Jones came out of the club together, and Donnie drove them back into New Orleans and dropped them off at their homes. They were talkative and cheerful. Donnie thought he heard Lineback say he'd won over five thousand dollars at blackjack. He tipped Donnie with a fifty-dollar bill when he left the limo.

Not to be outdone, Wilhemina Jones matched the tip as she stepped from the limo onto the cracked concrete driveway of her house behind the magnolias. Donnie thanked her and waited until she'd gotten inside and flashed the porch light before he put the limo in gear and drove away.

Back at Circe, Nordo told him that Stopps's wife had arrived and taken him home in their tan '99 Lincoln Town Car. Nordo seemed to notice and recollect the year, make, and color of every car he saw.

"Asshole was drunk," Nordo said. "Puked his guts

up in the bushes right over there while the missus sat in the car and rolled her eyes. Pathetic sight, man."

"He was already soused when I picked him up earlier in New Orleans," Donnie said.

Nordo shook his head and flashed a look of concern. "Fucking booze'll kill you. Guy'd have fewer problems if he'd smoke weed and lay off alcohol."

"Like you?" Donnie asked.

Nordo grinned. "Fucking right on," he said, and chucked Donnie under the chin with his forefinger. Made Donnie bite his tongue. Donnie wondered if Nordo would live to see age twenty-five.

He let Nordo park the next car that arrived, a sleek green Jaguar. It was fun watching Nordo stall until the driver had disappeared inside the club before he gunned the Jag's engine and made an unnecessary detour along the lot's perimeter before parking.

By the time Donnie got back to Julep that night and opened his apartment door, he was ready to sleep for about ten hours.

What he wasn't ready for was what happened, which was Donnie switching on the light and seeing that two uninvited guests were waiting for him.

They'd probably been waiting a while. Both their suit coats were carefully draped over the back of a chair. They were both wearing dark slacks and white dress shirts with ties that were too wide to be fashionable.

One of them, about six-foot-four and two hundred and fifty pounds, was standing leaning against a wall with his hands stuffed in his pants pockets. He was easily sixty years old but he looked fit enough to play pro football. The other was skinny and tall, though probably not much over six feet. It was difficult to judge his height because he was lounging on Donnie's bed like a pinup model, propped up on one elbow with his hand supporting his head. He was grinning toothily at Donnie and chewing a huge wad of gum with his mouth open so you could see it. He had thick blond hair well oiled and combed straight back, and was probably in his forties.

Neither man said anything. No sound in the room other than chewing gum popping as the lounger on the bed worked his jaw and grinned.

"Least you coulda done was take your shoes off," Donnie told the lounger, glancing at the man's boat-sized black wing tips gouging into the bedspread.

"Fuck you," the lounger said through his grin.

"Excuse him," the larger, upright thug said to Donnie. "He's short on manners. It's his one human failing, so excuse him."

"Fuck you," the lounger said to his apologetic partner. Lots of gum popping. Insolent as a teenager.

"It don't cost you anything to be polite," the huge man pointed out, unperturbed.

"Who are you guys?" Donnie asked.

"We're the ones that're here to take you for a ride," said the lounger on the bed. He scrunched his shoes around, deliberately making more smudges on the spread.

"A ride?" Donnie asked, remembering his conversation with Jules earlier that evening.

"A ride," confirmed the lounger. "Like in *Godfather Sixteen.*"

"Forget about it," Donnie said. "I saw that movie."

He hadn't noticed the apologetic giant, who'd been leaning against the wall, drift over until he was beside and a little behind him. Got a glimpse of what looked like a brown leather sap as it arced through the air to smack him hard behind the left ear.

"Excuse him," he heard the lounger say.

Donnie found himself facedown on the rough carpet, fighting to stay conscious and losing.

Old coiled springs squealed, and he was vaguely aware of the lounger getting up from the bed, then leaning close over him.

The strong, warm scent of spearmint.

The last thing Donnie heard as the darkness came was the rapid popping of chewing gum.

15

By the time they were down in the street, Donnie had regained consciousness, but his head still throbbed and he was groggy.

Their car was a gleaming black Cadillac with fins. It had to be an antique, but it still might have been manufactured yesterday. Donnie settled into the soft upholstery in back, the big man beside him, and marveled that the vehicle even had that new-car smell people always talked about.

"Some wheels," he said.

The monster in the suit beside him grunted.

The Caddy settled lower and pulled away from the curb fast, pressing Donnie back in the seat.

"She'll do a hundred before you can blink," said the lounger, who was driving. "And she's bulletproof."

"It's reassuring nobody can shoot us," Donnie said.

"We was, to be truthful, thinkin' more in terms of a bullet not gettin' out," the big man said. As he spoke he poked Donnie's ribs with what felt enough like a gun barrel to be taken seriously.

"Some people see bullets as clues," said the lounger, taking a corner fast enough to make the giant Caddy list like an ocean liner. "Ballistical science can match grooves from different barrels, identify the make of gun or the gun itself, even pick up fingerprints from when the gun was loaded."

"Not good to leave bullets layin' around," said the big one.

"There oughta be a law," Donnie said.

They drove west out of town, then made several turns, and Donnie lost all sense of direction in the dark. After about half an hour they were on a road running through dense woods. Donnie stole occasional glances out the window and saw gates and driveways that belonged to obviously expensive homes set back among the trees.

Finally the car slowed, then turned in on one of the drives and braked to a halt. After waiting for an iron gate to glide open, the lounger stepped on the gas and the Caddy accelerated smoothly along a winding drive bordered with tall pine trees and parked in front of what looked like an immense English manor house.

"What's all this about?" Donnie asked.

The giant said nothing. The lounger caught Donnie's eye in the rearview mirror, grinned, chewed, popped gum, and said, "I give up. What's it all about?"

When they climbed out of the parked car, Donnie got a better look at the house in the moonlight. It had a traditional stone foundation that gave way to red brick that reached halfway up the structure, then turned into yellow stucco beamed with rough-hewn wood and became English Tudor. There was room for more than one architectural style. The place was grand in a funky way and seemed to take up a little more ground than a football stadium. Ivy had climbed two-thirds of the way up the front wall, then fell in slender, brownish shoots away from the stucco as if it had weakened from lack of oxygen at such a height. What seemed like scores of window all had canvas awnings. Off to the left was a gleaming white frame guesthouse next to a lake. The main house's roof and endless dormers and gables blocked out much of the star-dotted night sky. To say the house was vast was an understatement.

"Parliament meet here?" Donnie asked, showing the bastards he wasn't afraid. Much.

"Such a wiseass," said the skinny lounger. *Pop*! went the spearmint gum. "I kinda like him."

"Shame," commented the burly one.

Isolated as the house was, there was no reason to conceal the gun. The big man removed it from his suit coat pocket and pointed it at Donnie, knowing his business and staying just far enough away that Donnie couldn't make a grab for it or suddenly rush inside the length of his arm and the barrel. The gun was a huge antique semiautomatic that could blow Donnie in half.

"Walk," said the gunman, given to monosyllables now that they'd arrived at their destination. He motioned with the oversize handgun.

The lounger, staying well off to the side, saw Donnie glance at him and opened his coat wide and held it to flash the checked butt of a gun stuck in his belt. Grinned a "way ahead of you" grin. That was okay; Donnie wasn't planning on doing anything sudden. Not at this point. He'd sized up these two as pros. Everybody here had seen the moves and knew the odds.

The lounger sprinted ahead and opened one of the ten-foot-tall front doors.

"In," said the big man.

In they went.

The place looked like the inside of a plushly furnished British hunting lodge. There was plenty of overstuffed brown leather furniture, a massive fireplace, trophy animal heads mounted on two walls. A deer, a leopard, a moose, and what was surely a bison gazed balefully down at Donnie with dark glass eyes as if wondering how it had come to this. On the other two walls were oil paintings of fox or game-bird hunting scenes.

"Know who lives here?" the lounger said.

"Hemingway?" Donnie ventured.

"He's dead," the big one said.

"Two syllables," Donnie said. "You're making progress."

"Know what I think?" asked the lounger through his grin. He chewed mechanically for a while, moving the wad of gum around with his tongue. When Donnie didn't answer, he said, "What I think is that you're wising off to try and impress on us that you ain't scared. But I think you're scared, all right."

"If you were going to kill me you wouldn't have brought me here," Donnie said.

The lounger backed away a step and appeared shocked. "Kill you? Nobody mentioned anything like that. We never intended to kill you. The thought never entered our minds yet."

"Kill him?" said a tall man who had just entered the room. He was wearing some kind of blue-and-red silk robe over a white shirt and dark pin-striped pants, and had on shiny black shoes. His deeply lined face was long and thin, with a pointed chin, downward-arced slash of a mouth so nearly lipless it resembled a knife scar, and sorrowful brown eyes. He looked more as if he were in his seventies than eighties, wasted by time but still large because of his frame. "What makes him think somebody's gonna kill him?"

"Hemingway," said the big man with the huge gun.

The old man raised gray eyebrows. "The writer guy?"

"The same," said the lounger.

"Hmph!" said the old man to nobody in particular. "Siddown," he said to Donnie.

Donnie did, in a large leather armchair that hissed and enveloped him in a way he didn't like. It eagerly accepted his bulk as if it had been waiting for him for a long time.

The old man sat on a matching brown leather sofa opposite him, crossed his legs in an oddly prim fashion, and studied him. The other two men lurked unobtrusively in the background like well-trained waiters or killers.

Donnie looked around and said, "You must like British things."

"The British got class," said the old man solemnly.

"That's their system," said the lounger in the background. "Class system."

The old man seemed not to have heard him. But he did say to Donnie, "The large man behind me is Army. The skinny chap with the mouth is Frankie Fayne."

"I can see why his nickname's Army," Donnie said, glancing at the huge man, who was now holding the gun tight to his thigh.

"That's his real name," the old man on the couch said. "My real name is Vito Cantanzano. That ring any kinda bell with you?"

"It doesn't sound British," Donnie said.

Vito grinned and looked over his shoulder at Frankie. "This bloke could keep up with you when it comes to smart-mouth remarks, Frankie."

"He's trying not to be scared," Frankie said.

"Sure. Can you blame him?"

"I could blame him for everything that ever happened to me," Frankie said.

"Maybe later," Vito told him. Glancing again at Donnie: "Did Mr. Wells give you any problems about comin' here?"

"Docile as a newborn infant," Army told him.

"How do you know my name?" Donnie asked, playing along.

Vito regarded him with eyes about as expressive as those of the mounted animal heads on the walls.

"We know lots about you. And we know things you should know."

"Oh?" Playing the innocent. "About what?"

"A bank was robbed in Buffalo seven years ago. Asshole who held it up carjacked a woman's minivan outside the place to get away. He ran over her after throwin' her outta the van."

"Vicious chap," Donnie said.

"The story mean anything to you?"

"He should have kept her for a hostage," Donnie said.

"You mean *you* shoulda."

"I wasn't anywhere near Buffalo seven years ago." The real Wells would say that one way or the other, Donnie figured. He was sure there was nothing in his information on Wells about a bank robbery where a woman was run over and killed.

"No, it's true, you weren't," Vito said. "But you were on the run an' alone at that time after another bank job in another city. Nobody really knows where you were. Bloody hell, *you* probably don't remember where you were."

Donnie didn't like the direction this was taking. "So?"

Vito shrugged elaborately and grinned. "So you were in Buffalo."

"Shuffled off to," said Frankie the Lounger.

Nobody seemed to notice.

"A man like me," Vito said, "with connections, I can easily put you in Buffalo at the time of that bank robbery. I can put you in the bank. I can make the gun traceable to you. I can put you in the room where they give lethal injections."

"You must have *some* connections."

"Do you believe that I can do that?" Vito asked earnestly.

Army was frowning at Donnie. The lounger had stopped chewing and was grinning in anticipation. Donnie knew how he'd be persuaded to believe Vito if he weren't already convinced.

"I think I do believe you," he said.

Vito nodded. "Splendid. It's important you know, you fuck with me and you'll surely come to grief." He got a pack of Camels from his pocket and with a quick, practiced motion stuck an unfiltered cigarette between his lips. "You smoke?"

"Not anymore," Donnie said, recalling that Wells had quit three years ago.

"It's kept me alive," Vito said, picking up a small bust of Winston Churchill from the heavy walnut table alongside the sofa. Churchill's head snapped back and a flame appeared. When Churchill was back on the table, Vito puffed contentedly and smiled at Donnie. "Now that we agree you were in that bank, we need to chat."

"In front of Frick and Frack?" Donnie asked, motioning with a thumb in the direction of Army and Frankie.

"Sure. They been with me a long time, and I trust them like I would my late sainted mother. They got their faults but they're honorable buggers."

Donnie, seeing that Vito was serious, said, "Good enough for me."

"I was at one time more active in what you might call business," Vito said. He leaned back farther in the sofa and took a deep drag on his cigarette. Smiled in a way almost sensuous. Here was a man who genuinely enjoyed smoking. "One of my interests was a certain club with a casino attached. When I sold that interest a few years ago to people who the orga— who someone I trust vouched for, I thought I had no worries. And I didn't. But what I got now is questions."

"Part of life, questions," Donnie said.

"Part of death, being a smart-ass," said the lounger.

"Such as," Vito said, through another cloud of smoke, "what the fuck is goin' on out there at Circe, old sport? The new owners, they redecorated everything an' enlarged the casino. They do a big business, but I got a suspicion there's somethin' more. I'm wonderin' what."

"Why?"

"No, what."

"I mean, why are you wondering?"

Vito smiled and nodded. "Smart as well as a smart-ass," he said. "In my position, even retired and in my golden years as it were, I need to be aware of what's goin' on around me. If somethin' don't ring true, I naturally wanna find out what's bloody wrong. Plus there's the stories I hear about some of the happenin's out at that place. And about things bein' found in the bog."

"Bog?"

"Swamp."

"Things?"

"Not livin' things."

Donnie figured Donnie Wells wouldn't be stupid about this. "You're scaring me, Mr. Cantanzano."

"Well, I just said you were smart. It ain't surprisin' you figured out you oughta be a tad ruffled."

"I gotta admit I have heard of you, but I thought you were—"

"No, I ain't. I'm just retired, is all. Still enjoyin' sex and cigarettes an' a good kidney pie. Not necessarily in that exact order, though."

"You look healthy, all right."

"Which it's my goal to stay."

Silence stretched not quite tight enough to break. The two men sat staring calmly at each other while Army and the lounger looked on.

At last Vito spoke. "You understand my meanin' in all of this, Don Wells?"

"People call me Donnie."

"So, does Donnie understand my meanin'?"

"Somewhat. But there isn't much I can tell you. I only been working the job out at Circe less than a week."

"Still, I got word you have a kinda insight into things."

Word from his nephew Nordo, Donnie figured. "Are you asking me to spy for you, Mr. Cantanzano?"

Vito blew a smoke ring and watched it drift toward the ceiling. "Askin'? I wouldn't say I'm askin'."

The lounger giggled.

Donnie thought it was time to bring it out into the open. "I've always been an independent operator, but I understand you don't say no to the Mafia."

"Not twice, generally," the lounger said.

This time Vito glared at him. "Frankie, do hold your tongue or I'll fuckin' cut it outta your head."

The lounger speeded up his gum chewing but obeyed and stood silently.

"That's right," Vito told Donnie. "You don't say no, an' you—meanin' me—don't ever really retire. I still got the connections. Got the big bite with the sharp teeth. You understand my meanin'?"

"Like the food chain," Donnie said.

"Uh-huh. I'm a shark and you're . . . whadda they call that stuff drifts in the ocean, old chap? Plaque, is it?"

"Plankton?"

"Yeah, that's it. Whales suck it in, whoosh, an' shit it out, wham! It can't get away, just like you. Little fuckin' particles, driftin' this way then that, ain't got a bloomin' chance. Just like you ain't, little fuckin' particle in the tides, this way an' that, movin' with the moon's attraction, whatever, you know? That clear?"

"How could it not be?"

"Good." Vito lit another cigarette from the stub of the first. "There's somethin' more I want you to do for me out at Circe," he said. "There's another employee out there, a kid. I want you to kinda look out for him. Nothin' obvious, but I want you should see that nothin' untoward happens to him." *Untoward.* That British thing was relentless.

"I'll need to know the bloke's name," Donnie lied.

"Name's Nicholas, goes by Nordo. He's a numb-brain, but if anything awful should occur to him out at that place, I would be mightily pissed off about it. I would act."

"Understood," Donnie said. "I know Nordo and like him."

"That's fine. An' needless to say, I don't want the lad to know about this conversation. It might shake his confidence."

"I doubt it," Donnie said.

"Well, maybe not. But he'd lose a certain amount of faith in me. I wouldn't like for that to happen."

"It won't because of anything I say," Donnie assured him.

"You got any questions?"

"One, is all. How come Nordo does this misplaced-love-child-from-the-sixties act, like he's just wandered outta Woodstock in a fog?"

Vito considered and nodded wisely, judging this to be a reasonable question. "His father was a fuckin' long-haired commie peacenik kinda bloke. Some of it rubbed off on Nordo, is all I can figure. Crept into the way he acts an' talks sometimes. A bit crackers, doncha think?"

"Uh-hmm."

"I'm hopin' the penny'll drop someday and he'll change, get some gumption an' backbone."

"Where's his father now?"

"Nicky's adopted. His present father of record runs a car dealership here in New Orleans. Mother of record is one of my sisters."

Donnie caught something in Vito's voice. "Your nephew Nordo was adopted by one of your sisters and her husband?"

"That's more or less what happened."

"Where's his real father? The peacenik bloke?"

"Ran off somewheres, I guess. Some time ago. Nobody's heard from him for years."

Donnie knew what that meant. "How about his real mom?" Donnie almost added *your other sister*, but caught himself.

"She was always a difficult kinda woman, an' not what you'd call a good mother. Not even a good family member. More the kind who got crazy ideas of her own. Always talked too much to the wrong people. Loved to travel an' was always goin' off on her own without tellin' anyone. She sorta just went travelin' an never came back. She's in the mountains, last I heard. Or maybe it's the seashore."

"Oh."

Vito shrugged. "But that's old family history, is all. Ancestral stuff every family's got. Like skeletons."

"In the closet?"

"Here an' there." Vito took a long drag on his fresh cigarette, then blew smoke out through his nose. "Army an' Frankie, they'll be around to see you now and then to sort of get reports about Circe. Nothin' in writin', you understand."

"Course not."

"You don't see them for a while, don't worry. They'll probably be seein' you."

"I won't worry about them," Donnie said. "They know how to make themselves at home."

"You want them to deliver you back to your place?"

"That'd be nice. It's a long hike just down the driveway to the road."

"We like the isolation out here," Vito said.

"So quiet you could hear a body drop," Frankie said, popping his gum.

"Does the lounger have to ride along?" Donnie asked.

Vito appeared puzzled, then smiled. "The lounger . . . I kinda like that. Frankie, Donnie here thinks you're a bloody lounger. One of them long chairs that fold up."

"That's what he'll do under stress," Donnie said, "fold up."

Vito laughed. "Oh, I don't think so. I know both my chaps here, an' they don't show the white feather. But you can call Frankie whatever you want, long as he don't object."

"I do," Frankie said.

"Don't matter," Vito told him. Then to Army: "See these two ruffians don't get into any kinda scuffle."

Without bothering to wait and see if Army had heard him, Vito stood up and walked slowly across the room.

"Everybody behave," he said at the doorway, without looking back. "Fuckin' behave."

Army moved closer, the big handgun at the ready. Donnie could see that the safety was off. Army stayed behind Donnie as the lounger opened the door and led the way through the cavernous hall and back outside where the car was parked.

"Sometime Mr. Cantanzano's gonna change his mind about that behaving remark, and that's when you're gonna find out what happens to wiseasses," the lounger said through his stuck-on grin.

"Is he really British?" Donnie asked. "Some kinda earl or something?"

"He's somethin', all right," Army said. "You're gonna find out what."

But Donnie already knew what. Despite the former Mafia capo's advanced age, Donnie didn't take Vito Cantanzano lightly. He remembered back more than ten years, the stories about a mass grave outside Baton Rouge. Nine dead bodies discovered in a landfill, none of them having died a natural death.

All of them with at least some slight connection to Vito Cantanzano, then the feared head of the Italian Mafia in southern Louisiana, confidant of Don Santo Trafficante, and reputed minor player in the JFK assassination.

Donnie knew the old man was far more dangerous than his two minions in the finned and floating Cadillac. He was in fact the force that held two thugs in check and lent some purpose to their meanness. He could do that not just because of what he was, but because of who he'd been and to some extent would always be. When the Caddy and Vito were young, they were both indeed something.

And it was obvious they both had plenty of miles left in them.

16

She wasn't throwing darts this time.

Friday evening Donnie followed coded instructions delivered in a phone call and met Sue Bristol at Other Rooms. She was seated alone in a booth along the wall, leaning forward with her elbow on the table, her chin cupped in her hand. She looked pensive.

The back of the lounge was occupied by half a dozen guys who looked like members of a work crew, drinking beer and gathered around the pool table, where two of them were playing what looked from a distance like eight ball. It was still early, and most of the customers and the noise in the place was around the pool table and at the far end of the bar. Peggy Lee was singing again. This time it was "Fever." Donnie decided somebody in the place had great taste in music.

"Corner pocket! Corner pocket!" one of the pool crowd shouted urgently.

"In your dreams!" somebody answered.

". . . when it sizzles . . ." Peggy was singing.

A glass and a bottle of Bass ale were in front of Sue. She was dressed in a yellow blouse and tight

Levi's. Her blond hair was pulled back tonight, held by an oversize, tiger-striped barrette.

When she noticed Donnie she sat up straighter, smiled, winked, and said, "Sit yourself down, sailor."

He slid into the booth to sit opposite her. "Am I the first tonight?" he asked, playing along.

"Not exactly. I had to chase three of those rednecks away. One of them offered to marry me."

"Think he was serious?"

"Dead serious. But not about marriage."

"It's probably the Peggy Lee," Donnie said.

"You better believe it."

A barmaid came over to the booth and Donnie ordered a Heineken. Sue ordered another Bass ale.

When they were both settled in with their drinks, Sue said, "They're with an oil rig crew."

"The pool shooters?"

"Yeah. That's what they told me. There are some working wells around here. Black liquid gold."

"Not just casino gold," Donnie said.

"That was my thought, but that's all it was—a thought."

She reached down on the seat beside her and lifted a small rectangular package wrapped with brown paper and secured with packing tape. Smiling, she placed it on the table in front of Donnie.

"A gift?" he asked.

"From Jules Donavon," she said. "From me, too, of course."

"You knew it was my birthday?"

"We knew it wasn't."

Donnie reached for the package.

"No need to open it here," she said.

He drew back his hand and stared at her. "What is it? A clock? A bomb? Slippers?"

"A plaster bust of Elvis Presley."

Donnie waited for more. There was no more. "You mean it?"

"Sure, I mean it."

"God! It's just what I always wanted!"

"It's pretty tacky. His upper lip is even curled."

"All the better."

"Another thing about it," she said in a softer voice, "is that if you broke it you'd find secured inside so they won't rattle a miniature recorder and body mike. The latest microtechnology. Donavon wanted you to have it, to use it when you thought the time was right. And by the way, the Elvis bust only looks like plaster; the stuff it's made of is practically unbreakable. You'll need a hammer to get inside. That way you won't get clumsy, knock it off the shelf, and have an embarrassing accident in front of the wrong party."

"I like that precaution," Donnie said. "And I have just the place for a bust of Elvis."

"Close by your Cabbage Patch dolls, I imagine." She peered closely at him over her glass of ale. "Are you really an Elvis fan?"

He nodded. " 'Hound Dog.' "

"It figures."

"You?"

"Huh?"

"An Elvis fan?"

"Not really. Oh, I like 'All Shook Up' a lot. I don't know why."

They both worked on their drinks. Donnie was trying to decide where the Elvis bust would look best in his apartment.

"You got anything for me?" Sue asked.

He glanced at her. "Fever all throoough the night," Peggy was singing.

"To take back to Jules, I mean."

He told her about his involuntary visit with Vito Cantanzano.

When he was finished, she sat back and stroked her chin thoughtfully, so delicately that her fingertips were barely touching flesh. Donnie had seen her do that before. He liked watching it. This was some woman.

"Things are getting kind of complex," she said. "They not only want you to spy for them, they want you to play bodyguard for Cantanzano's nephew."

"Yeah. But I'd be sort of bodyguarding Nordo anyway. He's a jerky kid who needs looking after. And whatever information I give Cantanzano and his obsolete enforcers shouldn't do much harm and might prompt some information in return. They play by rules so old they're prehistoric, but some of them still apply. Vito and his men might even prove useful somewhere along the line."

"You're talking about using the Italian Mafia as an ally," Sue said uneasily.

"They won't know it," Donnie pointed out.

She stared levelly at him with her wise blue eyes.

"I gotta tell you something, Donnie. You stay legal or you'll lose me on this."

"Legal is what I'm about," he assured her.

"There's some talk about you in the Bureau, mostly by assholes. The word is you go independent and play off the game board now and then."

He started to speak.

She raised a finger so he'd be quiet. "Think, now. Don't tell me you don't. Don't ever goddamn lie to me."

"What I was gonna say," he told her, "is that those assholes are jealous. They think undercover agents get all the press and glory anyway. And since I had the movie and books, then the *Falcone* TV series about me, it eats at them all the more that they're plain vanilla. If they understood long-term undercover they wouldn't feel that way. The way your own life somehow gets misplaced somewhere along the way."

"I know what it's like," she told him.

"That's why I mentioned it to you."

"I understand. What I'm saying is, if you do start playing with wild cards, I don't want to know about it."

"Your career," he said. "You have ambition."

"Something wrong with that?"

"No. I won't screw things up for you. Put you on the spot where you might have to lie."

"That's what I'm warning you about. Telling you straight-out up front. I won't lie for you and jeopardize my future, Donnie."

"You would, I bet. But you won't have to."

She laughed hopelessly and shook her head. "God-damn men!"

"We invented Bass ale," he pointed out.

"Oh, you've got a couple of accomplishments and interesting uses."

She kept saying things like that, keeping him off balance. Maybe they meant something. Or maybe she was more interested in his reaction than in him, reassuring herself that he was professional and disciplined enough not to take the bait. He hoped so. He wanted *her* to be as professional and disciplined as Jules had said. He thought he hoped so, anyway.

"Any news on the Marla Grant murder?" Donnie asked.

"None. The local law hasn't come up with anything, and the Bureau can't openly investigate her murder any more than we can Frank Allan's or Lily Maloney's. We don't want anyone at Circe to get a whiff of Bureau presence here in Julep."

"What about *your* presence?" he asked her. "I wouldn't describe you as unnoticeable."

"Which is why it's plausible that we'd be sitting here talking. Far as anyone knows, I'm just a lonely lady hanging around this place from time to time, and you're hot from prison and chatting me up."

"Easy to believe," Donnie admitted.

"If it's to our advantage," she said, "later on we can make it look as if you've scored. But it'll only look that way. Keep in mind this is all gonna be professional."

"Professional's what's kept me alive," he said.

"Uh-huh. That and staying legal." She leaned forward slightly and started to slide out of the booth. "I'll pass on to Donavon everything you told me. Anything else before we part?"

"No, that's it."

"I really did turn three of those oil crew rednecks away. Should I slap you in the face to make this conversation look like another failed pickup?"

"Not unless you want to get slapped back," he said. She wouldn't know he didn't mean it. Maybe she'd back off a few inches, stop ragging him.

She grinned as she stood up from the booth. "I'm liking you more and more."

Donnie wondered, What the hell am I dealing with here?

But Jules had vouched for her. Maybe she was a little odd. Maybe the job had made her that way. Maybe it had made him that way. He relaxed.

"When you leave here, don't forget Elvis," she cautioned him.

"Thanyouverymush," he told her.

She gave it a lot of hip swish as she strolled from the lounge. For the pool players, he guessed.

"Damn!" one of them said from back by the table. "How'd I miss that shot?"

17

"Dumb fuck," Mitki said to the man he'd just escorted from Circe.

Donnie and Nordo were standing near the kiosk. The man Mitki was gripping by the elbow and had just ejected was a pudgy guy of about forty with a jowly face and his receding red hair in a buzz cut.

Donnie remembered him arriving in a black BMW. He'd been drunk, barely able to stand when he climbed out from behind the wheel. The petite brunette who'd been in the passenger seat came around and helped to support him. She was younger than he was, wearing no makeup, and with the careless, fresh-faced look of a college girl more interested in studying than dating. The pudgy guy winked at Donnie and patted the girl's rump in a way that made Donnie sure she wasn't his daughter.

"He gonna be okay?" Donnie had asked her.

"Don't worry, he'll be all right."

"Right as fuckin' rain," said the man, accepting his parking stub and awkwardly stuffing it into a side pocket of his gray suit coat.

Donnie ignored him and looked at the woman, thinking that if she fixed herself up she'd be a beauty.

"All he needs is a few cups of coffee in him," she said.

"Casino," said the man.

"Coffee first, Harry," said the woman who wasn't his daughter.

"Coffee's for mornin'. This is evenin', i'n it?" He stared at Donnie, brow knitted in confusion.

"Evening," Donnie confirmed.

"Coffee and something to eat, then," the woman said. "Let's go inside, Harry."

"Inside hairy what?" He winked lewdly.

"Dammit, Harry!"

Donnie didn't like this. "You sure he'll be—"

"It'll be okay," she said, a little angrily this time. Then to Harry: "Do as you're told, baby. For me."

"For you," he'd said, and kissed her forehead sloppily, leaving a sheen of saliva above her left eye.

She was nowhere in sight now. Harry could have used her.

Mitki sneered at him and yelled, "Get this asshole's car, Nordo. Be quick about it."

Nordo ambled over with deliberate slowness and held out his hand for the parking stub.

Harry looked bewildered.

"Right-hand coat pocket," Donnie said.

Mitki fished in the pocket for the ticket stub, then yanked it out so fast the pocket tore and hung in a triangular flap.

"Meshed up mu besht shuit," said Harry, staring at the ruin hanging on his hip.

"Goddamn rag anyway," Mitki said. He released the man, watched for a moment to make sure he'd be able to stand up by himself, then backed away a few feet. "C'mon and move, Nordo; this fucker's putting out enough fumes he might explode if somebody tosses a cigarette near him."

Nordo was doing his cool casual walk to get the parked BMW.

"Where's your friend?" Donnie asked Harry. "The woman you brought here."

"Where's Sally, Harry?" Mitki asked with a sneer.

"Fuck her!" Harry said. "Name ishn't Shally anyway."

"It was supposed to be a joke," Donnie said. "You know, the movie . . ."

"Not funny," Harry said, squaring his shoulders.

"Where she is is in the bar," Mitki said. "He and the cunt had an argument. She's in a snit and not coming out."

"Don't talk 'bout her like that," Harry said. He took a step toward Mitki, but Donnie grabbed him and held him back. Mitki was smiling in anticipation.

"This guy's too drunk to drive," Donnie said. "He'll kill himself and somebody else."

"Who gives a fuck?" Mitki said.

"I'll go in and talk to the woman, see if she'll drive him."

"Stay outta the club," Mitki said.

"Don' wan' her," Harry proclaimed. "She an' me're quits! Maybe I'll look up Shally."

Mitki grinned at Donnie "See? He wants us to mind our own business."

"Ver' true," Harry said.

"Bolt wouldn't like it if this guy plowed into something with his car on the way home from here," Donnie said.

"Fuck you all," Harry said, and began running in a zigzag pattern toward the parking lot. His legs and arms were pumping at a rate suggesting his forward movement should have been a lot faster. He threw his left leg out at almost a right angle with every step. Harry had never been fast, even sober.

Donnie started to go after him but Mitki grabbed his arm and pulled him back.

"Let the jerk go live his life," Mitki said.

"He gets behind the wheel of that car and he might end his life and somebody else's. He's so drunk he doesn't even know what planet he's on."

"Not our business. We're not the highway patrol or astronomers."

Nordo hadn't parked the car, so he was having a little trouble finding the right black BMW. Donnie and Mitki watched as Harry caught up with him. Harry hastily tipped Nordo with a bill that almost fluttered to the ground before Nordo caught it and handed over the car key to Harry. Harry dropped the key, picked it up, then stumbled on toward his car. Nordo shrugged and plodded toward the portico.

"That had to be the last bill he had," Mitki said. "He lost big at roulette, started raising hell. Said he was financially ruined. The cunt tried to calm him down and he slapped her in the face. High-postage bitch wouldn't put up with it. She didn't say a word, just spun on a spike heel and walked away."

"I still say she oughta be driving," Donnie said.

"Doubt if she would even if you asked her. Probably lost interest in him if he really is out of money. Any woman—"

The muffled pop wasn't very loud, but Donnie and Mitki both recognized it.

They began walking fast toward the black BMW parked in the far row where Donnie had left it.

Nordo saw them and stopped. He realized where they were headed and reversed direction to fall in beside them.

When they got close to the car they could see that the driver-side front window had gone milky except where it was patterned wildly in red.

"That *asshole*!" Mitki said.

"We should have gone in and gotten the woman," Donnie said.

Mitki didn't bother telling him to shut up.

When they reached the car, Mitki carefully opened the passenger-side door and they looked inside.

Harry was slouched down limply in the seat with his head thrown back. His mouth was open wide as if he were silently screaming. There was a blackened hole not quite as big as his mouth in his right temple. On the seat beside him was a large-caliber revolver.

"Jesus!" Nordo was saying over and over. "He, like, shot himself. Shot himself. Jesus!"

"Forty-five-caliber Magnum," Donnie said.

Mitki slammed the car door closed. "Both of you shut the fuck up."

The three men stood silently. The night was sultry and quiet. Now and then the whine of a truck passing on the distant highway reached them like a far-away moan.

"You better go get Bolt," Donnie said.

Mitki shook his head no. "I got authority to act. Some things Bolt don't need to know or wanna know."

Donnie looked at the rows of cars opposite the shattered window. "Looks like the bullet angled up after it went through his head then the window. Nothing else looks like it was hit."

"That's a break," Mitki said, "but not much of one." He swiveled his head to peer behind them. No one else had emerged from the club. Apparently no one else had heard the shot, or recognized it for what it was if they had heard.

Donnie and Nordo watched as Mitki reached across the car's interior, grabbed Harry's limp body, and pulled it over into the passenger seat, knocking the gun to the floor. Grunting with effort, he propped the body against the seat back and strapped it firmly upright with the safety belt. Harry's ruined head bowed so that his chin rested on his chest, jowlier in death than in life. He looked as if he were asleep but having a hell of a nightmare.

Straightening up, Mitki said, "It's dark. Drive fast and it'll look like he's sleeping even if somebody does glance at him."

"Whaddya mean, *drive*?" Nordo asked.

"You can't do what you're thinking," Donnie said.

"Why not?" Mitki said. "There ain't much blood on the seat. Nobody else has touched the gun."

"The woman—"

"She's still inside. Far as she knows, it'll be like we say. No reason not to believe us. I escorted him outta the club, he got in his car, then drove on outta here. All that needs to be done is for somebody to drive him to a nice quiet spot where nobody's around, wipe down the steering wheel and gearshift for prints, then move him back behind the wheel."

"What about the blood on the passenger seat, and the fact that blood's been smeared around?"

"This thing don't have to be perfect," Mitki said. "We got certain connections in law enforcement."

"This isn't a bright thing to do," Donnie warned him. "It'll look like possible homicide. You talk murder and your connections come unplugged in a hurry."

"You talk *their* murder and they plug in tighter."

Nordo was staring at him, his eyes wide.

Mitki stared back and grinned. "You're it, Nordo. Get in the car, drive it to a secluded place about a mile away, off the road in among some trees. Then do what you have to and hike back here. It'll look like the asshole drove to a quiet spot, brooded about losing his money and his girl, and got so depressed he shot himself. Wouldn't be the first time somebody took the fast exit after losing big at the tables."

"Then why not let it be that?" Donnie asked. "Right here in the parking lot?"

"Because there *is* no gambling here," Mitki said.

"Any publicity is something we don't need." He crossed his beefy arms. "Nordo, get in the car."

"Not on your life," Nordo said. He tried his cocky grin but it was shaky. "I don't remember anything like this being in my job contract."

"I'm not leaving you a choice."

"No way, man! I ain't getting in no car and taking a stiff for a ride, even if it is a Beamer."

"Oh, really? Then let's say the asshole was so upset he shot the parking-lot attendant before roarin' ass outta here and killing himself."

Nordo swallowed hard and backed away a step.

"Fuck this! I'll do it," Donnie said. He started to walk around to the car's driver's side.

Mitki's big hand closed on his arm, scrunching the material of his parking valet's uniform, digging into muscle. The guy had a grip like a grappling hook. "I said Nordo does it."

"You want it done right?" Donnie asked, looking him in the eye. "I think you do. There are a couple of dozen ways to fuck this up. I think you want it done right."

He saw the light of resolve dim in Mitki.

"Bolt won't want this coming back on him," Donnie said. "That's the reason you're doing it. So it makes sense you wanna do it without screwing up. Who's your best choice, Nordo or me? Who would Bolt choose? Who would he want *you* to choose?"

Mitki released Donnie's arm. "Do it, then, Donnie. And do it right or you pay."

"We all pay," Donnie said.

"Jesus!" Nordo said.

"I'll drive him a couple of miles away and take the gun with me when I leave him. It'll look like he was killed by a hitchhiker, nothing to do with gambling losses. I'll do it right enough you won't have to use your police contacts."

Mitki looked thoughtful for a moment, then grinned with every tooth. "Now that is a fucking good thought, Donnie."

"I thought that was what you were suggesting."

"I was. It took you goddamn long enough to catch on. Nordo'll drive along behind you and give you a lift back here. And take your valet uniform jacket off before you go. That way nobody'll connect you with the club if something happens to go wrong."

Mitki was cooking now.

"Have Nordo wait fifteen minutes so he doesn't accidentally pass where I turn off," Donnie said. He wanted to keep Nordo as far away as possible from what was going to happen.

Donnie knew he was walking the edge here himself, making a suicide look like murder. Better than the other way around, he thought. He was sure Jules Donavon and Whitten would see it the same way and cover for him. It wasn't a good time for Circe to have a customer blow his brains out over gambling losses, and here was Donnie's opportunity to ingratiate himself with Bolt as well as make points with Cantanzano.

"Don't drive too fast, and remember to watch for me waiting by the side of the road," Donnie told Nordo.

"I'll make sure Nordo does his part," Mitki said. "You make sure you do yours."

Donnie stripped off his valet's jacket and handed it to Nordo, who looked at him as if in a daze. The sight of Harry's body slumped in the BMW was still vivid in his mind. Donnie had to close Nordo's hand around the jacket to keep him from dropping it.

"Kid's got no balls," Mitki said.

Nordo came out of his trance and glared at him, then tossed the jacket over his shoulder, holding it snagged by the collar with one forefinger. He was into his casual act again and looked like a young Frank Sinatra in an early publicity photo.

Mitki shoved him in the back to get him moving toward the portico, then got beside him to keep him walking. Neither man looked back as they picked up the pace, striding in step with each other, receding figures in the dappled shadows between the rows of cars.

The bright lights of the portico and club entrance lay ahead of them like safe harbor and redemption.

Donnie went the other direction and got in the car with the corpse.

18

Harry had put the key in the ignition but hadn't started the car. Donnie was glad he didn't have to fish in the dead man's pockets.

A .45 Magnum bullet through the head will stop a heart in a blink; there wasn't much blood on the seat. After climbing in behind the steering wheel, Donnie started the engine. He'd wipe the key after parking the car. The steering wheel was leather or something much like it and probably wouldn't take prints well, but he'd wipe that, too. Then the inside and outside door handles. He'd touch nothing else he'd leave behind.

Then he thought of the broken, milky window. It might attract attention even on the dark, sparsely traveled highway.

Using his knuckle, he pressed the power button, and the milky glass complete with blood and bullet hole sank down into the door until it jammed, leaving about an inch showing. That would be good enough. Had to be.

Donnie looked around to make sure nobody was leaving or arriving at Circe.

A car turned in off the highway and headed up the long drive. He sat watching its headlights. When it braked to a halt beneath the portico roof he saw that it was a black SUV about the size of a house. A man in a white shirt climbed down from it, and Nordo handed him a parking ticket.

Donnie waited until the man had entered the club before knuckling the BMW's headlights on and pulling out of the parking lot.

He drove.

It was better with the window down. The car's interior had smelled like blood and gunpowder and death. The hot breeze whirled the scents of violence around and carried them out into the clean night. Donnie wished his fear would fly with them, but it stayed, a stubborn passenger like the dead man.

Only four cars passed him coming the other way on the highway. Donnie hit the high beams when they got close, making sure the drivers were momentarily blinded so they wouldn't notice the bloody edge of the window or the passenger with his head sunk down on his chest. One of the drivers justifiably gave him an angry, fading blast of the horn. *Don't blame you, buddy.*

A little over five miles out from Circe, Donnie slowed the BMW and rolled along the shoulder for a while, then saw a clear spot and turned off into the dark, high grass.

He parked behind a cluster of tall pine trees, out of sight from the highway, and switched off the headlights.

Except for the stars and a sliver of moon, darkness

surrounded him. And silence. Almost. Far, far away a dog was barking.

Donnie untucked his shirt and used its tail to wipe the key and ignition switch, then the steering wheel. Also the window and headlight controls and gearshift, to be on the safe side.

Carefully he leaned to the right, bringing his face unnervingly close to Harry's ruined head, and was able to reach the pistol lying on the car's carpeted floor. Straightening up, he tucked it in his belt and climbed out of the car.

The car's interior light was startlingly bright. Donnie hurriedly wiped inside and outside door handles and kicked the door closed so it would go out. It was on some kind of timer and stayed glowing for five or ten seconds. Then it winked out and he could barely see Harry sitting inside the car in the darkness of forever.

Donnie backed away from the car, hesitating, calculating, making sure he'd forgotten nothing. Thinking about what he was about to walk away from.

Dead man, shot through the head.

No gun.

Window with bullet hole, lowered, obviously after death.

Conclusion: murder.

Motive: the theft of gambling winnings at Circe?

Not a chance. Too many people knew Harry had walked away from the tables a big loser.

So maybe Harry had picked up a hitchhiker and they'd gotten into an argument. Or he'd tried to rob somebody himself to recoup his losses and failed miserably. Maybe this, maybe that. Questions without answers.

Which was the way Donnie wanted it.

Satisfied, he turned away from the car. He realized that the faraway dog was quiet now. He hadn't noticed when it had stopped barking.

What else might he not have noticed?

A warm breeze blew in from the west, but it touched his perspiring flesh and made him shiver. In the faint moonlight he followed the tire tracks in the tall grass back to the highway.

He'd walked along the highway in the direction he'd come from for only about five minutes when he saw approaching headlights and moved back away from the gravel shoulder.

The lights belonged to a white limo.

Donnie stepped out where he could be seen and the limo passed him, then pulled to the side of the highway. Its backup lights came on and it reversed about a hundred yards to where Donnie was standing.

The driver-side tinted window glided down and Nordo looked out at Donnie. His eyes held a touch of wildness and he wasn't smiling. "C'mon! Climb in, man!"

Donnie walked around the limo and got in back, where he'd attract less attention when they arrived back at Circe.

Nordo negotiated a neat U turn, then lowered the glass partition behind the driver's seat and glanced back at Donnie. "This is some heavy shit, man!"

"Tell me about it," Donnie said.

"But it's not like we killed the guy or anything. I mean, like, he's dead either way."

"That's how I figure it," Donnie agreed, letting Nordo talk himself down. Nordo had probably been thinking hard about this, trying different rationales on for size, all the time he'd been driving to pick up Donnie.

"Damn shame, man. But he did it to himself."

"No doubt about that," Donnie said.

"No reason a lot of other people have to suffer for it. I mean, hell, they find him in the parking lot at Circe and there'd be a lotta bad publicity and shit and the cops might close the place down, put a lotta people outta work."

"You and me," Donnie said.

"And, I mean, we didn't do anything to deserve it, man."

"Neither one of us."

"I bet the guy's wife'll get more insurance money, seeing as how he was murdered instead of killing himself."

Wonderful! Donnie thought. He didn't mention to Nordo that the woman who'd arrived with Harry and was last seen sulking in the bar might not be his wife. And not everyone carried insurance. A guy like Harry, he might have cashed in his insurance policy and gambled away the money long before he cashed in his life.

"It's like we're doing a good deed," Nordo said, "though that's not how I feel about it now."

"Maybe you'll feel that way later."

"You think so, man?"

"Sure," Donnie lied.

"It's still against the law, though, what we're doing."

"Lots of things are against the law," Donnie said. "You smoke weed, you break the speed limit, you help an abused woman get a bigger insurance settlement. . . . You might go to jail but you can still go to heaven."

"I'm, like, thinking more about not going to jail," Nordo said.

There was some honesty left in him, Donnie thought.

"Everything go okay back there?"

"Perfect," Donnie said. "Don't worry, Nordo. Want my advice, when you park the limo back at Circe, put what happened tonight out of your mind. Then later let it back in slowly, a little at a time and in the right way, so you can handle it."

Nordo drove silently for a while, then glanced in the rearview mirror at Donnie and grinned. "I'm gonna take your advice, man."

"Good."

"I won't forget this, Donnie. I mean, what you did for me, volunteering to take care of . . . what happened. I'll pay you back someday, I swear."

"Someday, maybe," Donnie said, knowing there was no maybe about it.

It was a shame, he thought, gliding along in the limo on the dark highway, how in his world people used each other so selfishly. He'd been doing it and having it done to him for a long time now. So long that he wondered occasionally if people in the out-side world used each other that way.

He thought probably they did, but it made him feel no less soiled or lonely.

19

It had been a hell of a night, but it wasn't over.

Donnie noticed the old finned Cadillac parked a few blocks from his apartment on Barrack, so he had a pretty good idea what to expect when he opened his door.

They weren't bothering to surprise him. The lights were on, and Army was standing leaning against a wall with his arms crossed. Frankie the Lounger was on the bed again, this time lying on his back with his ankles crossed and his fingers laced behind his neck. It was the way Donnie often lay in bed and thought, staring at the ceiling. Maybe that was why it particularly bothered him, seeing Frankie like that. As if it were his ceiling. His bed.

Without moving, Frankie gave Donnie a sideways look. "You got a cat?"

Donnie stepped all the way into the apartment and shut the door. "No. Why?"

Frankie popped his wad of spearmint gum, moved his hands out from behind his neck, then drew a length of coarse twine from a pocket and held it up for Donnie to see. "You had a cat, I was gonna kill it in front of you. Impress on you that we could do somethin' like that to you, that we were serious about our dealin' with you and you better take it serious. Kill your fuckin' cat right in front of your own eyes. Wrap this twine around its throat and strangle it slow."

"I'm glad I don't have a cat," Donnie said.

Army shook his huge head and looked somber. "Excuse him," he said. "I'm always makin' excuses for him."

"Why don't you shoot him?"

Army shrugged. "He's an old friend. You gotta learn to overlook faults in your friends, you wanna get along in this world. So Frankie's not perfect. You got friends that strangle cats, don't you?"

"I guess so," Donnie said.

Nobody moved or said anything for a while. A cicada was making a lot of noise in the big tree outside the window. There was a swishing sound as a couple of cars passed down on Barrack Street. Let the silence build. Donnie knew when not to talk. He was good at not talking. The only guy in the country who knew better than Donnie when not to talk was the snappy dresser who hosted that quiz show where people tried to win a million dollars. It was a time to be respectful, when people were so close to their dreams. Even if sometimes the dreams were nightmares.

"Why we're here," Frankie said, "is for you to give us whatever information you learned so far out at Circe."

"I haven't had time to learn much of anything."

Frankie shifted his gum around in his mouth. "You're supposed to make the time. You was supposed to have figured that out, that we meant for you to be proactive. See, that's why I wish you had a cat."

"Sorry, no pets," Donnie said. "Not even a goldfish."

"You got no heart?" Army asked.

"I got no pets."

"Fish make nice pets," Frankie said. "You get hungry you can eat them."

"Frankie," Army said, "go easy on the animals. You know I like 'em."

Donnie hoped Frankie the Lounger would push it too far and get Army mad at him. But he didn't argue or make another animal remark, despite Army's obvious value as a straight man.

Pop! went Frankie's gum, as he suddenly sat up and swiveled around to sit on the edge of the bed, sending a whiff of spearmint wafting through the room. Upright, he began to chew in earnest with his mouth open. *Pop! Pop! Pop!*

"So what did you find out, Donnie?" Army asked.

"They speak some Russian out there."

"That don't surprise us," Frankie said.

"What were they saying?" Army asked.

"I don't know. I don't speak Russian."

"You sure it wasn't Cajun they was speakin'?" Army asked.

"What's Cajun?"

Frankie stood up now and widened his toothy grin, never letting up on the gum chewing even as he spoke. "I think this dickhead is toying with us, Army. We came here to toy with him, and he thinks he's gonna toy with us."

"Thinks wrong."

"All the way down the line." *Pop! Pop! Pop!*

Before Donnie had a chance to move, Army came away from the wall in a hurry and had him from behind, pinning both his arms to his sides.

Still grinning, Frankie walked over and punched Donnie three times in quick succession in the stomach.

Donnie could take a punch there and had been prepared for it, but the three blows still took the wind out of him. He bent over, making it seem he was hurt more than he was, and made a big show of trying to catch his breath.

When Army released him, he sank to his knees on the carpet.

"It didn't surprise us that you learned nothing worth shit," Frankie said, standing looking down at Donnie. "And the reason we didn't cut off some of your fingers is 'cause for you to be any good for us you gotta be in shape to keep workin' out at Circe. Otherwise you'd be a fuckin' bleedin' mess."

"Is that British?" Donnie asked. "Bleeding mess? You learn that from your boss?"

Frankie kicked him.

Donnie bent low with his head against the carpet, turning turtle like when he was a kid picked on by a gang. Knowing he had no choice but to take what was coming. Telling himself, Screw them; he could take it.

But nothing else happened. They didn't want to mess him up too much. Wanted him able to look spiffy in a valet uniform and park cars.

"You shouldn't have kicked him, Frankie," he heard Army say. Army's large hands gripped Donnie gently by the upper arms and he helped Donnie to his feet. "There I go havin' to make excuses for my friend again," he said apologetically.

"Fuck this guy!" Frankie said. "Hey! I mean, fuck him!"

"See, he's gettin' all worked up," Army told Donnie. "That's what he does when he fucks up and maybe kills somebody. Then it's too late to make excuses."

Donnie stood bent over, listening to Frankie's gum pop, smelling spearmint and not liking it.

"Fact is," Army told Donnie in a gruff but soft voice that begged for understanding, "you gotta work harder out there at Circe. Do what you can to learn some things we might like to know, just like Mr. Cantanzano asked you. You think you can be more cooperative and hold up your end of the bargain now?"

Donnie nodded. "I think so."

"You'll do your best anyways, okay?"

"Sure. Team player."

"That's what we like to hear." Army released Donnie, who managed to stand by himself. "Hear what he said, Frankie? Team player."

"Better be the fuckin' right team."

"Aw, Frankie . . ."

Pop! went Frankie's gum. "I'm gonna bust his

157

kneecap. I don't see why this loser can't park cars with a limp."

"No! We're done here, Frankie. We had our say and made our impression, just like Mr. C. asked."

" 'Told,' you mean."

"Told. I meant he told us, Frankie. Instructed us. You wanna *tell* him any different?"

"Not tonight."

"We're goin', Frankie. I hope you feel better, Mr. Wells."

"You die and you won't hurt no more," Frankie said. "I recommend it to you, Wells."

Donnie watched them move to the door and open it.

As they went out, Frankie glanced back at Donnie and grinned. "Shoulda had a cat."

20

When Donnie reported for work the next afternoon, an uncommonly polite Rat told him that Mitki wanted to see him.

Mitki, disturbed over a lunch of what looked like an entire haunch of some unfortunate animal, was also unusually polite. He told Donnie that Mr. Bolt wanted to talk to him, then interrupted his lunch to escort Donnie to Bolt's office.

Mitki was shooed away with a flick of Bolt's hand as soon as they entered the office. There was a faint scent of burned tobacco present, still strong. Donnie thought someone might have been smoking a cigarette in the office very recently. He saw a faint haze of smoke up near the ceiling. Though there was an ashtray on a corner of the desk, it was clean, and Bolt wasn't smoking.

Bolt didn't bother with the busy-man-interrupted act this afternoon. He ceased what he was writing in a leather-bound book on his desk and leaned back, smiling, still holding on to a fancy green fountain pen.

"You put in a productive shift last night," he said

smoothly. A civilized way to refer to body-and-blood work.

Donnie shrugged. "I thought that was why I was hired."

A door behind Bolt opened. It was set in the wood paneling so Donnie hadn't realized it was there.

A tall, rawboned man with almost colorless hair combed straight back stepped into the office and closed the concealed door. He was about sixty, wearing a neat tan suit, a beige shirt, and a brown tie with a green pattern in it. He advanced a few more feet into the office and stood observing Donnie without smiling but without appearing hostile. Donnie observed him back. He had angular, pleasant features, his face tanned and deeply lined. Slate gray eyes that suggested they'd seen a lot. A slight bump on the bridge spoiled an otherwise perfect nose above a well-formed mouth and firm chin. The man seemed perfectly at ease and had the rugged but worldly look of an educated farmer.

Bolt stood up behind his desk. "This is Mr. Drago," he said to Donnie. "Mr. Drago, Don Wells." He motioned with his arm as if from where he stood he could move the two men and close the distance between them.

Drago cooperated and stepped toward Donnie.

Donnie moved toward him and they shook hands. Drago's hand was unusually large. His grip was strong, like a manual laborer's, but smooth as a lounge lizard's.

"Mr. Wells," he said through his amiable smile, "I'm told you are a man with nerve and self-possession. A useful man."

"I try to do what I think needs doing," Donnie said, letting himself show pleasure at the compliment.

"You make it sound simple, and perhaps it is. But for so many people it is impossible. Thoughts and fears intrude. Most people either lose sight of what needs doing, or they lose the ability to do it. Only a few persevere."

"I guess we're talking about the secret of life," Donnie said with grin.

"Certainly one of them," Drago said. Without taking his eyes off Donnie, he removed a cigarette from a gold case and lit it with a gold lighter. He hadn't asked if anyone minded if he smoked.

"I guess I'm still trying to figure out some of the other secrets." Donnie backed off a bit.

"That's a process that continues all through life," Drago said. "The trick is to solve the riddles as they come at you, before it's too late."

"I suppose that's true," Donnie said. He believed it.

Drago drew on the cigarette, exhaled, and flicked ashes on the carpet. That explained the clean ashtray. He used thumb and forefinger to pick a fleck of tobacco from his lower lip. "I wanted to meet you. I make it a point to meet employees who've indicated they might have a bright future."

"Now that we've met, I hope you're not disappointed," Donnie said.

"Not at all. You seem wary of me, respectful but not afraid. That's the proper attitude, and it's not a contrivance. I know men's souls; I can judge them at a glance. I do not find you wanting, yet I don't find you perfectly fathomable. That could be a good thing.

It might mean you have useful depths." He smiled and shrugged in the elegant tan suit. "Or it could be a bad thing, that you have this unfathomable quality." He glanced at Bolt, who was still standing behind the desk, looking wary but respectful. A contrivance, Donnie thought. He read envy in Bolt and would bet Drago also saw it.

"I've been in places where it paid not to be fathomed," Donnie said.

"And where you were under constant scrutiny. Though you're a risk taker, I don't expect you to return to prison this time."

"Last night ought to tell you I haven't reformed."

Drago smiled. "Oh, it would be a shame for someone like you to reform. Your talents seem to suit exactly your role in life."

Donnie sure hoped so.

"While you haven't reformed," Drago said, "you've obviously become smarter with time."

"I'm sure I was careful enough last night."

"You were. Your work was checked after you left." Drago went to the desk and stubbed out his cigarette in the crystal ashtray. He drew a deep breath and exhaled, this time without a haze of smoke. "I wanted to tell you personally that your actions of last night were noticed and appreciated at the highest levels. We reward performance." He glanced at Bolt. "Mr. Wells deserves a generous bonus, Ewing."

"I think so, too," Bolt said too quickly.

"Thanks," Donnie said, nodding to both men. "I was only doing my job, and will again when I'm called on."

"Ah!" Drago said with a wide grin, teeth yellow but even. "Initiative."

"That's one of the reasons I hired Mr. Wells," Bolt said.

"A man gets older," Donnie told him, "he wants to move ahead in life."

Drago nodded. "Some men get older. They live as long as God intended. Others . . ." He shrugged. "I understand, Mr. Wells. Your intentions are commendable and duly noted."

Without a good-bye to Bolt or Donnie, he turned around and went back through the door in the paneling. Donnie wouldn't forget the almost invisible, well-fitted door. It might be necessary someday to prevent it from serving as an escape route for Bolt.

Bolt remained standing, staring at Donnie. He said, "You made some points where it counts."

"I hired on to play the game."

"You sure you know what the game is?"

"I'm learning the rules."

"And fast," Bolt said. "Harry Lomer's body was discovered in his car early this morning. Didn't make the papers yet, but it was all over TV news. They interviewed his wife, who said he'd lost some money gambling and was in a bad mood when he'd left her after a minor argument. She had no idea why anyone would want to kill him. She didn't say anything about his drinking too much. Didn't even mention the club."

"A woman who believes in keeping up appearances," Donnie said.

"And one who knows when to keep her mouth shut even if she might be suspicious about the circumstances of her husband's death. Probably by now she doesn't care how or why he died and is looking at the practical aspects of her situation. Some women are like that. They don't really shine until one way or another their husbands leave them."

"Finding themselves alone doesn't leave people much choice."

Bolt looked at him closely, maybe catching the plaintive note in his voice and wondering about it.

"Maybe she's learning the rules, too," Donnie said. "A generous bonus might be a good idea for her, even though she's not an employee."

Bolt smiled and nodded. "You do indeed solve the riddles as they come at you." He sat back down behind his desk and began writing again with his fancy green fountain pen in his leather-bound book. "Thanks again, Donnie. You can expect your bonus with your next paycheck."

Bolt didn't look up after speaking. The only sound in the office was the faint scratching of the pen point on paper.

Donnie knew that was the end of the meeting and he had nothing else to say that would be of the slightest interest to Ewing Bolt.

Nothing he wanted to say, anyway.

But what he'd eventually say in court would be of plenty of interest to Bolt.

There was no riddle in that, other than whether he'd live to say it.

21

When Donnie got home from work that night, he opened his apartment door to a mess.

Drawers were hanging open. His clothes had been yanked from the old wardrobe hangers and dumped on the floor. The mattress was sitting on the box spring crookedly. A corner of the carpet was turned up. The easy chair's cushion was propped in a corner, sliced open so the batting was bulging out. A lamp was on its side on the floor, still glowing as Donnie had left it when he'd gone in to work that afternoon. A vase that had been on a shelf was beside the lamp, unbroken but upside down. Elvis was okay, didn't even look as if he'd been moved.

Donnie methodically straightened up the place, making mental notes as he went. Nothing seemed to be missing. Anything whoever searched the apartment might have found would only have substantiated his identity as Don Wells. He was beginning to feel better; the search might be a good thing for him, solidifying him with whoever had done the deed.

But there were two questions in Donnie's mind: Did they find something he and the Bureau had somehow overlooked? And who had done the searching?

He left the chair cushion till last, then placed it with the sliced side down on the easy chair and sat down on it with a bottle of Heineken from the kitchen. He'd noticed that even the contents of the refrigerator had been moved around. Whoever had conducted the search had been thorough.

When the bottle was empty, Donnie got up from the chair and left the apartment. He walked down to the 7-Eleven, called Jules Donavon on the public phone, then bought a shrink-wrapped cheese Danish and a carton of milk.

Back in the apartment, he ate the Danish but decided against the milk and had another beer.

The snack didn't work. He was exhausted but remained too uneasy to sleep. Instead of going to bed, he switched on the old TV and ran through the channels, settling on one showing the old John Wayne western *The Searchers*. Though he'd seen the movie several times, he watched Wayne hunt for years for the Indians who'd abducted his young niece. Obsessive bastard fixated on his mission. Donnie could understand it.

He got tired before Wayne did and gave it up. Decided to get some sleep. He pushed himself out of the easy chair and turned off the TV.

The lock on the apartment door seemed to have been picked and still worked okay, for all the good it did. After fastening the brass chain lock and wedging a chair under the doorknob, Donnie went to bed, looking forward to tomorrow.

He didn't sleep well at all. Most of that night he spent astride a horse, roaming an endless desert in search of something elusive and dangerous.

He had no luck, though he searched until late the next morning.

Both of them this time.

At Chicken Vittles.

Sue was behind the steering wheel of the plain white Taurus sedan parked under the chicken-and-ax sign. Jules Donavon sat alongside her, only about a foot away from the red plastic tray hooked over the almost-down window of Donnie's Honda. It was easy for Donnie and Jules to talk to each other between bites of hen burger or extra-crispy chicken fingers. No one in the three other cars parked for curb service looked suspicious, and the diners who'd decided to leave their cars and eat inside didn't seem to be paying any attention to them. Even if Donnie was being followed, this would hardly attract attention, a stop for a curb-service lunch.

"You said on the phone you've been busy," Jules said around a bite of hen burger. Beside him, Sue munched french fries and watched Donnie.

"That guy Harry Lomer they found murdered in his car yesterday," Donnie said, "I'm the one who left him parked there."

Jules stopped chewing and stared at Donnie. Donnie was pretty sure he saw Sue smile slightly.

"He lost big and committed suicide outside the club," Donnie said. "Mitki ordered him moved."

"Why'd you wait to mention it?" Jules asked.

"It's not the kind of thing you talk about over the phone."

"Or maybe you were trying to make up your mind whether you can trust me," Sue said.

"I went close to the line," Donnie told her.

"Some would say you crossed it."

"I don't think he did," Jules said. "Only smudged it. What Donnie did is a technical violation of the law, but he's an undercover agent who acted to preserve the investigation. There's a larger issue here."

"A dead suicide makes for a crime site," Sue said, "and Donnie altered evidence."

"She's right," Donnie said. "But you two know the reasons I did it."

"We can put the information in our report," Jules said, "but in a way that makes it clear it was justified. After all, making a suicide look like murder is quite a different thing from if it were the other way around."

Sue looked over at Donnie and nodded. "Okay. But the locals will be pissed if they find out."

"Now give us the details," Jules said. He was clearly irritated at having to defend Donnie. He and Donnie both knew Donnie owed him one.

Donnie explained exactly what had happened with Harry Lomer. Then he told Jules about his meeting yesterday with Bolt and Drago.

"This is just what we need," Jules said, an edge of excitement in his voice. "Drago might be the thief-in-law who runs the show."

"He has that kind of respect and fear from Bolt," Donnie said. "Something else, Jules. When I got home from work last night I found somebody'd tossed my apartment. And they didn't neaten up before they left."

"What about Elvis?" Sue asked.

"Dead. Not a suspect," Donnie said.

Jules glared at him.

"Elvis is okay," Donnie said. "They couldn't have found out about the hidden wire."

Jules took another bite of hen burger and chewed thoughtfully. Donnie dipped a chicken finger into honey-mustard sauce and took a bite. Chewed. Waited.

"You think the Italians mighta tossed your place?" Jules asked.

"Maybe, considering the way it was done, without even refolding my socks. Cantanzano and company don't strike me as subtle. Or particularly skillful."

"They were dangerous men in their day," Sue said.

"Now they're semiretired," Jules said. "Not so active but still dangerous. Doing it by rote."

Donnie said, "My impression is that Vito's mainly worried about his nephew. Other than that, he's curious about what's happening at Circe, and whether he should lever himself into it somehow. Scouting the territory and looking for the main chance is habit with him."

"That we can use," Jules said. "You can spy *on* them while spying *for* them."

Donnie had played that game more than once.

"My guess is it was the Russians who searched my apartment," he said. "Checking me out more closely because of Drago's interest in my work. And they might want to be blatant about it, remind me how vulnerable I am."

"We'll check Drago out just as closely. Our databases or Interpol's might have something on him. He have a first name?"

"Just *Mister*," Donnie said. "He's that kind of guy."

"Which is what makes him interesting."

Donnie took a sip of Diet Coke through a plastic straw. Swallowed a bit of something solid that momentarily stuck in his throat. Hoped it was chicken. "What about Marla Grant?"

"I was about to ask you the same question," Jules said.

"There's been no mention of her at all out at Circe."

"Nothing here, either. The locals are still investigating. We are, too, but in ways less obvious. Other than Frank Allan's lighter found near her body, there's no connection between her and Allan."

"There has to be. And it's probably the key to what's going on out at Circe. Mind if I nose around on the side? I'm in the best position to recognize two plus two."

"You are. You're also in the best position to get your head lopped off. If the wrong people notice you in the presence of anyone who knew Marla Grant, you'd better have a damned good explanation ready."

"I do," Donnie said. "My furnished apartment. Since the place was wrecked and might not feel safe anymore, I'd logically consider moving, seeing a real estate agency that handles rentals."

"Or maybe you can see the dentist Marla worked for if you get your teeth knocked out," Sue said across the car.

She was smiling, but Donnie nodded. "Julep's a small place. Wouldn't be that much of a coincidence. There aren't that many real estate agencies or dentists here."

"Risk seeing one but not both," Jules advised him.

"I'll start with the one that doesn't require dental work."

"Sounds like he's determined to see both," Sue said.

"He's that way sometimes," Jules told her. "Determined to the point of fixation. Like a truculent twelve-year-old who's seen too many John Wayne movies."

"Hound dog," she said.

"You'd think different about it if Indians ever abducted you," Donnie told her.

Jules stared oddly at both of them.

Donnie started the Honda and tapped the horn to get the carhop's attention so she'd pick up his tray with her tip on it.

"You gonna take those chicken fingers home to eat?" Sue asked.

Donnie handed Jules the grease-stained cardboard container to pass across the car to her. "You two can share them. I don't like the image they conjure up."

22

Donnie had made sure he wasn't followed on the drive to Chicken Vittles. He made doubly sure before stopping at a drugstore where there was an outside public phone barely visible from the street.

He parked some distance from the phone and walked to it, scanning the parking lot. Nothing unusual: an elderly couple emerging from a Cadillac, the woman waiting while the man carefully locked the car; a kid learning to skateboard over near some unoccupied benches; a mother with two preschoolers pushing out through the automatic doors with a flurry of smiles and motion.

When he reached the phone and had fed it enough coins to reach Grace's number in Florida, Donnie was glad to see a white minivan park so that the view from the street was closed off entirely.

Grace answered on the second ring and he identified himself.

"You okay?" She knew he wouldn't have called unless it was necessary. They both knew that sometimes the necessity came from within.

"Yeah, okay. I needed to hear your voice."

"I'm glad you called when you did," she said, a trace of Spanish still in her cadence and phrasing. "I was about to go down to the beach."

Donnie pictured her sitting on one of the old aluminum webbed loungers they sometimes dragged down to the surf to rest on or sunbathe on between swims, her long dark hair moving with the wind, her tan, compact body.

"You there, lover?"

"Here. Wish I were there."

"Will you be soon?"

"I don't know. I hope so. I guess that's why I called."

"You don't need an excuse. Not an excuse for anything with me."

"I know. It's what keeps me going sometimes."

"If it didn't," Grace said with a low laugh, "you'd find something else."

"Not somebody else, though," Donnie said. "How are things there? What are you doing?"

"Things are good enough, considering you're not here. I was bored, decided on a swim, when you called. I've been spending more time on the beach, sometimes just sitting and watching the waves come in. Yesterday the dolphins were swimming just offshore. They reminded me of you. They look something like sharks but they're not."

"They stay alive by looking like sharks. It scares away a lot of potential predators."

"Is that true?"

"I don't know. Maybe."

"I wish you were here with me, lover. We could watch the sunset together."

"Someday soon," he said. And he wanted to be with her on the beach near her cottage so keenly that it was an ache. "I'd better hang up," he told her, knowing the stupidity, the danger, of torturing himself this way.

"I wish I could be there to take care of you."

Donnie couldn't answer around the lump in his throat. He replaced the receiver in its cradle and stood for a long moment in the shade by the phone.

Grace hadn't asked why he had to hang up. Hadn't asked where he was. She knew better. He'd made sure of that. The safest way for both of them was for her not to know. The safest way was also for him never to call. But now and then he found not calling impossible.

It made the tightrope act that had become his life more bearable, knowing that she missed him as he missed her, that he knew exactly where she was on this planet of countless miles and people.

That she didn't know where he was sometimes made him so lonely he felt as if he might be poised on the edge of an abyss.

And he was.

23

"You should come see something," Mitki said to Donnie as soon as Donnie had changed into his parking valet uniform at Circe.

Donnie said nothing as the big man lumbered out of the tiny locker room, then led the way along a narrow hall. Mitki had on a dark chalk-stripe suit and a gold silk tie today, and he looked like a bear that had eaten a banker and stolen his clothes.

They went through a door and Donnie found himself standing in the casino. It wasn't yet open. The colorful rows of slot machines were glowing but silent, the roulette wheels still, the blackjack and poker tables covered with white throw cloths. The usual bright lighting was also reduced, changing the color of the carpet from rust to brown, dimming the usual glitter of the bottles and polished glasses behind the curved bar with its inset video poker screens. There was nothing but dimness behind the brasswork windows of the cashier cages. Along the far wall a man was working on a disassembled slot machine. By day, unoccupied, the casino had a slightly seedy, mundane look to it, as if the workings of a dazzling but simple magic trick were visible. It wasn't yet showtime.

Mitki led the way across the plushly carpeted casino to another door near the cashier cages. With his hand on the knob, he paused and turned toward Donnie.

"Mr. Bolt says you should see this," he said. He was smiling in a way that bothered Donnie. "Says you should be a spectator and not interrupt."

"Mr. Bolt gonna be there?" Donnie asked.

"Naw. He don't like the sight of blood so much anymore."

Mitki pushed the door open and stood aside so Donnie could step through ahead of him.

They were in a large, unfinished room with gray cinder-block walls and some partly assembled bleacher seats. A small auditorium, actually. Donnie figured it was set deep in the hill behind the casino. Light was provided by fluorescent fixtures hanging by chains from the iron ceiling girders. Brown metal folding chairs were stacked along one wall. A gray metal office desk, with another on top of it upside down, was against another. Large cardboard boxes and unpainted wooden two-by-fours were on the floor near the desk, material for more bleacher seats. Spacious as the auditorium was, the surrounding dimness made it seem smaller, and it smelled faintly of stale perspiration and of terror, giving Donnie a claustrophobic feeling.

In the center of the auditorium was a small boxing ring with the posts and corner sections of the ropes wrapped in blue padding. In the ring, at opposite corners, stood Nordo and Rat. Nordo was wearing Levi's, a white T-shirt, and red-and-white jogging shoes. Rat had on gray sweatpants and was shirtless and barefoot. His short, round torso was hairless and with a weight lifter's definition. He was a barrel with muscles.

Donnie looked at the ring, then at the dozen or so men standing around it. He recognized a couple of guys who tended the grounds, and a thin black man named Len who was a parking valet on shifts when Donnie wasn't working. This was the first time Donnie had seen him close up. Len had broad cheekbones, a receding hairline, and a mottled, crinkled scar along his neck, as if he'd been hanged and survived. He returned Donnie's stare with a careful, blank expression. The other three men Donnie didn't recognize. They all had on suits and ties, were in their fifties, and looked like respectable citizens. Donnie doubted if they were.

"What we got us here," Mitki said to Donnie, "is a portable ring. Mr. Bolt is considering putting on boxing matches sometime in the near future, letting the patrons place bets on the outcome. Just like in Vegas."

"I sense a difference," Donnie said.

"Well, this is a kind of trial run like we have now and then. It's not so much boxing or wrestling as it is fighting no-holds-barred."

"And no referee," Donnie pointed out.

"I'm sorta that," Mitki said. "At a certain point when I figure time's up, I ring a bell for the contestants to stop. One of them's always gladder to hear it than the other."

"How many rounds does the fight go?"

"I decide that, too. But not ahead of time."

"So there are no rules."

Mitki put on a confused look. "You must not have been listening. I just told you the rules."

None of the other men had said anything. Len and the groundskeepers were deliberately looking anywhere but at Donnie. The three guys in suits were ignoring him in a different way, as if they really didn't consider him important enough to acknowledge his presence.

Donnie turned his attention to the ring. There were no seconds. The only men in the ring were Rat and Nordo. Nordo looked scared. Rat looked eager.

"You really want to do this?" Donnie asked Nordo.

"I really don't wanna get my ass fired."

"He didn't follow instructions or use common sense worth shit last night," Mitki said.

"So suspend him without pay for a few days."

"Nope. That'd set a terrible precedent. The other employees, they see or hear about something like this, they got a clearer idea where they stand, what their choices are. We frequently ask our personnel who don't live up to expectations to engage in a little athletic contest. It's all in the spirit of keeping up morale, you might say."

"I did the best I could, man!" Nordo implored from the ring.

Mitki didn't bother answering him.

Donnie knew the real reason why Nordo was in

the ring instead of speeding away from Circe in his car. He couldn't bring himself to lose face in his family, both his real one and his Mafia family. Vito Cantanzano wouldn't look favorably on a nephew who'd cut and run, who hadn't done his job because he was a coward. Maybe fighting Rat in a ring, with a time limit, was preferable to what might happen to him in the hands of Army and Frankie the Lounger. Fate and heredity had trapped Nordo. Short of stepping in at the last second to save Nordo's life, Donnie figured he had no choice other than to let this thing play out.

Nordo's face was twisted with fear as he stared down from the ring at Donnie. They both knew there was nothing Donnie could do to help him. The rock was about to meet the hard place. Nordo knew exactly where he was.

Donnie nodded to Nordo as if to wish him luck, then stepped back a few feet for a better view and stood with his hands in his pockets.

"Everybody's here," Mitki said. He walked over to a timekeeper's round bell mounted on the side of the ring. There was a small silver hammer dangling near it on a silver chain, the kind of classy touch that helped make blood sports respectable.

Rat saw him approaching the bell and began moving around in his corner, tensing his chunky arms and throwing them back and forth across his body with his elbows out, loosening up for action. Nordo stood motionless and stared at Rat.

"Kind of a mismatch," Donnie said softly.

"Who said anything about a match?" Len whispered beside him. "More like Christian versus lion."

Mitki lifted the silver hammer and tapped the bell. A harsh clang echoed off the block walls.

Rat grinned, hunching his sloping shoulders and tucking in his chin so his neck expanded, and immediately advanced on Nordo.

Mitki said, "Gonna be fun."

If you're the Marquis de Sade, Donnie thought.

24

Nordo wandered a few feet toward the center of the ring, then stood looking frightened and confused, an expression on his face as though he'd just mistakenly gotten off a bus in the wrong end of town.

As Rat got near him and hunkered down lower with his fists balled, Nordo assumed a straight-up boxing stance reminiscent of those old daguerreotypes of John L. Sullivan. Donnie winced, knowing what was going to happen to the kid.

It did.

Rat faked a jab to Nordo's head, then ducked even lower and slammed a right-hand punch into Nordo's midsection that doubled him over like an envelope flap. He fell so fast that Rat's next punch, a nasty left hook, buzzed over his head and found nothing but air.

Nordo lay on his side with his knees drawn up and appeared unconscious.

Mitki tapped the bell.

"End of round one," he said, when Donnie looked over at him.

"After five seconds?" Donnie asked. "Why not count ten over the kid and call it a fight?"

Mitki grinned. "You call *that* a fight?"

He had a point, Donnie had to admit. But would it ever be a fight?

"Nobody said anything about Marquis of Queensberry rules," Mitki reminded Donnie.

"Even so," Donnie said, "I don't think there's anything in them about beating up parking valets."

"I've seen fights," Mitki told him, "that lead me to believe the boxing commission would approve of this one."

Nordo rolled over and struggled to his knees, then to a standing position. He swayed and held a hand to his left side, looking around in a daze, then staggered in the general direction of his corner. He was kind of crab-walking, a little bowlegged and veering crookedly off to the side.

Rest between rounds was optional, too. Mitki put hammer to bell.

Clang!

Here came Rat again, smiling in anticipation behind his raised fists. Nordo seemed not to have heard the bell and was unaware of Rat's approach.

"Turn around!" Donnie yelled at Nordo, who glanced at him, then looked over his shoulder. Donnie fought the impulse to climb into the ring and help Nordo.

When Nordo saw Rat, he grimaced in fear and his eyes darted from side to side. There was nowhere to run. Nowhere to hide. No time to get to the ropes and climb out of the ring even if Nordo decided to dash for the door.

He turned to face Rat, his loosely clenched fists at his sides, as if resigned to what was about to happen.

Rat hit him hard in the side of the neck with a right cross. This time instead of falling, Nordo sagged against Rat and held on with both arms wrapped around him. Nordo's eyes were blank and his jaw was slack, as if he felt nauseated and might vomit.

Rat began tattooing Nordo's body with punches, but at such close range and in Nordo's desperate embrace, he couldn't summon much power.

Being able to withstand the barrage seemed to work a change in Nordo, though he still clung to Rat like an exhausted lover. Some kind of love. Nordo shifted position slightly and poked a finger hard into Rat's eye. Again. First one eye, then the other. As if in the midst of pain and chaos Nordo had suddenly discovered something downright fun.

Donnie couldn't believe it.

Rat backed away, rubbing one eye while he squinted the other. A tear ran from the open eye; Donnie knew Rat's vision had to be blurred.

Nordo tried to kick Rat in the testicles but missed. Tried again and got a kneecap.

Rat went down.

Nordo's lips were curled back to expose gums and teeth. His eyes were wild. The kid had finally gotten angrier than he was afraid. Found something inside himself that Rat hadn't figured was there. Probably Nordo hadn't figured it, either, but there it was. Donnie had seen this kind of thing before and wondered how far it would take Nordo.

Rat rolled his stocky body over, did a sloppy push-up, and got to his hands and knees, one eye still clenched shut. Nordo kicked him in the ribs, causing Rat to roll again onto his back. Nordo screamed, leaped high, and landed on Rat with both feet. He began to run in place on Rat, lifting his knees high, stomping hard on Rat's stomach, chest, neck, the side of his face.

Mitki, dumbfounded, stood paralyzed watching this, then realized where it was going and rang the bell.

Rang it again.

Nordo didn't pay any attention.

Donnie looked at Mitki, shrugged, and mouthed *No rules.*

Everyone gathered around the ring was shouting now, some of them jumping up and down as Nordo was doing. A few of them applauded and cheered. There were a couple of enthusiastic high fives. It was exactly the show for this crowd.

Mitki had seen more than enough. He scampered up into the ring, grabbed Nordo, and flung him toward a corner.

Nordo bounced off the ropes and came at him.

Mitki barely avoided a wild roundhouse swing and shoved him away again.

Donnie figured he had a chance to stop this now. He climbed into the ring and got a bear hug on Nordo to stop him.

Nordo was still revved up and strong. He slipped away and grabbed Mitki from behind by the ears.

Mitki yelled and shook his head, but Nordo hung on.

Donnie got behind Nordo and clutched his wrists. "Let go! Dammit, let go, Nordo!" He was helping Mitki. Who at Circe could bitch about that?

Donnie kept a slippery grip on Nordo. Nordo just as determinedly maintained his hold on Mitki's ears. The three men lurched backward across the ring, almost tripping and falling, and finally Nordo released his grip on Mitki.

Mitki stood cupping his palms to his ears. "You little bastard!" He advanced on Nordo. "Hold on to him, Donnie, if you know what's good for you!"

Donnie was trying to figure out what to do when he saw that Rat had crawled over to his corner. The human stump was on his feet now, turning around in a crouch, blood trickling from his nose and down his chin to stain his chest. He was holding a knife in his right hand and glaring through puffy, reddened eyes.

"Watch out, Mitki!" Donnie yelled. Confusion was the best tactic here. Quickest response, anyway.

Mitki, who was never Rat's target, spun around and saw Rat, who ignored him and darted past him in an effort to get at Nordo. Dumb kid saw him and didn't even move. In fact Donnie, holding him in check, felt Nordo's body actually strain toward Rat.

As Rat lunged with the knife, Donnie yanked Nordo backward and stepped in front of him.

He danced sideways away from the flashing blade and grabbed Rat's wrist, strengthening his grip as he wrenched the arm around behind the broad back. He turned Rat's palm up and bent his hand back toward the wrist.

Somehow Rat managed to hang on to the knife. Donnie could feel its sharp point flick over his own wrist as Rat tried to maneuver it so it drew blood.

Rat's thick wrist was slippery with sweat. Donnie knew he couldn't hang on to it much longer. The arm would break free soon. Then the knife blade would find flesh.

Donnie moved closer to Rat, crouched low, then straightened up, bending the arm up and up toward the center of Rat's back. He felt the arm slip from its shoulder socket and heard Rat's high-pitched scream.

The knife dropped to the canvas mat.

Donnie pushed Rat away and at the same time kicked the knife out of the ring. A man leaning with his elbows on the ring apron twisted away, avoiding the knife.

Mitki and Nordo stood staring at Donnie.

Rat was leaning back into the ropes, gripping his limp arm, his face screwed up in pain. He was pale. He wasn't screaming now, but Donnie thought he heard him whimper.

Nordo moved toward Rat and began to scream again. "Asshole! You're an asshole, man!"

Donnie grabbed Nordo around the waist with both arms and pulled him back. It was working until Nordo planted a heel and found leverage to resist. Again Donnie was amazed at the kid's strength.

Mitki stared at Donnie, his eyes wide.

"Want me to turn him loose?" Donnie asked.

Mitki growled, then said, "No. Just get him the fuck outta here!"

Donnie had to drag Nordo from the ring, down to the floor.

As he pushed him ahead toward the exit, the dozen or so spectators quietly moved aside. They were all looking at Nordo with something like awe mixed with confusion and admiration. It was as if a fifty-to-one horse out of a truck from Texas had just won the Kentucky Derby.

"I'm gonna kill that little rodent bastard!" Nordo was mumbling in his rage. "Gonna fuckin' kill him, man!"

"Maybe later," Donnie said, knowing with a sad wisdom that more likely it would be the other way around.

25

"You continue to impress," Bolt said to Donnie the day after the Nordo–Rat fight.

They were in Bolt's office, Bolt seated behind his oversize desk, the sun searing the green expanse outside the window. Donnie, seated facing Bolt, noticed a large bird, probably a buzzard, circling in the distance beyond the trees. He hoped it wasn't an omen.

"I figured it'd do no one any good if Rat killed Nordo," Donnie said. He averted his eyes from the circling bird, back to Bolt.

Bolt smiled, looking like a mature, kind uncle. "Are you sure he would have?"

"I'm sure it was the second time he'd have killed Nordo if I hadn't interrupted. They don't play well together. My sense of Rat is that sooner or later he kills people he doesn't get along with."

"Possibly you have him pegged," Bolt said. "Why do you suppose he's that way?" He seemed genuinely curious.

"Seeking closure maybe," Donnie said. "Or maybe he's stupid."

"Probably the latter," Bolt said, not picking up on

Donnie's sarcasm. "Still, a man like that has his uses."

"Like being expendable," Donnie said. When Bolt didn't smile, he knew he'd gone too far. "When the time is right," Donnie added.

"When it's decided," Bolt said. He fixed a level stare on Donnie. "More precisely, when *I* decide."

"Sure," Donnie said.

Bolt's gaze became less intense. He swiveled slightly in his desk chair, this way and that, while seeming to look inward, as if trying to formulate something in his mind before speaking. "I called this meeting, Donnie, to let you know your efforts to be an acceptable employee are noticed, and they're paying off. That's the American dream and the American way. Organizations work on incentive, and this one is no exception. The incentive is that when you do well, you move up. You've done well."

"Thanks, Mr. Bolt." Donnie playing it straight.

Bolt the great American continued: "By way of you moving up, slight changes will go into effect. There might be certain tasks you'll be asked to perform or in which you'll be included. They aren't to be discussed with anyone afterward. A man with your background should understand that."

"I understand it very well."

"I was sure you would. Are you willing to advance to that sort of level and job description as a Circe employee?"

"Of course." Donnie hadn't actually heard a job description and didn't have to. "That's why I'm here. A man reaches a certain point, he sees the larger issues. He no longer wants to be an independent operator."

"And you're at that point?"

"I am. I've done a lot of time inside the walls. I don't want to do more. Better to have the protection of being part of something larger."

"I admire your candor," Bolt said, "almost as much as I admire your adroit dishonesty. Just so long as I can recognize one from the other. And make no mistake, I can."

"Sir?" Donnie thought here was the time to be transparently naive, reassure Bolt that he could indeed see through Donnie's phoniness and feigned misunderstanding.

"Recognize one from the other, as you well know. It's an essential skill." Bolt made a steeple with his fingers and peered over it. He loved doing that. "Now I'll be candid with you. Rat won't forget what you did to him, and he'll attempt to get back at you."

"I figured that," Donnie said.

"Losing face is unacceptable even for a man named Rat. But here comes the candor: I'm not sure I can hold him in check. Rat is a genuine nutcase. He has periods of emotion and unreason. Mitki can control him better than anyone, but even Mitki occasionally loses his grip on the leash. Then Rat runs wild."

"Can I kill him if I have to?" Donnie asked.

Bolt smiled. "Of course not. I would never under any circumstances condone violence against another human being." He stood up behind his desk and buttoned his suit coat, his way of dismissing Donnie.

Donnie nodded and stood up also. He, too, could recognize one from the other.

At the door, Donnie paused and turned around to face Bolt, who'd sat back down at his desk.

"What about Nordo?" Donnie asked.

Bolt raised his eyebrows inquisitively.

"I mean, is he fired?"

"No reason he should be," Bolt said. "If I were going to fire him, I wouldn't have bothered having him disciplined."

Donnie drove into New Orleans before work the next day, but instead of meeting with Jules, he followed instructions and joined Sue for lunch at the Court of the Two Sisters.

They sat at one of the courtyard tables and ate good Cajun food from the buffet. She had her blond hair pinned back and was wearing tight jeans and a powder blue blouse. The filtered sunlight brought a pink flush to her complexion. Anyone observing them would deem it perfectly logical that Donnie would want to be with her for reasons other than business.

A jazz quartet was playing softly, far enough away from the table that it didn't interfere with conversation, at the same time making their conversation impossible to hear at the other tables.

"What is that?" Sue asked, looking up from her salad.

"A truffle, I think," Donnie said, glancing at what he'd speared with his fork.

"I meant the music."

"Oh. 'Take Five.' Old one by Dave Brubeck."

She popped a tiny cocktail tomato into her mouth. Lucky tomato, Donnie thought. "I like it," she said.

"The salad?"

"The music."

Donnie had already filled her in on what had happened between Nordo and Rat, and his later conversation with Bolt. She hadn't reacted. He knew she was mulling over what he'd said, even as she listened to jazz and squished cocktail tomatoes between her molars. Odd woman, but interesting. He hoped Jules was right about being able to trust her. He knew that now a corner had been turned and there wasn't any choice.

Over ice cream for dessert, Sue said, "What happens if you get put on the spot out at Circe? Told to do something you can't? Not borderline like the Harry Lomer thing—something you really can't do?"

"Like kill someone?" Donnie asked.

"Like kill someone."

"I won't, obviously. The trick will be to put on a good show and stay credible, not jeopardize my own life or the integrity of the operation."

"Some trick."

"I've done it before."

She grinned at him. "I know." She took a last bite of ice cream, licked the spoon, then pushed the bowl away. "I'll pass what you said on to Jules, Donnie. Now I'll pass something on the other way. The Bureau's traced Ewing Bolt."

Donnie sat forward. The more he knew about Bolt, the better he'd be able to play the dangerous game at Circe.

"He burned to death in a house fire forty-five years ago in Whaling, Connecticut, when he was two years old."

Donnie knew what that meant. The man calling himself Ewing Bolt had stolen the real Bolt's identity, using the birth certificate of a person who'd died as a child so the ID wouldn't conflict with that of anyone living. With the birth certificate, available upon request from public records, he'd obtained a library card perhaps, then with two pieces of identification some minor credit cards, club membership cards, anything that wouldn't require a Social Security number. It was the standard way for someone to construct a false identity.

"We think Bolt is actually a member of the Canadian-Russian *Mafyia* who entered the U.S. illegally. Somebody often described by the Russians in Canada as a 'criminal authority.' The Russians have moved into Canada in a big way and no doubt have forged alliances with the Russian Mafia in the U.S."

"No doubt," Donnie said. The euphemism "criminal authority" was another way of saying "Don" or the more common U.S. term for an old-guard Russian crime kingpin, "thief-in-law." Thieves-in-law still ran much of Russian organized crime and were respected and feared, often becoming advisers even when they became less active and turned over the reins of authority to younger and more vicious men. Managing an illegal casino like Circe might well be where a thief-in-law would spend the late and lush phase of a criminal career. Still, he would work under the direction of an active thief-in-law still close to the center of power. That would probably be Drago.

"This criminal authority got a name?" Donnie asked.

"Grigory Petrov. Said to be a bad, bad boy but smart and very smooth. He ran a gambling and drug-marketing operation in Toronto before disappearing from Interpol's and the RCMP's radar screens two years ago."

Donnie was ahead of Sue. "Fingerprints?"

Sue smiled. "A partial of a Petrov print is on file. Ring finger, right hand. What Jules wants is for you to obtain something bearing Bolt's fingerprints, including the finger we can match."

"Are there warrants out for Bolt-Petrov?"

"No. That's where the smart and smooth come in. He and his attorneys managed to keep him clean. Of course, he could be picked up for illegal entry into the U.S., but it would be a waste to hang such a minor tag on him."

Donnie agreed. Sending Petrov back to Canada, then maybe to Russia, would be like arresting a serial killer for littering and giving him a slap on the wrist. "What about Drago? Any information on him yet?"

"Nothing. You sure you saw him?"

"He was no illusion, and whoever he is, he's even higher than Bolt in the mob hierarchy. Bolt damn near does everything other than kiss his ring."

"We're staying on it, Donnie. If Drago can be traced, we'll do it. Having *his* fingerprints wouldn't hurt, either."

"He doesn't seem to come around very often, but I'll try."

Sue was staring at him. "If Bolt said you'll be elevated in the organization at Circe, you'll be using the wire, won't you?"

"Yeah. That's why I have it."

"Be damned careful with it, Donnie. The people you're playing with—"

"I know," he interrupted, thinking of Lily. Frank Allan. Marla Grant.

Sue nodded, her smile sticking but turning sad. "So I'll tell you again anyway: Be damned careful."

The waiter arrived with their check, and she leaned across the table and reached for it.

"Brunch is on the Bureau," she said. "They owe you plenty for what you did in New York. By the way, they ever thank you for that?"

"In a hundred little ways," Donnie said.

She didn't say anything as she plunked down cash for the meal, counting out a generous tip. The expression on her face suggested she was wondering whether Donnie was serious or being sarcastic.

He couldn't help her with that one.

26

Dr. White's office was outside the Quarter, in a yellow brick-and-stucco building with a lot of roses around it and a parking lot that had been laid out around a huge live oak that shaded most of the cars. As he got out of his car and walked toward the building's entrance, Donnie couldn't help wondering how long the tree had stood, what events had occurred around it. The past was everywhere in New Orleans, with a reach into the present.

"She was a sweet woman," said Dr. White. "And a smart one, but without a lot of complications."

He was a fortyish, handsome man with boyish features and a mop of curly black hair. Like a lot of dentists, he smelled like cloves.

Donnie had decided to drop in on him before leaving the city. First he'd bought some basic items to facilitate a disguise—easy enough to do in the French Quarter. A shop on Dauphine specializing in Mardi Gras costumes sold him a pretty realistic false mustache and a pair of glasses with clear lenses. The guy behind the counter tried to talk him into a Groucho Marx outfit, but Donnie refused the baggy pants and checked coat and opted for the wire-rimmed glasses and more conservative mustache.

Back in the Honda, it took him only a few minutes to affix the mustache, comb his hair differently, and put on the glasses. He smiled into the rearview mirror. The change in his appearance was more than good enough for what he had in mind.

He'd introduced himself to the doctor as Don Grant, Marla Grant's cousin.

Dr. White was standing near a dentist's chair and a contraption that looked as if it took X rays. He'd left the tiny room's door open, and there were muffled voices and what might have been the sound of someone getting his teeth polished, but they still had reasonable privacy. "Marla lived in Julep," he said, "but spent most of her time here in New Orleans because this was where she found work. I started my practice originally in Julep, and she worked for me there. When I moved the office here to enlarge my patient pool, she came with me."

"Long way to commute," Donnie said.

Dr. White shrugged his shoulders inside his white smock. "Not really. Lots of folks drive here from Julep to work. Sometimes they stay the weekend."

"Did Marla ever do that? Stay the weekend?"

Dr. White looked oddly at Donnie. "You ask curious questions for a cousin."

"The family's curious about Marla's death. Like you said, she was a sweet woman. And apparently not very complicated."

"What I meant was that she led a simple, honest life. She didn't put on airs or manipulate people."

"So who'd want to kill her?"

"No one that any of her friends can think of."

"What about her, uh, romantic life? I mean, did you ever meet anyone she was seeing socially?"

"A man? No. Marla dated occasionally but definitely wasn't interested in getting involved. She was ambitious, said this was the time of her life when she wanted to get ahead in some kind of career."

"Meaning real estate?"

"I guess so," Dr. White said. He shot a glance at a wall clock that looked like a giant molar. "I don't think I've got all the answers you want. Have you talked to the police?"

"Some," Donnie lied.

"They could probably tell you more than I can. All I know is Marla was a wonderful, loyal friend and employee. And not the sort to lead a double life."

"Why do you say double life?"

"That's what the police seem to think, that she had some kind of secret vice or fetish." Dr. White shook his head. "That's New Orleans for you. Believe me, Marla wasn't the type to be a dental receptionist by day and a dominatrix by night. Besides, when would she find the time, what with her real estate work? That's the direction she was moving in, where she could make more in commissions than the salary I could afford to pay. Residential real estate."

"She sold for one of those big franchise agencies, didn't she?"

"No. A local realtor. Monet. Spelled like the painter. You oughta talk to someone there."

"Maybe I will," Donnie said. "I remember someone from the agency at the funeral."

"I don't remember you from the funeral," Dr. White said.

"I wasn't there long. I hate funerals, especially if they involve someone I was fond of."

A short, dark-haired woman wearing a smock like the dentist's stuck her head around the corner. She was rather pretty but wore a fierce frown of the sort that had probably over the years forged the cast of her features—a slow-motion version of the childhood warning come true. "A Ms. J. Stodner is here, Dr. White."

He nodded. "Thanks, Sophie." She disappeared.

"Marla's replacement?" Donnie asked.

"Temporarily," Dr. White said. "I'd better see to my patient."

"Thanks for talking to me. I wanted to get . . . well, a better sense of Marla to carry with me when I went back home."

"Where is home?" Dr. White asked, definitely suspicious.

"East," Donnie said.

"Where east?"

Sophie saved Donnie, poking her head around the corner again, wearing a deeper frown. Not a woman to mess with even if she was an underling. "Ms. Stodner's waiting, Doctor."

"She run the place?" Donnie asked, when Sophie was finished admonishing her employer with a look.

"Thinks so," Dr. White said with a smile. He accepted Donnie's hand and his thanks again, rather tentatively.

Donnie left the office figuring the dentist would forget him by the end of the day. Or maybe he'd mention the visit to the police. Let the police wonder about Marla's cousin.

It was always good to follow the advice of your dentist. Donnie got in the Honda and drove to a newspaper machine. He should be able to get Monet's address from the classified ads for houses.

Monet Real Estate was a small operation with an office in a strip shopping center near Magazine Street. It seemed even smaller inside, until a door opened behind the reception desk and Donnie caught a glimpse of rows of gray steel desks in a well-lit room, each with a computer monitor on the left-hand corner.

A matronly receptionist with a helmet of blue-gray hair and a syrupy Southern accent expressed her grief and horror about what had happened to Marla. She gnawed her lower lip in thought when Donnie asked who might have known Marla best at the agency.

Finally, leaving a wake of perfume smelling strongly of lilacs, she ushered Donnie through the door that had briefly opened, then to one of the desks. She introduced him to a thin, consumptive-looking man who was bald on top but had long, thick black hair curled above and over his ears. The receptionist said his name was Ron Rucker. She told Rucker that Donnie was "Marla's grieving cousin from the East," and went back to her desk on the other side of the door.

"I was about to leave town for home," Donnie said. "Thought I'd drop by and talk to someone about Marla. The family's going to miss her."

"We'll miss her here, too," Rucker said. He was perched on the edge of the desk, perspiring slightly as if he'd been doing physical work. The other people in the office, half a dozen women, were seated in their desk chairs writing or using their computers.

"Are you one of the other agents here?"

"Sales manager," Rucker said. "I was just finishing cleaning out Marla's desk. Not Marla's, strictly speaking. She shared it with another part-time agent."

"Oh? Who would that be?"

"Sandy Scofield. But they didn't know each other all that well. Didn't spend a lot of time in the office. That's because they're both—or *were* both—active salespeople, working in the field."

"Field?"

"That's anywhere there's a house to be listed or sold," Rucker said.

"Ah!" Another woman entered the office and scurried frowning past them to a corner desk. She had nodded curtly to Rucker, all business. "What I thought," Donnie said, "is that maybe you could give me some little thing here to remember Marla by. You know, her personal fountain pen or something."

"You're lucky you came when you did." Rucker motioned with his head toward a cardboard box on the floor near the desk. "Most of this stuff was gonna be thrown away." He squatted so it looked like his pants were going to burst their seams and rummaged through the box's contents, presumably taken from the desk drawers assigned to Marla. "No fountain pen," he said, standing up, "but here's her listing book if you want it. It's full of notations written by her."

Rucker handed Donnie a thick book with page after page of photos and information on houses for sale.

"Those aren't only properties listed with Monet," he told Donnie. "These books are put out by a regional service and list most of the houses for sale in the area."

"This'll do fine," Donnie said. "I appreciate it." He tucked the book beneath his arm. "Listen, is there anything you can tell me about Marla? I mean, I'm not trying to play cop, but the family's naturally curious about the criminal aspect of this. Marla sure wasn't the type to have the kind of enemy who might kill her."

"None of us really knows that, though, do we?" Rucker said. "Sometimes in the military you find out even you can kill if you have to."

"You look too young to have been in Vietnam."

Rucker smiled. "Desert Storm. Not a long war, but a bad one." He moved his head from side to side, as if shaking off memories. "But you're right; it's hard to imagine anyone wanting to do . . . what was done to Marla. She seemed like an open book, and wasn't the type to lead a double life."

"You're the second person to tell me that," Donnie

said, "about the double life. And she had a twin sister, you know."

Rucker shrugged. "Deuces wild." Then in a more serious tone: "What I meant, why I joked, is because any notion of Marla being mixed up in some kind of intrigue involving a twin sister seems absurd. If you'd known her, you'd understand. She was very much the new American career woman. That was pretty much her focus all the time."

"Maybe something all too American happened to her."

Rucker looked thoughtful. "That *is* the kind of society we seem to have become. Actually I never knew Marla had a twin. Or even a sister. She never mentioned it."

Donnie wondered what else she might not have mentioned.

He shook hands with Rucker, sneaking another glance at the contents of the cardboard box. Nothing but listing sheets, a tape dispenser, box of paper clips, half a dozen stubby pencils. The usual detritus of fractured employment.

"Thanks for taking the time," Donnie said.

"Here, wait!" Rucker said, withdrawing his hand from Donnie's and stooping low again. "Take one of her cards." When he straightened up, he handed Donnie a white business card. It was slightly oversized and had a color photo of Marla in the upper left corner. She was smiling and had her hair artfully mussed and looked nothing like the woman in the morgue photo.

"She was beautiful," Donnie said, shaking his head sadly.

"They all are here," Rucker said. "At least in their company photos. The business has been pretty much taken over by women. They love to sell houses and they're good at it, and they all have glamour shots taken for their business cards and newspaper ads. They look more like a bunch of soap-opera stars than real estate agents." He laughed and glanced around. "Hell, the old guys who used to man these desks never even thought of putting their pictures on their cards. And it's a good thing. They were an ugly bunch."

Donnie laughed with him, slipped the card into a side pocket of his sport jacket, then walked away with the bulky listing book still tucked beneath his arm.

As he was leaving, the graying receptionist was seated holding a phone to her ear. She smiled but looked at him as if he might be stealing company property.

"Marla's," he said with a return smile, pointing to the listing book with his free hand.

"Ah, Mr. Monet . . ." she was cooing into the phone, as Donnie pushed open the glass door and went outside.

My listing book now, he was thinking.

Also thinking how good it would feel to get rid of the glasses and mustache.

27

When Donnie opened his apartment door that night after work, the light came on and he was face-to-face with Elvis Presley.

He'd barely had time to think about that when a hand grabbed his shirtfront and yanked him all the way inside. He staggered and went down on one knee.

As he was straightening up to see who belonged to the pants and shoes he was looking at, something hard slammed into the back of his head.

Donnie was facedown flat on the carpet. As he lost consciousness he saw again Elvis's pale features and realized someone had struck him in the head with the white mock-plaster statuette of the King.

The statuette with the microrecorder and wire concealed inside.

He prayed Elvis hadn't shattered from the force of the blow.

". . . headbreak hotel," he heard an amused, taunting voice say.

He knew whose.

Then he knew nothing.

*   *   *

Until pain.

One hellacious headache.

". . . shouldn't ought have hit him," Army was saying.

Donnie didn't open his eyes. He was careful not to reveal in any way that he'd regained consciousness.

Something was softly humming . . . an engine. Vibration. Motion. He was in a car.

Donnie did a careful mental check of his body parts. Aside from his throbbing headache, he didn't have much feeling in his arms, which were twisted around behind his back, bound at the wrists, cutting off circulation. Legs, everything else, felt okay. He was slouched sideways in plush upholstery in a corner of the car. Plenty of leg room. A large car. Army's voice had come from his right, and Donnie's left shoulder was against hard, cool metal as well as the softness of the upholstery. Since he was on the left, he was in the backseat and Army wasn't driving.

Donnie smelled mint. Heard chewing gum pop.

Frankie the Lounger, whose voice Donnie had heard as he lost consciousness, must be in front at the wheel.

Donnie cautiously eased his left eye open to a narrow slit.

Darkness, passing headlights, the back of Frankie's head. They were in Vito Cantanzano's yacht-sized black Caddy. Nobody was sitting alongside the Lounger, so it was just the three of them in the car.

"Mr. C. don't like it if you bring him a bruised bundle unless he asks," Army said.

Pop! More mint scent. "We'll say Sparky here put up a struggle," said the Lounger.

"*You'll* say," Army told him.

Pressure on Donnie's left shoulder increased against the inside frame of the door as the car made a tight right turn. He let his left eyelid close as brighter light flickered across his face.

They drove for a while, which was fine with Donnie. It allowed more time for his headache to abate somewhat. Wasn't helping his arms much, though. They were getting more numb by the minute.

Donnie knew their destination, so he waited until the car stopped before opening his eyes.

They were parked before Vito Cantanzano's sprawling, bastardized English Tudor mansion. The shrubbery concealed low-lying lights that illuminated the winding walk to the front porch and door with its brass lion's-head knocker. A medieval-looking porch light with lead-framed yellow glass was glowing a welcome to guests.

Sort of a welcome, anyway, Donnie thought.

Army waited without moving while Frankie the Lounger climbed out of the Caddy and opened the rear door, almost causing Donnie to tumble out. Or so Donnie made it look.

"Sparky here is still a bit woozy," Frankie observed.

"And has a headache, I betcha," Army said, as he maneuvered his bulk out the other side of the car and walked around to help Frankie support Donnie.

"Kinda jag-off that deserves a headache, you ask me," Frankie said around his chewing gum. "Maybe if I slap him a good one in the head again it'll go away, you think?"

"Do *you* think? Ever?" Army asked.

Frankie answered with a barrage of gum popping.

"Now stand up straight like a good lad," Army said, as he gripped Donnie beneath the armpits and hoisted him off his feet. He set him back down with unexpected gentleness, as if he were a doll whose limbs should have automatically adjusted so he could stand.

Donnie made it seem to work, managing to stand alone while Army unfastened the ropes that bound his wrists. The feeling in his arms began to return immediately, with something between a tingle and an ache. He actually felt alert and strong enough to bolt into the night, but he decided that wouldn't be wise. He suspected why Cantanzano wanted to talk to him. The aging don would surely know by now about the fight out at Circe involving his nephew Nordo.

Donnie was ushered into the room made up like a mock hunting lodge where he'd first met Vito Cantanzano.

This time Cantanzano was seated in the leather wing chair with his legs crossed casually. He was wearing a pale blue silk robe, or dressing gown, brown leather slippers, and a midnight blue ascot with a silver star pattern. In his right hand was what looked like a glass of port. When he motioned to Donnie to sit in the identical wing chair opposite his, Donnie noticed that the robe had leather elbow patches, and there was no shirt with the ascot, just pale flesh and gray chest hair. Another of Cantanzano's awkward attempts at upper-echelon British class.

"You wanna glass of port?" he asked, playing the gracious host.

Donnie said he did, and Vito nodded to Army. Donnie sat quietly and watched while Army went to a marble-topped sideboard and poured port into stemmed crystal. After replacing the decanter, he walked slowly over as if he were an English butler and handed the glass to Donnie. Donnie thought for a moment that Army might bow at the waist, but he didn't. Donnie was disappointed. He sampled the port. It figured to be expensive, and it tasted that way. He swallowed, then moved his head experimentally, hoping the drink would help the pain above the base of his neck. *Ouch!*

"Whazza matter?" Cantanzano asked. "The way you're frownin' . . . You a chap's got a migraine?"

Frankie the Lounger and Army were staring deadpan at Donnie. He saw no point in getting Army in trouble with his boss.

Donnie nodded. "Up late the last couple of nights. Too much Elvis Presley."

Cantanzano's long, sad face broke into a seamed grin. "Hey, you a fan of the King?"

"Sure," Donnie said.

"Me, too. Ever been to Graceland?"

"Sure," Donnie said again, lying hard and remembering a TV special he once saw on Graceland, former home of the King, which was now a tourist attraction. The Travel Channel, he thought. "Some bathroom!"

"Yeah." Cantanzano looked wistful. "Terrible to have all that money and class and die young."

"Terrible to die young," Donnie said.

"Lucky guy had all that money and class and ass," smart-mouth Frankie said. "Word is he was some swordsman with the ladies."

"Do get the fuck outta here," Cantanzano said with proper gentility. "The brace of yous."

Frankie appeared puzzled.

"He means the two of us," Army said, and gave him a shove toward the door. Frankie glared at him but went.

When Donnie was alone with Cantanzano, the old man took a sip of port, sighed, and looked at him. "You did real good the other night."

Donnie knew it was the right time to hold his silence.

"I mean the thing with Nick."

It took Donnie a second to realize he meant Nordo. "I don't mind that much looking out for the kid," he said. "I like him."

"You went way beyond just lookin' out for him," Cantanzano said. "Not only last night, but in that other matter, the guy that shot himself. You're a standup chap."

Donnie wondered how the old don knew about the suicide, how Donnie had taken Nordo's place in moving Harry Lomer's body and making suicide look like a hitchhike murder. About Nordo's violent run-in with Rat in the ring. Had Nordo told him?

The Harry Lomer thing was the kind of knowledge that shouldn't be spread around if there was no reason.

"You saved the boy twice over."

"Nordo was doing okay in the ring with Rat," Donnie said. "When he had to, he went to the well and got what he needed. You should be proud of him."

Cantanzano smiled proudly. "I am. Him and me, we got the same blood." Another sip of port. "Breeding tells."

"It did that night," Donnie said.

"Rat woulda killed Nick if you hadn't stopped him."

"Could be."

"Way I hear, Rat's a man likes his cutlery, and he ain't known for his restraint."

"The way Nordo was going," Donnie said, "he mighta taken the knife away from Rat and fed it to him."

Cantanzano actually laughed out loud with glee.

"I mean, I had to hold the kid back. Turns out he's got cojones like beach balls!"

Cantanzano laughed louder and choked on a sip of port. "Sure he does," he said when he was finished coughing. "Whaddya expect?"

"I can't say I was surprised," Donnie said, piling on the points. "Still, it was nice to see. I mean, him taking the play away like that."

"No fuckin' gutless freako flower child like his father, that one, eh?"

"Not that one."

"He still okay out there, you think?" Cantanzano asked.

"Yeah. He's better off than he was before. Less likely to get fucked with. The boss, Ewing Bolt, doesn't intend to fire him. I'd say Nordo did some fast growing up the hard way."

"They do get older while you ain't lookin'."

"One day they're playing hopscotch; next time you look they're stomping someone's face."

"That's the best way, eh?"

"Sure," Donnie agreed. He wondered if Cantanzano meant best way growing up, or best stomping technique.

"It might be that we got you by the short hairs and you got no choice," Cantanzano said, "but that don't keep me from havin' you collected and brought out here so I can thank you personally when you do good."

"Nice of you," Donnie said, knowing the irony would be lost on Cantanzano.

"Kinda chap I am."

"That's your reputation."

"No shit?"

"What I've heard."

Cantanzano threw back his head and downed the rest of his port as if it were cheap booze in a shot glass. He raised an arm and wiped his mouth with the silk sleeve of his robe, but with a certain delicacy Donnie found amazing. "Well, you been thanked."

Donnie waited a few seconds, until he was sure Cantanzano was going to remain seated, then stood up. He hadn't seen Cantanzano give any kind of signal or press a button, but he heard the door open behind him. Reflected in the glass of a framed fox-hunting scene, he saw Army and Frankie come back into the room and stand politely side by side.

"You're gonna be delivered back to where you were collected," Cantanzano said.

Donnie nodded, then walked over to be ushered out by the two waiting thugs.

"And don't strike him blows on the head no more," Cantanzano added. "Nor do anything else untoward."

Frankie momentarily stopped chewing gum, fixing a hard look on Donnie.

"He didn't tell me about it," Cantanzano said. "I knew, Frankie. You gotta learn better." He suddenly gripped a glass ashtray, drew back his arm, and hurled the ashtray at a large, obviously expensive vase halfway across the room. His aim was unerring. The vase shattered, its delicate glazed flower pattern reduced to a dozen jagged pieces after the violent crash. "The rule is, you use muscle only when I tell you. You two buggers bloody forget that again, you're gonna fuckin' come to an unfortunate end."

Frankie went even paler but remained silent as he and Army pushed Donnie out through the doorway, then followed and flanked him closely.

Back in the Caddy, as they were pulling out of the driveway, Army, sitting beside Donnie but talking to Frankie, said, "I warned you about head-bangin' when it ain't called for."

"I wish the old man hadn't busted that vase. He

oughta stop breakin' up good things just because he's mad. It's a bad habit and it's gettin' worse."

"Mr. C. breaks things to make his point," Army said, "when he's trying to stop somebody from screwing up all the time. I guess it makes him feel better, too, but mostly it's to stop a fuckup from fuckin' up."

Frankie straightened out the car and smacked the steering wheel with an open palm. "Hey! Fuck you and your warnings! Fuck that old man and his orders!"

"Ease up, Frankie," Army said calmly. "The walls have ears."

Pop! Pop! Frankie was chewing frantically. "Fuck the walls! I wanna tell you, *double fuck* the walls!"

"Hear that, walls?" Army asked Donnie.

"Heard it," Donnie said.

In the front seat, Frankie barked a falsetto laugh. "Listen, Army, push comes to shove, you think Cantanzano's gonna believe that chunk of dog meat back there instead of me?"

"Yeah," Army said.

Frankie the Lounger fumed quietly, wishing he hadn't asked the question, knowing Army might be right.

Progress, Donnie thought, rubbing the golf ball–sized lump at the base of his skull.

In his business, progress.

28

"It's this way," Mitki said to Donnie by the parking kiosk at Circe. "Rat don't forget, ever. He's got this Chinese thing about saving face."

A warm wind blew in from the line of dark cedar trees off in the distance, carrying the smell of the swamp. "He isn't Chinese," Donnie said, "and he hasn't got a face worth saving."

Mitki put on a pained expression. "You talk like that, it'll only make things worse. It'd be better all around if you left the area. Safer for you."

Donnie, wearing his neat tan parking valet uniform, watched a car approach the entrance to Circe's long driveway. It didn't turn in. "You're Rat's friend, so why are you warning me?"

"This isn't any warning; it's a threat. You don't leave the area, you're gonna leave the world. I told you, Rat don't forget. Nobody's ever got by with him what you did. Sooner or later he's gonna do you, and he's gonna do that little asshole Nordo."

Donnie knew what was going on here. He remembered Jules telling him not to underestimate Mitki or assume he was without guile. Only his sadism kept him from attaining a higher position in the mob.

"What you're worried about," Donnie said, "is that Rat's gonna act out of turn, get him and you in trouble with Bolt and whoever's over Bolt."

Mitki raised his eyebrows. "Over Bolt? What's that supposed to mean?"

"Only an idiot would think Bolt owns and operates this place. There have to be money men. Investors."

Mitki took his time lighting a long greenish cigar. The fetid swamp breeze snatched away the smoke he blew in Donnie's direction. Mitki puffed on the cigar, then removed it from his mouth and held it out to the side and observed it the way George Burns used to do. When he looked at Donnie he was wearing a Burnsish little smile. Suspicious, though. "I never knew you were knowledgeable about business."

"What I'm saying is you don't have to be knowledgeable about business to figure the setup here. Or to figure why you're worried you can't control Rat."

"Maybe control's got nothing to do with it. Maybe I want you to get outta here and prevent trouble because I like Rat."

"Means nothing to me. I don't like Rat."

"I can understand that. I don't like you."

"We aren't getting anyplace with this conversation," Donnie said. "You want me and Nordo to hit the highway, and it's not going to happen."

"I didn't say a word about Nordo. What do you care if that little prick stays around here and gets his ears cut off?"

"I guess I like Nordo the way you like Rat."

Mitki gave a kind of half growl, half chuckle and shook his head. "Well, I'd say it's your funeral, only it takes a body for there to be one of those. People that cross Rat, they tend just not to be there one day."

"I guess I'll have to settle for a memorial service," Donnie said.

Mitki laughed. "Nobody remembers or mourns fuckheads like you. You been a lost soul all your life, and after you die you're just a little more lost and nobody cares or even sees much difference in it." He blew smoke again in Donnie's direction before spinning on his heel and walking away. This time the breeze cooperated.

There was something in his words, some reflection of truth, that bothered Donnie more than he liked to admit.

Maybe Mitki said something to Rat about the conversation, because late that night, when things at Circe were winding down, Rat approached Donnie and Nordo. He was wearing black slacks with a thousand pleats that made him look even rounder than he was, and a red T-shirt. His arm Donnie had injured was in a flesh-colored sling, but no hard cast. Not broken, just dislocated, along with some torn muscle and strained tendons. Must be sore as hell.

Donnie, who'd been sweeping up around the kiosk, leaned on the broom handle.

But Rat didn't so much as look at him.

"You smokin' weed again, asshole?" he said to Nordo.

"Unfiltered Camels, man." Nordo smiled and

flicked his cigarette so it bounced off Rat's thigh in a little shower of sparks. A little higher and it could have set all those pleats on fire. Donnie wished the kid would back off a little but knew it wasn't going to happen. He was riding high and liked the feeling. Mitki was right about the recipe for trouble that had been cooked up the night of the fight.

No time was wasted. Rat scrunched up his round little features in his fat head and moved on Nordo.

Nordo, flushed with bravado, assumed his exaggerated John L. Sullivan boxing stance.

Blood was going to flow here. Bones were going to break.

Nordo's blood. Nordo's bones.

Donnie had to move fast. He leveled the broom handle and jabbed its tip hard into Rat's damaged arm.

Rat gave a high-pitched yowl and backed away.

He switched his attention to Donnie now. His entire body was throbbing like a locomotive building pressure and power for a charge.

Then he drew a deep breath that puffed up his neck like a toad's and exhaled longer and louder than Donnie would have thought possible. Somehow Rat had found temporary self-restraint.

"Your time'll come," he said. "Both of you. You think I put up with the kinda shit you dished out the other night, you're makin' a fatal mistake."

"You're a fuckin' fetal mistake, man," Nordo told him.

"You an' me are gonna be together in a place an' time where your smart mouth won't help you," Rat said. It was ugly, the way he smiled. "I always even the scales."

"You're, like, too fat to even any scales," Nordo said.

It didn't get to Rat. The smile stayed. He had something in mind and was satisfied to mull it over. For now.

"I'll see you guys in hell," he said. "Least you'll think it's hell."

Holding his injured arm, he went back into the club. He was hunched over slightly and walking with a hitch in his stride. He'd sustained plenty of damage the night of the fight, injury to more than his pride and his arm.

"Whaddya think he means?" Nordo asked. "That remark about seeing us in hell?"

Donnie shrugged. "Who knows? He wants to save face, like the Chinese."

"He ain't Chinese, man."

"He thinks he is," Donnie said. "Chinese enough, anyway."

Nordo grinned and fired up another unfiltered Camel, then strutted toward the parking lot.

Feeling pretty good, Donnie thought, watching him stepping out like there were a band behind him. Cocky as you could be only at his age. High enough tonight he didn't need to smoke weed. High enough to fall hard.

29

Donnie was awakened at eight o'clock the next morning by a phone call. His bedroom window was open about six inches and a warm breeze had pushed into the room and was caressing his bare right leg, which he'd extended out from the light sheet that covered him. He'd been dreaming about being trapped in a maze, pursued by a giant rat. Fat rat. Had a front paw in a sling.

It was a relief to wake up.

He said a sleepy hello into the receiver and waited for a reply, but got only the staticky hiss of the phone connection.

After about ten seconds Mitki's voice said, "Don't come into work till about five o'clock tonight, Donnie. You ain't gonna park cars. Mr. Bolt's got a different job for us tonight."

"Us?"

"You, me, a few close friends. And some new playmates you're sure to like."

This was what Donnie feared. He couldn't let himself be put into a position where he'd have to be party to someone being injured or killed. Bureau undercover agents weren't authorized to be criminals, not even agents like Donnie Brasco. Aside from the professional and moral implications, there were legal considerations. Events that unfolded from the time Donnie arrived in Julep would, if things went as planned, eventually find their way into a courtroom. The evidence couldn't be compromised.

"What kinda job is this gonna be?" he asked Mitki.

"There's no point you knowing that ahead of time. You'll only worry your pretty head. Wear dark work clothes. Bring some gloves. And make sure there's plenty of gas in that junk pile car of yours."

"So what's the deal, we taking a trip?" Donnie the curious. Who wouldn't be, being awakened from a sound sleep by a phone call like this?

"We're all on a kinda trip, don't you think? Everybody in this cesspool world."

"Listen, you wake me up when I've had about four hours' sleep and lay all this crap on me. Now you go all metaphysical when I ask you for a little more information. I think you owe me that."

"You got all the information you need."

"Am I supposed to bring anything else? Maybe a casserole?"

Donnie waited. "Hey!"

But Mitki had hung up rather than trade sarcasms. Done it softly and soundlessly, with uncharacteristic subtlety. Unsettling.

Work clothes. Gloves. Full gas tank.

All Donnie needed to know.

Like hell, it was.

Donnie reached for the phone to call Jules, then thought better of it.

He got dressed, then went outside into a morning bright enough to hurt his eyes.

There was Mrs. LaValierre, the elderly widow from the ground-floor apartment in the same building as his, coming toward him on the front walk. She was carrying a plastic grocery bag with some celery stalks sticking out of it. She nodded and smiled with Southern charm and hospitality. Donnie smiled back but had no time to dawdle and enjoy the day.

"Are you adjusting nicely to the neighborhood?" Mrs. LaValierre drawled.

"Very well, thanks."

"I knocked on your door the other day, thought I heard you moving around inside, but since you didn't answer I naturally assumed you were otherwise occupied."

"I must have been, not to hear, but I'm sorry I missed you."

Donnie stepped aside to let her pass, then hurried on before their conversation could take deeper root.

He steered the Honda through a McDonald's and ate an Egg McMuffin and sipped coffee while he drove to the other end of town and a small shopping mall he remembered seeing. He had to vary the origins of his phone calls, avoid patterns. At this stage of the game, a lot of eyes might be watching him.

His own eyes had been watching the rearview mirror, and he'd deliberately timed some traffic lights so he'd just made it through the intersections as they flashed red. Almost but hadn't quite run the lights.

No other vehicle showed in his mirror. He was reasonably sure he hadn't been followed.

In the center of the mall were some public phones halfway down a narrow tile hall that led to the rest rooms. Donnie sat on a hard steel seat before an end phone and called Jules. He had a morsel of food lodged between his molars and could still taste the Egg McMuffin, was still hungry. Another cup of coffee would be good, too. As if he needed more nervous stimulation.

"I got the call to duty above and beyond," he told Jules when the connection had been made. He repeated the instructions relayed to him by Mitki.

"Any ideas?" Jules asked, when Donnie was finished.

"I don't know enough about what's going down to have any that I trust, but there are two I don't."

"That gonna stop you from suggesting them?"

"Nope. What do you think about me tipping off Vito Cantanzano about some kind of operation being run out of Circe tonight?"

Jules hummed tunelessly into the phone, thinking. He did that sometimes when he had to make a move. As if he thought better with his own musical accompaniment.

"It'd stir the pot," Donnie said, prodding Jules.

"So go ahead and stir," Jules said. "What's untrustworthy idea number two?"

"Tonight might be the time for me to wear the wire."

"It might also be the time they'd think to check you for a wire."

"Yeah," Donnie admitted, "but this is all about taking chances. It'd be good to have some solid evidence of whatever's gonna happen tonight."

"Not if you find yourself an active participant."

"We both know I can't afford to be that, even if it means blowing my cover and terminating the operation."

"What if it means terminating you, Donnie?"

"There's usually a way to avoid that."

"Final answer?" asked Jules.

"Yeah. I've already phoned a friend. So give me the million dollars."

"So wear the wire," Jules said. "But be extra careful, Donnie. It occur to you that you're maybe being set up? Like Lily and Frank might have been?"

"Lots of things have occurred to me. I try to push them out of the way."

"I know you do." Jules's voice was slow, thoughtful. "I don't much like this, Donnie."

"Neither do I, but there it is."

"You seriously gotta keep yourself clean on this. And, uh, make sure you get a good angle. Get close enough for the mike to pick up what's being said." Jules for you. Now that they were committed to using the wire, he wanted good evidence, whatever happened to Donnie. "Remember, what's on that tape will play in court someday."

"We hope," Donnie said.

"Yeah, we do that a lot. We're deeper into enemy territory here. Walk carefully and watch your back."

"I thought you'd say that, about watching my back. You always do, somewhere along the line."

"It figures in with the hope part," Jules told him. "And the friend part."

After hanging up the phone, Donnie walked down to a menswear store. It wouldn't be a bad idea to make a purchase, give himself a reason for having driven to the mall, just in case someone had managed to follow him.

He remembered reading in the Don Wells file that Wells had favored argyle socks, so Donnie bought a couple of pairs. Another piece to the disguise, to his new identity that had become his other self.

As he paid the clerk and carried the folded paper bag containing the socks out of the shop, he actually felt kind of smug. This new remnant of Don Wells that he could hide behind made him feel oddly more secure.

As if a pair of socks could make a difference.

Argyle, at that.

When he got back to the apartment, he decided to break the Elvis statuette and remove the microrecorder and miniature microphone.

But he stopped cold and stood still before the bookshelf.

Not liking what he saw.

What he didn't see.

Elvis was gone.

30

Donnie stood staring at the empty space on the shelf where the bust of Elvis had resided. He'd gotten used to the thing, seen it and yet not seen it, and he realized it might have been missing for days without his having noticed.

He recalled Mrs. LaValierre mentioning that she'd heard someone in his apartment. Might that have been when the bust was stolen?

The pertinent questions cascaded through his mind. Who had taken it? Why? Had they discovered the microrecording equipment inside?

Elvis was expendable. There was no way to know or have access to what was inside without breaking the statuette. And there was some kind of padding to prevent any rattling around. It was possible that whoever had stolen Elvis, for whatever reason, didn't suspect there *was* anything inside it.

The other thing that was possible, Donnie couldn't let himself think about right now. The operation out of Circe was on for tonight, and he still had to tip off Vito Cantanzano and the remnants of Julep's Mafia organization. It was probably too late to contact Jules or Sue Bristol and arrange for another wire. And considering what had happened to Elvis, maybe it wouldn't be a smart thing to do anyway. Mitki and Rat were a couple of cutups eager to play. Especially Rat.

Donnie would be a lot more comfortable tonight knowing he wasn't wearing a wire.

A lot more comfortable if he could keep convincing himself the Elvis statuette was somewhere safe and unbroken.

But he knew comfort was seldom part of the equation. Wasn't he the one who'd told Jules the job was all about taking chances?

When Donnie arrived at Circe at five that evening he was wearing Levi's, a black pullover shirt, a black windbreaker, and his well-worn dark blue–and-gray New Balance jogging shoes. In a pocket of the windbreaker was a pair of new brown jersey work gloves.

Mitki, wearing a navy blue jogging suit and running shoes, was standing near the entrance. He came down the shallow steps to meet Donnie, quick and sure on his feet, moving with the bulk and lightness of a pro linebacker.

"C'mon with me around back," he said immediately, and led the way around the side of the building.

They went through a wide, open sliding gate set in a high chain-link fence topped with razor wire. It was the first time Donnie had been in that part of Circe's grounds. There was a large garage for storing vehicles and maintenance equipment, and an area of gravel and cracked shells that made for a driveway and turnaround.

Donnie was surprised to see an eighteen-wheel tractor-trailer parked there, its diesel engine idling and sending vaporous dark puffs of smoke from twin chrome stacks behind its dusty blue Kenworth cab. The trailer had a bulky refrigeration unit mounted in front up near the roof so it was slightly higher than the top of the cab. It was the kind of rig used for hauling frozen meat or produce. The air and electrical lines running between cab and trailer were hooked up, making the truck ready to drive, and the refrigeration unit could be heard humming away between deep bass beats of the throbbing diesel exhaust.

The black van that had dogged Donnie and laid down the oil slick that led to his harrowing off-road adventure was parked nearby. Near the back of the van, Nordo was standing talking to Len, the lean African-American who worked the opposite shift as parking valet. Neither man had on his valet uniform. Like Donnie, both wore dark clothing. Nordo, in fact, looked like a throwback to the days of serious roving motorcycle gangs, with skintight Levi's, a waist-length black leather jacket with the collar turned up, and black boots. He seemed to have an extra gob or two of grease in his slicked-back black hair, too.

He noticed Donnie and nodded, then lit a cigarette with a match he ignited with a thumbnail. He absently flicked the burned match away in a long, smoking arc and didn't bother watching where it landed. Cool, Donnie thought.

"What's Nordo doing here?" Donnie asked Mitki.

"Going with us, is what he's gonna do."

"You mean he's included in this job tonight?"

"Sure. Ain't he part of our big corporate family?"

This Donnie didn't like. There was no way Nordo would be taken into the inner circle and trusted to act in concert with Mitki, Rat, and associates. Ewing Bolt might like the kid enough to keep him parking cars at Circe, but he wouldn't send him along tonight. Unless . . .

"Mr. Bolt know about him going?" Donnie asked.

Mitki smiled meanly at him. "Privates don't ask colonels what generals know."

"I'm interested in what the general might *not* know," Donnie said.

"Ain't nobody interested in your interest."

The van's passenger-side door opened and Rat climbed out, then swaggered over to the idling truck. He climbed onto the running board, holding himself balanced with his good arm, and said something to the driver, who was only barely visible to Donnie in an outside mirror. Then he hopped down off the truck and walked over to where Donnie and Mitki stood. He seemed not to see Donnie.

"We're set to go," Rat said. "Should be dark when we get there."

"Get where?" Donnie asked.

"Where we're going," Mitki said.

"Asshole asks dumb questions," Rat said.

Mitki sighed. "It would fuckin' figure." He waved a big arm and motioned for everyone to gather around him.

When they had, Nordo stood near Donnie and whispered, "Gonna rock 'n' sock tonight, man."

Donnie assumed Nordo thought what was about to happen tonight was a stroke of good fortune, that he was going to learn a lot in the next few hours to tell his uncle Vito. Never figuring he might not be able to tell anybody anything, being in the dead state. Enthusiasm instead of common sense. Donnie knew this was how old men got young men to fight wars.

On the other hand, he was older than Nordo, and he was going.

"As you know," Mitki said, "I'm in charge of the party, and Rat is second-in-command. Either of us give you the word, you act like good soldiers. When we pull outta here, everybody stays behind the truck. Follow loose-like. We don't want this to look like no goddamn convoy." He stared hard at everyone as they nodded that they understood. "When we get to the staging area," he said, "there'll be more instructions."

He was holding his gloves in one hand and slapped them on his thigh. Either he had a military background or he had seen a lot of war movies. "Let's mount up now. Nordo and Len'll go with Donnie in Donnie's junk pile over there. Rat and me'll go in the van."

As everyone walked toward his assigned vehicle, Donnie realized one reason why he might have been invited along. Not only might this be a test, but they needed another car and driver. Either the van was loaded with something or they were going to pick up more troops at what Mitki had referred to as the staging area.

The tractor-trailer revved up with a throaty roar and maneuvered toward the gravel-and-shell driveway that would cut into the road near the main drive. The van fell in behind. Eating dust until they reached the county road, Donnie took third place in the Honda.

Nordo sat alongside him in front. Len was in back. Nordo was humming under his breath, probably didn't even know it. A nervous reaction. Sounded like music from *Grease*. Donnie, feeling as if he were about to tilt at windmills, thought it should be *Man of La Mancha*.

"Any idea what's in the truck?" Donnie asked.

Nordo continued humming.

"I don' know nothin' about nothin'," Len said from the back of the car.

"What's all this about?" Donnie asked, goosing the Honda a little to keep up with the others. "I mean, where the fuck we going?"

"Those two things are part of the nothin' I know nothin' about," said Len.

Donnie got the idea.

Nordo was wearing his cocky toothpaste-ad grin. He really did know nothing.

They hit the main highway and increased their speed to the legal limit.

Donnie figured it would probably be the last legal thing they'd do that night.

31

They drove north on 55 into Mississippi, their head-light beams yellow in the soft, warm night.

Near McComb, they took a state highway west. Bugs died against the windshield with regularity, sounding almost like light rain.

The big truck's running lights were easy to follow in the night. Donnie drove the Honda in silence. Nordo suggested getting some good rock or rap on the radio once, but Len and Donnie had both met the suggestion with open hostility. Though quiet, Len seemed plenty nervous. Donnie hoped it was for the right reasons.

The truck slowed and veered to the right. Directly ahead of Donnie the van's brake lights flared.

He slowed the Honda and followed the other two vehicles up a small, unpaved cutoff to a clearing in the dark woods. The hard earth was rutted, making the battered old Honda buck and rattle. Donnie hoped its last off-road jaunt had only loosened things and not done any lasting damage.

The van's headlights winked out, as did the truck's lights. Donnie killed the Honda's lights. The dust and insects dancing in the yellow beams disappeared.

Mitki and Rat got out of the van and walked toward the center of the clearing. As Donnie was climbing out of the Honda, he saw the truck driver open the Kenworth's door and swing down from the tractor.

The only sound in the quiet, moonlit clearing was that of the ticking, rhythmic rumble of the idling diesel. It was like a ponderous clock that seemed to be marking time.

"We wait now," Mitki said simply. "And we keep the noise down."

For the next five minutes no one said anything. Faint moonlight made its way through the overhead branches, creating shifting, dappled patterns of shadows on the ground as the evening breeze moved the leaves.

A slight rustling sound made Donnie turn.

Two men in camouflage hunting garb, carrying shotguns, emerged from the woods. They held the guns casually slung in the crooks of their arms, as if they were plenty familiar with them, and they moved easily and silently, obviously used to being in the outdoors.

At first Donnie thought the plan had hit a snag, but Mitki and Rat didn't seem surprised to see the men.

One of the hunters, a beefy redhead with an unkempt beard, nodded to both of them.

"Well?" Mitki said impatiently. "You got a voice?"

The other hunter, whipcord lean inside his baggy fatigues, and with a hatchet face and shrewd eyes, spat off to the side. He made it a point to take his time answering.

"We're pretty much by ourselves here," he said in a smooth Mississippi drawl that dripped insolence from every syllable.

"Make sure it stays that way," Mitki told him.

"If we see or hear somebody," the redhead said, "Carl or me'll use a turkey call to warn you."

Mitki stared at him, then turned around and looked at the men who'd driven out from Circe. "Anybody know what a turkey sounds like?"

"Gobble, gobble," Nordo said with a grin.

"I know," Len said, serious, still nervous. "I used to hunt wild turkey up near my dad's place in Georgia."

That seemed to satisfy Mitki. "Be sure the turkey makes plenty of noise," he told the redheaded man.

"Gobble, gobble," the man said.

Mitki glared at him. "Was that some kinda insult?"

"Only if you're a turkey," the other woodsman said.

Mitki turned away, and the two hunter-lookouts faded back into the dark woods in opposite directions.

"Those boys are local," Mitki said to no one and everyone. "They're kinda independent, but they're reliable, and they know the area 'cause they roamed it for years. They'll let us know if anyone happens along here, and as long as they *don't* let us know, you can relax and do your work without fucking up."

He'd barely finished speaking when a low rumbling sound made its way through the woods.

"That's a diesel," the truck driver said.

"I didn't think it was a goddamn turkey!" Mitki told him.

Light and shadow played over the trees; then the woods went dark again. The rumbling changed tone, got lower and louder, and a massive rectangular black shape emerged from the night. Another tractor-trailer.

As it rolled into the moonlit clearing, Donnie saw that the cab was a red Peterbilt, not a blue Kenworth like the one that had driven here from Circe.

What was identical about the trucks were the trailers.

The second truck pulled alongside the first. Air brakes hissed, and it slowed to a stop.

"What's in the trailer?" Donnie asked, pointing to the first truck, figuring at this point Mitki might be willing to provide an answer.

"Chickens," Mitki said.

"What's in the second truck?"

"Chickens."

Rat got into the van and reversed it so it was closer to the trucks. Then he got out and walked around to open the back of the van. "You guys unload these," he said. "The truck drivers'll show you where to put 'em."

Donnie, Nordo, and Len walked over to the van. Donnie saw that there were four rectangular concrete slabs stacked on the floor in back. It was a good thing the van had a reinforced suspension that would handle all that weight.

They dragged the heavy slabs from the van and carried them to where Mitki directed. The slabs were about two feet square and rough enough to cut through Donnie's cheap brown jersey gloves. He guessed they'd been poured just for this onetime purpose.

Following Mitki's instructions, the three men placed the slabs flat on the ground beneath the front ends of the trailers on both sides.

Both truck drivers got to work, cranking down the supporting jacks for the trailers so that they rested on the concrete slabs and wouldn't sink into the soft earth when the cabs were pulled out and the trailers lost their front-end support. Then they unhooked the electrical and air lines behind the cabs. It didn't take Donnie long to see what they were up to. The cabs were about to exchange trailers.

Truck doors slammed shut, diesel engines roared, and the cabs lurched out from beneath their trailers. The front of each trailer dropped about six inches, but the slabs distributed the weight, sank into the earth, then held. The drivers were experienced, and, free from their burdens, the cabs were nimble in capable hands. They managed a neat crisscross maneuver to change places. Then the cabs were backed in so each was hooked up to the trailer that had been the other cab's.

While Donnie and Nordo cranked the supporting jacks back up, the drivers busied themselves reconnecting air-brake and electrical lines.

Donnie stepped away from the second trailer and saw that Rat had backed the van close to it. The trailer's doors had been opened, and Len was busily unloading something from it, then transferring it into the back of the van.

"Fifty of them," Mitki said. "Keep count with him,

Rat. We're s'posed to get exactly fifty chickens, and only the ones that are marked."

"Damned things are cold, even through these gloves," Len said.

Rat gave his little rodent-squeal laugh. "That's because they're froze, dumb fuck. Nordo, get your ass over here and help Len."

"I don't like handling dead chickens," Nordo said. "Even if I got gloves."

"Who the fuck asked you if—"

A sudden sound like an abrupt death rattle broke the silence of the woods.

Again. This time louder and more like a rock being raked hard over a metal washboard.

Everyone stood frozen in midaction.

"What the hell was that?" Mitki asked.

"Turkey," Len said. "Only it wasn't no turkey."

32

Rat heaved the trailer's left door shut so hard it caught Len's fingers, mashing them where steel met steel just beneath a hinge. Len screamed. Both truck drivers raced toward the cabs, paunchy men surprisingly fast. Donnie caught a glimpse of Mitki running around the front of the van to pile in behind the wheel.

"FBI!" a voice shouted. "Stay where you are."

A gunshot cracked through the night.

Now figures darker than the night were emerging from the woods all around the clearing.

"C'mon!" Donnie yelled to Nordo, who was standing paralyzed and the only body not in motion. "To the car!"

A motor roared. One of the big diesels. The black van backed up in a semicircle, leaning almost far enough to tip over, the drive wheels spraying dirt and grass.

Len was screaming louder now, trying desperately to free his hand. The trailer beside him pulled away; then air brakes hissed and it jounced to a halt so fast the back end lifted and fell heavily.

Gunfire erupted from every direction. Rat was suddenly in front of them, aiming a pistol at Nordo. Donnie leaped forward and elbowed Rat hard in the face, and he dropped the gun and fell back.

Headlights and taillights came out like stars. Lights were flashing all over and around the clearing. Everything was a maelstrom of noise and confusion, glare and deep shadow. Time became compressed, the way it does in crisis and action, when death is dancing close. Through his terror, Donnie trusted training and instinct.

He had to shove Nordo into the Honda's passenger seat. Then he vaulted onto the hood and swiveled down on the other side, had the door open and leaped in and gripped the steering wheel. Seconds. It had all happened in seconds.

The key was still in the ignition. Donnie twisted it almost hard enough to snap it off. He could feel the vibration of the engine starting but couldn't hear it over the surrounding noise.

". . . fucking *right* where you *are!*" a voice shouted over a bullhorn. It seemed to come from above. Branches were waving like excited arms, sending crazy shadows over everything. Donnie thought he could hear helicopter rotors thrashing a background beat to the clamor.

"Didn't you hear him, man?" Nordo asked in a stunned voice.

Donnie didn't answer. He had the car in gear and was roaring toward a break in the clearing. The main road might be blocked, so he zigzagged among the trees, ran over some thin saplings that rattled beneath the car, and bounced up onto the unpaved road a hundred yards beyond the clearing. The outside mirror on the passenger side cracked and dangled crookedly.

"They're, like, goddamn shooting at us!" Nordo screamed.

Donnie hoped not. Prayed that the raiders were well briefed and would recognize his car.

A flashing red light appeared directly in front of them, jiggling slightly as it headed toward them. Donnie leaned forward to peer more closely through the windshield. He saw that the light was mounted on the dashboard of a big SUV that was bearing down on them fast.

Donnie switched on the Honda's headlights and flashed them. Maybe the desperate signal would work if the SUV's driver couldn't make out the Honda in the dark, wouldn't know the car's driver was friend and not foe.

The SUV's headlights came on high, blinding Donnie.

Old-fashioned game of chicken now.

Both vehicles picked up speed and roared toward an inevitable collision.

A crash would be inevitable if neither driver lost his nerve and swerved, chose a tree to hit instead of high-speed steel.

"Ease the fuck up!" Nordo was screaming. "Donnie! C'mon, man!" He tried to grab the wheel but Donnie knocked his arm away.

"That thing'll run over us like we ain't there!" Nordo shouted. He made a whimpering sound, then clenched his eyes closed and began to wail.

But at the last instant, the blinding high beams framing the flashing red light in front of them darted to the side.

The Honda sped past inches from the other vehicle, engine snarling as if in triumph. It swayed and rocked in the SUV's windy wake, and Donnie had to fight the light little car to keep from spinning out.

"We did it!" Nordo yelled. "We fuckin' did it, man!"

Donnie gripped the wheel hard, wondering if his heart would ever slow down.

They didn't see another car the rest of the way to the county road. Donnie wondered if that was an accident or by design.

On pavement now, he pushed the Honda harder, up to ninety on the narrow, dark road.

Nordo sat staring straight ahead with wide eyes, his hands squeezing his knees. "We could, like, maybe slow down now, don't you think?"

"Not a chance," Donnie told him, shuffling the wheel through his hands to take a banked curve. The trees were very close on each side of the road, the tips of their low branches sometimes whipping the car's fenders as it fishtailed, then recovered on sharp curves.

From the drive out, Donnie remembered a straight stretch of road to the main highway. It would be an opportunity to build distance between the Honda and any pursuers.

Rubber squealed as the car came out of what he figured was the last tight curve, and he increased their speed. Edging the tach needle close to the red line, he mashed the accelerator to the floor.

The little car raced up to a hundred miles per hour, then a hundred and ten, twenty.

"Holy shit!" Nordo said. "What's under the hood of this pile of junk?"

"Apologize," Donnie said.

"This fine automobile," Nordo amended.

"I did a little custom work on the engine," Donnie said calmly. "I like a fast car. You never know when you're gonna need one."

"We sure needed one tonight," Nordo said. He glanced over at Donnie and flashed his smart-ass grin. His cockiness was back in full force, as if it came and went whenever a switch was thrown.

On the interstate, Donnie slowed to the legal limit and settled back in his seat. The car was still running smoothly, though the wind sang where it rushed around the dangling outside mirror.

"What was all that about back there, man?" Nordo asked.

"Whatever was in those trucks," Donnie said.

"Chickens? Frozen, yucky, skinned chickens? I didn't even like touching them!"

"Plucked chickens," Donnie corrected. "The chickens weren't skinned."

"Whatever," Nordo said.

"You'll never make much of a cook."

"I'm into the eating part of the game. But it'll be a while till I scarf down chicken again."

"I don't know what it was about," Donnie said, "other than chickens." He could think of possibilities, but he didn't want to share them with Nordo.

"You see that asshole Rat?" Nordo said. "He was

gonna fuckin' shoot me, man! Probably thinking it'd be blamed on the cops or everyone'd think it was a stray bullet."

"Probably," Donnie agreed, thinking Nordo had gotten something right tonight.

"You're a helluva driver," Nordo said, clapping Donnie on the shoulder. "You could even teach me a thing or two."

Or more, Donnie thought.

But didn't say.

Nordo suddenly let out an exuberant whoop, startling him. "Hooo, boy! We did it, man! Like, left their sorry asses back there in the dust!"

Donnie couldn't help grinning.

"Let's get some tunes on the radio, okay, Donnie?"

"Why not?" Donnie said, and rolled down the window while Nordo fiddled with the radio.

A hot engine running smooth. Music and warm wind, blowing all the way in from Donnie's youth.

Maybe Nordo did know a thing or two.

Back at Circe, Donnie parked the Honda at the far end of the lot.

As he and Nordo trudged toward the entrance, Ewing Bolt emerged from where he'd been standing in the shadows of the kiosk. He was wearing dark slacks and a white or cream-colored sport jacket with a white shirt and pale tie. If anything troubling or exciting had occurred tonight, it seemed not to concern him.

He strolled about a hundred feet out from the building to meet them.

"I heard there was trouble," he said. His voice was level but concerned.

"Plenty," Donnie said.

"Give me your version."

Donnie related what had happened in the clearing.

Apparently it dovetailed with whatever else Bolt had been told. He kept nodding slightly as Donnie spoke.

"Everyone got out more or less okay," Bolt told them. "I got a call from Mitki. Rat's arm is reinjured, and Len's hand got mangled somehow. They're on the way back here in the van."

"What about the trucks and the drivers?"

Bolt shrugged.

Donnie knew the truck drivers didn't make much difference, wouldn't have been in on any details. They'd only been instructed where to jockey their trucks. And whatever the fate of the drivers, the big tractor-trailers couldn't have gotten far from the clearing without being pulled over.

"So what do you want us to do now?" Donnie asked.

"Go home, both of you. Lay low, then come in to work whenever you're scheduled. Like nothing's happened."

"I don't get how things went sour," Nordo said. "Somebody must have, like, tipped the FBI."

Bolt smiled in the moonlight made red by neon glare. "The safest bet in Circe tonight is that that wasn't the FBI."

He removed the last cigarette from a pack and lit it, then dropped the empty pack on the ground and slid his lighter back in his pocket. He nodded good night to Donnie and Nordo and began walking back toward the club.

Donnie figured Bolt was right about the raiders not being FBI. He began thinking that when he'd heard almost everyone had escaped. The show had seemed plenty good enough to be convincing, but Bolt hadn't been completely fooled. Mitki, Rat, Len, and maybe the truck drivers had almost surely escaped because it was in the plan. Just as Donnie and Nordo had made it back.

Donnie stooped and picked up the empty cigarette pack Bolt had dropped, looked at it, then shook his head.

"Thought there was one left," he said, absently slipping the empty pack into his pocket.

He'd handled it carefully, knowing the cellophane wrapper could be almost as good as glass in revealing fingerprints.

33

Before driving to meet with Jules about last night, Donnie decided to phone Monet Real Estate and try to catch Sandy Scofield at her desk.

He was lucky. In the middle of her voice-mail message, she picked up. "Hello! Sandy Scofield here."

"Ms. Scofield, Mr. Rucker gave me your name. I'm Don Grant, Marla Grant's cousin. When I was in the office a while back and talked to Mr. Rucker, he told me you knew Marla pretty well."

"I thought you were the Blanchards. The two-story colonial Blanchards."

"Not me. Can I have a few minutes of your time, Ms. Scofield?"

"About Marla?"

"Yes."

"Okay, but I won't have much to say. Marla and I worked together on some listings, but we didn't know each other very well. Not that we didn't get along. Marla got along with everyone."

So I've heard, Donnie thought. "Did she ever mention anyone named Frank Allan?" he asked.

"A male friend? No. Marla was unattached and

not looking. I do know she hadn't had a steady boy-friend for over a year."

"Did she date?"

"Wouldn't have told me about it if she did. This is a business office, and ours was a professional rela-tionship. No girl talk, if you know what I mean."

"No girl talk at all? Only sales contracts and mort-gage rates?"

"Exactly." She sounded as if she meant it. Donnie knew if he ever wanted to sell a house in New Or-leans or Julep he'd call Sandy Scofield. "Did Marla ever mention the name Frank Allan?"

"Not unless he was a buyer or seller. Or maybe he was someone she met at one of the conventions."

"In New Orleans?"

"Sure. There've been two this year. One a nation-wide convention, the other for Midwestern and South-ern realtors."

"Both in the French Quarter?"

"Where else?"

"What goes on at these conventions?"

"There are panels, luncheons. People network. That's what they're really about, networking. That's why I said maybe Marla met this Frank whatsisname at a convention."

Donnie could imagine conventioneers networking by going on a gambling excursion to Circe. "Do you know if Marla gambled?"

"Gambled? You mean like with cards and dice?"

"Yes."

"Ha! Not Marla. What she did mostly was work.

She was ambitious, like me. Anything wrong with that?''

"No, no . . ."

"I really have to go, Mr. Grant. I'm sorry about Marla."

Donnie managed to keep her on the phone another five minutes, pumping her for information. But she had none of any importance to give.

He thanked her for her time and told her good-bye, and she told him again, with more feeling, how sorry she was about Marla. She couldn't imagine who'd want to harm Marla. Everybody liked her.

Donnie tried to remember a murder victim, other than mobsters, that he hadn't heard everyone had liked.

Jules had chosen one of New Orleans's better restaurants for their meeting this time. A light rain was falling in the French Quarter when Donnie parked on Chartres and walked around the corner and down St. Louis, staying beneath awnings as much as possible.

The restaurant was comfortably cool and dry after the warm dampness outside. Donnie, wearing dark slacks, a blue shirt, and a light tan sport coat, brushed droplets of rain from his shoulders and saw Jules sitting at a table near the back. It was just 11:30, early enough and rainy enough that most of the Sunday brunch crowd hadn't yet arrived, and there were few enough diners in Nola to allow privacy.

Donnie nodded to the maitre d', then threaded his

way between white-clothed tables and sat down opposite Jules.

Jules had a menu and a glass of white wine in
front of him. Today he was dressed like a business-
man from Boise—or an FBI agent: blue suit, white
shirt, red tie with a pea-sized knot. But there was his
jaunty black beret hooked over the back of the chair
next to him.

"You've gotta try the Creole tomato napoleon
here," Jules said, tapping the menu with a fingertip.

Donnie looked at him, wondering how he could
stay so fit and still indulge his joy of eating. "The *F*
in FBI doesn't stand for *food*, Jules."

"Also doesn't mean that when you're in a city like
New Orleans, you can't take advantage of what it
has to offer. And the way I see it, you earned yourself
a good meal, Donnie. Maybe the sautéed veal. I had
it once and would again, only there's too much that's
great on this menu."

When the waiter came, Donnie ordered pizza and
a beer. Jules winced.

"Should have gone with the veal, Donnie."

Donnie ignored him, wishing he'd shut up about
the sautéed veal. "Ewing Bolt doesn't think it was
the FBI that broke in on the operation last night,"
Donnie said.

"Clever Ewing Bolt. You don't really think the Bureau would have made such a mess of things, do
you?"

"It happens," Donnie said.

"The Bureau was there, but we were last on the

scene, as planned. Picking up the pieces, you might say."

So Bolt was wrong. Or only half-right. The FBI had been there, only later than he'd assumed.

"I thought Nordo and I got away from the scene last night because the Bureau gave us room to run," Donnie said.

Jules sipped wine, then smiled. "Only the SUV that let you pass was Bureau. Before that, you were on your own."

"I'm glad not to have known that last night."

"We didn't queer the operation right away for good reason. It seems Vito Cantanzano might be retired, but he can still muster the troops. We got word ahead of time. What's left of the Julep Italian Mafia tried to take over that shipment of chickens."

" 'Tried?' "

"We got both trucks last night."

"Just trucks? No bad guys?"

"Only some low-level Mafia soldiers who aren't talking and have high-powered attorneys who'll see that they won't."

"Everyone from Circe got away," Donnie noted.

"Because Cantanzano's troops weren't nearly as interested in them as they were in the chickens."

"What am I missing?" Donnie asked. "Should I try to buy a KFC franchise?"

"You don't need a business on the side, Donnie. Anyway, what made these frozen chickens valuable is that there were smuggled diamonds inside some of them. The driver was in on the deal with Circe. Bolt sent a second trailer full of frozen chickens to be substituted for the one carrying the chickens containing the diamonds. The diamonds were stolen from a certain African country in turmoil. They were scheduled to head for Miami, then to Europe, to purchase black-market plutonium to aid a breakaway Russian state's efforts to become a nuclear power. That's not going to happen now. Not yet, anyway. Circe's cut was a small part of the shipment that was to be loaded into the van."

"Fifty chickens . . ." Donnie said, remembering overhearing Mitki instructing Nordo and Len.

"Sounds about right, depending on the size of the diamonds inside them." Jules took a sip of wine and swished it around in his mouth before swallowing. Who'd guess he'd been a tough kid in a part of New Jersey where Thunderbird was the vintage of choice? "The van managed to flee from the scene last night, with Mitki and Rat in it. The other Circe employees escaped in the darkness of the woods. The Bureau got there just in time to confiscate both trucks and a lot of frozen chickens."

Donnie knew the Circe van was allowed to escape, even though transfer of most of the marked frozen chickens had taken place. To have stopped it and arrested Mitki, Rat, or any of the others would have imperiled Donnie's mission at Circe. It was a mission more important than a cut of a single shipment of smuggled diamonds, however profound their intended use. Bolt and company could have their fun, and their diamonds, for now.

"Something else," Donnie said. He handed Jules the cigarette pack Bolt had carelessly tossed away last night outside Circe. "Bolt's—or Petrov's—fingerprints should be on it."

Jules smiled and slid the cigarette pack, itself in a plastic pouch, into a pocket of his suit coat. "This should be confirmation of his true identity, maybe an early exhibit in his trial. But what about the mysterious Mr. Drago?"

"Haven't seen him again. You know how it is, Jules. His kind keeps its distance, stays as clean as possible."

"Even when murder's involved."

"Especially when."

The food arrived, and both men were silent until the plates were laid before them and the waiter had departed. Then Jules told Donnie again he should have ordered the sautéed veal. Donnie ignored him.

"What about the wire?" Jules asked. "I'm assuming you wore it last night. It should be at least a start on building the case against Circe."

"I wasn't wired last night."

Jules paused with his fork inches above his plate. "Oh?"

"I need to talk to you about Elvis."

Donnie told him about the missing Elvis Presley statuette that contained the microrecording equipment.

"That could be serious," Jules said, "or your thief might be a fanatical Elvis fan who lives in your building. What about the old lady you mentioned? Your downstairs neighbor and unofficial busybody. Maybe she's the nosy type who has apartment keys and picks up souvenirs."

"Mrs. LaValierre? Possible but I doubt it. And she'd be more likely to steal a bust of Lawrence Welk."

"Was anything else taken?"

"I don't think so," Donnie said.

"Beethoven."

"What?"

"We should have made it Beethoven," Jules said. "There are busts of Beethoven all over, and nobody steals them."

"Beethoven next time," Donnie said.

"No. I'll get another wire to you, Donnie, and you decide where to stash it."

Donnie figured his pizza had cooled enough to eat, so he used a fork to pry up a slice.

Terrific. He had to admit Jules knew how to find the best restaurants.

"I think Rat was going to kill Nordo last night," he said, after washing down the bite of pizza with beer.

Jules picked at his tomato napoleon and seemed to mull that over. "I'm afraid the kid's on his own," he said after a while.

"I'm going to try talking Cantanzano into pulling him away from Circe."

"That'd be okay," Jules said, "as long as you think Nordo's of no more use to you at Circe."

Donnie didn't want to think too hard about that one. Nordo might be of future use, but not if he were dead.

"I don't think Cantanzano will pull him," Jules said.

"It's worth a try."

"Sure, Donnie. If anything, it'll prove you got a real concern for Nordo, get you in tighter with the old man. What you got going with him oughta be working on trust by now as well as fear. You know how it is; guys like Cantanzano, once you get them to trust you like a long-lost son, they're set up for the fall."

Donnie took another sip of beer and didn't like how it tasted. "Jesus, what a business!"

"We both knew what it was when we got into it. Think of it in terms of the end justifying the means."

"Isn't that how the bad guys think?"

Jules sipped his wine and made a little dismissive motion with his head. Oddly French. Or maybe it was the nearby beret. "There are bad guys and bad guys, Donnie. Some of them are complex and think things through. Others just take because they want. How do you see Ewing Bolt?"

"Underneath the polish, he's simply a taker," Donnie said.

"And Mitki?"

"That, but also something more, even though he doesn't have the polish. Wheels between his ears are always turning."

"Rat?"

"An impulsive killer held in check by Mitki. Not even a taker. A destroyer."

"The worst kind," Jules said, "because they're unpredictable."

"The Mitkis are the most dangerous," Donnie said, "until you get them figured out. And sometimes you never do."

After the main course, Jules talked Donnie into trying fried apple pie à la mode for dessert.

Donnie found nothing to complain about.

Feeling as if he'd overeaten, but figuring maybe it was worth it, he left the restaurant first. Outside on the sidewalk, the rain had stopped but there was a damp breeze made cool by the nearby river. Donnie hunched his shoulders slightly and stuck his hands in his jacket pockets.

His right hand closed on what felt like a business card. He drew out the object and looked at it.

A business card, all right. Marla Grant's. He hadn't worn the jacket since the day he'd stopped in at Monet Real Estate.

As Donnie studied the card's touched-up photograph that made Marla Grant look like a show-biz beauty, something occurred to him.

He immediately went back inside the restaurant.

Jules was just standing up from the table. Donnie went to him and showed him the card.

"Impressive," Jules said. "She looks even more attractive than her other photos taken before she was killed. Women real estate agents, they get an excuse to get their picture taken and all try to look like movie stars nowadays."

"That's what Rucker said."

"Rucker?"

"Sales manager at Monet Real Estate, where Marla Grant worked as a part-time agent. Has Frank Allan's wife seen one of her business cards?"

"I doubt it."

"Show her this one. Maybe she'll recognize Marla Grant after all."

Jules stared at him, then smiled. "I understand what you're thinking."

"Undercover agents often carry photos in their wallets to make it look like they have family or girlfriends," Donnie said. "It helps make them seem more authentic. Obviously they don't carry photos of the real people they love. They choose strangers, from photographs that come with new picture frames, or from garage sales, or magazine photos, places like that. I think it's possible Frank Allan came across one of Marla Grant's business cards and impulsively picked it up. He probably cut the card in half, making the photo wallet size. My guess is he got the card in New Orleans during a recent real estate convention. Didn't figure the agent lived in Julep. She'd be from New Orleans at the closest. He might not even have bothered looking at what the card said, just wanted the photo to flash now and then. Never figured he'd be asked about it in any detail."

"But he was asked about it," Jules said. "In plenty of detail. And he couldn't answer."

"Then someone from Circe spotted Marla Grant in Julep, or maybe even in New Orleans, and figured she was Frank Allan's love interest. She might know what he knew. Pillow talk. They had to find out how much, if anything, he'd told her, then kill her to silence her."

"Poor, poor woman," Jules said. His features were knotted with compassion. He was squeezing the black beret in his strong right hand as if trying to extract juice from it. "She couldn't have told them anything, no matter how hard she tried."

"Which is why they worked on her so long before killing her."

"Bastards!"

"Show Frank Allan's widow the photo, Jules. My guess is she'll ID Marla Grant. She'll tell you she saw the same photograph in her husband's wallet before he was killed, part of his fake family or galaxy of friends. Part of his cover."

"Then what?"

"You figure it out."

Donnie knew Jules already had, that he just didn't want to say it. But Jules would have to be the one. Both men knew where this was probably going. But decisions like the one that might be coming at them were Jules's job, not Donnie's.

Ends and means in a business that chewed up people as if they were the sautéed veal.

34

It took a full ten minutes after Donnie was back in his apartment for him to notice that things were different.

Barely, almost imperceptibly different.

Objects that he'd deliberately set just so had been moved. The handle on the coffee mug he'd left on the dresser was now pointed another direction. The belt buckle on the pair of pants he'd left folded on a chair was now on the bottom instead of the top. In the bathroom, the toothbrush and toothpaste tube were still lying parallel to each other on the washbasin, but the tip of the toothbrush handle was no longer touching the glass.

There was little else Donnie could put his finger on, but the sense, the feel of loss of symmetry, was there.

He opened and closed drawers, examined furniture leg marks on the carpet, stood for a long time peering into the refrigerator, the medicine cabinet. There was no doubt in his mind that the apartment had been thoroughly searched by an expert. One so good that it took another expert to realize a search had been conducted.

Donnie stood in the middle of the bedroom, looking around, listening to a car pass outside on Barrack Street, wondering what the search meant. Maybe it was a good thing that Elvis had been stolen. Or maybe what was found inside Elvis had prompted the search. Possibly the search had been a routine check on Donnie by one of the factions that thought they had him on a leash. But it was also possible that suspicions about him had been aroused by recent events.

Donnie didn't know what to think of the search. He did know he didn't like it.

It didn't seem likely that what was left of the Italian Mafia in and around Julep would toss an apartment so expertly. And Mitki or Rat would most likely make it a point to leave the place a mess, to let Donnie know a search had been made so he could stew about it.

Donnie knew there was another possibility, and it sent a chill up his spine.

Marishov.

Always there was the possibility that the cunning, legendary former KGB hit man had finally found him, was at last ready to close in for the kill. Donnie had caught glimpses of him during the past few years, had a vague idea what he looked like—young, slim, fair, features almost delicate enough so that if necessary he could pass as a woman, making him all the more dangerous.

Marishov had come close to killing Donnie twice, which would only whet his appetite for success. He was a proud professional who wouldn't accept failure. It was nothing personal, and it wasn't merely business. It was murder as a craft—a craft Marishov had elevated to an art.

Something else for Donnie to think about on some level, every second.

He sat on the edge of the bed and picked up the phone, then pecked out Vito Cantanzano's unlisted number that had been in the information provided by Jules.

A voice that sounded like Army's answered.

"I want to speak to Vito," Donnie said.

"Who's callin'? Is this who I think it is?"

"He'll want to talk to me," Donnie said.

"Is this Wells? Donnie Wells?"

"You know it is, Army."

"Sure. I just wanted to hear you say it. Hold on, I'll go see if *Mr.* Cantanzano wants to talk to you."

Donnie watched the sweep of the second hand on his watch. Almost a full minute passed before Army returned.

"Mr. Cantanzano wants to know where you got his private phone number."

"I overheard Frankie mention it," Donnie said.

"That what you're gonna tell Mr. Cantanzano?"

"Sure. If he asks."

"It's a fuckin' lie."

"Maybe. It could be I found the number on a slip of paper that fell out of one of Frankie's pockets. Or maybe it was one of your pockets."

"*My* pockets? You got no honor, Wells."

"Only if you assume I'm lying," Donnie pointed out. "Cantanzano might not make that assumption."

Army was quiet for a few beats before replying. "That fuckin' Frankie."

"Am I gonna talk to Mr. Cantanzano?" Donnie asked.

"He's gonna talk to you. In person and soon. A car'll be there in a little while to pick you up out in front of your apartment."

"How do you know where I'm—"

"Caller ID," Army said, and hung up.

Donnie thought technology could be scary when it got out in front.

Frankie the Lounger drove silently as the old black Cadillac glided through the streets toward the Cantanzano manor house. Army was also unusually quiet. Other than the low hum of the motor, the only sound was the occasional popping of Frankie's spearmint chewing gum.

It wasn't long before Donnie found himself seated across from Cantanzano in Vito's imitation of England. Vito was wearing his silky powder blue dressing gown with the elbow patches and soft leather slippers, and was seated relaxed in his oversize brown leather armchair. This time there was a red silk ascot with a gold coat-of-arms pattern neatly folded about his throat. His left hand was resting lightly in his lap. His right hand held a stemmed brandy snifter. Every inch the English gentleman, except that he was a Mafia thug risen high.

Army and Frankie were standing like mismatched bookends flanking the room's double doors. They looked as if they'd very much like to leave.

"You give me a tinkle right on the phone like that," Cantanzano said to Donnie, "at my unlisted number. You're a chap's got a lotta balls."

"I had a lotta help from the operator," Donnie said.

"My understanding was, they ain't supposed to give out unlisted phone numbers."

"You have to know how to talk to them."

"And you know how?"

"If they're women," Donnie said. Don Wells, showing a little of the sexual braggadocio mentioned in his folder.

Cantanzano regarded him through narrow dark eyes. Then he turned his head slightly so he could see Army and Frankie. "You two buggers leave us alone unless you're called. This is gonna be a private chitchat."

Donnie watched as Army and Frankie walked out and closed the door behind them. Neither man had looked his way, though Army might have smiled slightly. Donnie was glad he'd used the phone company to let them both off the hook, so to speak. It did no harm to pile up debt that might be called in later, though it probably didn't mean a thing to Frankie.

Leaning forward in his chair, Vito said, "You want some brandy?"

Donnie politely declined with thanks.

"You save Nicky's ass again?" Vito asked, settling back again in soft leather.

"I think so," Donnie said. "Rat was gonna shoot him."

"I heard about that little adventure in the woods."

Donnie knew Cantanzano had more than heard about it. He'd unexpectedly planned and executed a part of it that went wrong, though it was unlikely he'd been anywhere near the action. He'd no doubt been busy establishing an alibi for that time. One the law couldn't break without breaking the code of the Mafia that went back into time to Sicily and still was in play.

"Didn't hear about Nicky almost gettin' nailed, though," Cantanzano said.

"It happened fast, but it happened."

"There any doubt in your mind about it? I mean, what happened coulda been just like you say, but are you positive that blackguard Rat was really gonna do Nicky?"

"I'm positive. That's why Nordo—Nicky—was included in the operation, so he could be set up for the kill, and how he died would be vague. That's how goons like Rat and Mitki do things when they're complicated—cause even more complications so what really went down can never be sorted out."

"I know how it bloody works," Vito said with a graceless wave of his snifter. Donnie believed him.

"I came here to ask you to pull Nicky out of Circe," Donnie said. "I can't keep saving him. If he stays, he'll be killed."

"Nicky's got somethin' to say about that."

"He doesn't have a chance against the kind of goons out at Circe."

"He's my nephew," Vito said. "My blood. Like

royal blood, in a way. Breedin' tells. He's a stand-up chap. Tougher'n you might think."

"He's plenty tough," Donnie said. "He's also plenty young."

Cantanzano sniffed his brandy without sipping it and seemed to think that over.

"Nicky stays at Circe," he said finally. "If he gets killed, you get killed."

Donnie knew any argument would be futile. In fact, it would be taken as a sign of weakness. Keeping his poker face, he merely nodded.

Cantanzano must have pressed a concealed button in or around his chair, because the doors opened and Army and Frankie the Lounger came back into the room.

"Donnie, here, tells me he wheedled my unlisted phone number outta the operator," Cantanzano told them calmly. He suddenly hurled the brandy snifter against the wall near Frankie, shattering the delicate crystal and staining gold-flocked wallpaper. "I don't fuckin' believe him."

Army and Frankie didn't move. They'd turned a few shades paler. Frankie's mouth was stuck open, his wad of spearmint gum visible.

"This kinda fuckin' thing happens again, somebody's gonna come a cropper." Cantanzano picked up a china figurine of a cavalier on a rearing horse, no doubt very expensive. He drew back his arm and the cavalier zipped across the room and exploded against the stone fireplace. Donnie's eye followed it, and he saw Elvis on the mantel.

"My apartment was searched," he said to Cantan-zano. "Are you responsible?"

"Naw," Cantanzano said. He saw where Donnie was looking. "Frankie seen that Elvis statue and knew I was a fan of the King, so he lifted it from your place and brought it here to get in my good graces. Dumb fuck." He picked up a ballpoint pen from the table next to the armchair and threw it at Frankie. It bounced off Frankie's shoulder. Frankie didn't move or change expression.

"All of you," Cantanzano said, "get the bloody hell outta here! Go on! Withdraw!"

Donnie followed Army and Frankie out of the room without a word, wondering how much time would pass before Cantanzano hurled and broke Elvis in a fit of temper and found the wire con-cealed inside.

He thought about it as he sat in the back of the Cadillac on the return ride to his apartment. It both-ered Donnie a lot, the way things were going lately. But it didn't really surprise him. Every operation came unraveled eventually, because basically it was a lie. Every one of Donnie's impersonations, his roles, seemed to have a genetic life like a real person's—only shorter.

And Donnie Wells had been alive for quite a while now since his death.

35

Donnie reminded himself of his mission. He was to discover what the Russian Mafia was doing at Circe, and find out who had killed Lily and Frank Allan—and now, Marla Grant. And his information would have to result in convictions in court. In every operation came a time to press, to take chances not dreamed of at the beginning. Donnie knew that time had come at Circe. He could feel it like hot breath on the back of his neck.

He used the public phone in back of DQ and informed Jules it was time to use the OR team—or at least one member.

"I need C. J. to analyze the alarm system at Circe and clear a path for me," Donnie said. "There has to be information—hard evidence—in Circe that we can use, something that might hurry things along."

Jules didn't answer right away. "You'll be taking a helluva chance, going into a place like that. A legitimate casino's got sophisticated security devices like Fort Knox. Imagine what someplace like Circe might have. Could be anything from land mines to tiger pits."

"That's why I want C. J. You have any doubt he could find a way through land mines and around tiger pits and into Fort Knox without raising an alarm?"

Jules laughed. "Since you put it that way . . . But C. J.'s in Virginia on a terrorist case. I'll call Whitten and see if I can pull him, see when he can get here."

"I'd like to go in soon," Donnie said.

"You sound nervous."

"I think of it as anxious, Jules. I have a feeling my cover's slipping and we're operating on limited time."

"Speaking of which," Jules said, "you ever hear of Al Gundi or Harry Meyers?"

Donnie took a few seconds to shuffle through the mental index files of years, too many years meeting the wrong kind of people and pushing his luck. "Never," he said confidently. "Neither one of them."

"They've heard of you, in a way. They're old partners in crime with Don Wells. Teamed up with Wells on several bank robberies in the eighties in California. They tried to contact him in prison last week, but we sidetracked them. We're assuming they think Wells is still alive inside the walls."

"Why would they try contacting him? Wells had lots of time left on his sentence."

"They mighta wanted to visit him, get certain information from him. Gundi and Meyers are screwups and were never in the same league as Wells. The guy was an expert at robbing banks, Donnie. And as that kind of operator goes, he had a pretty good run."

A run that led to him dying in prison, Donnie thought. "So what are Gundi and Meyers up to?"

"No good, is all we can figure. The thing is, Gundi belongs to the auto club and requested one of their travel maps. That's how we found out about the trip."

"Trip?"

"When they requested the map they gave their starting point and destination. Gundi and Meyers seem to be driving cross-country from New York to New Orleans."

"Coincidence?"

"Possibly. Or maybe they heard of a Don Wells in and around New Orleans and want to see what's going on. They might think Wells somehow got out of prison."

"Are you still tracking them?" Donnie asked.

"As well as we can. We more or less have tabs on them right now, and they haven't reached New Orleans. But we have to keep them in mind, figure them as a factor somewhere along the way. We might be able to apprehend them in New Orleans, come up with something flimsy to hold them for a while. But you know how that works. We'll have to turn them loose sooner than we want. Hell to pay, then."

Donnie knew who'd pay hell.

"If they find their way to Circe," Jules said, "all bets are off, in a manner of speaking."

"I admire the way you keep your sense of humor," Donnie said, "no matter how bad things look for me."

" 'Cause we're friends."

Donnie knew that in an odd way Jules was right.

The things people did to remain sane in an insane world. "Any information on Drago?" he asked.

"Not a scintilla. And after a lot of looking. Whoever he is, a thief-in-law or just a common thug, he has to be in the country illegally. Probably came across from Canada, like a lot of the Russian mob."

Donnie knew the dearth of information added to the likelihood of Drago being prominent in the Russian mob hierarchy. The upper echelon of Russian crime figures had ways of purging their records in the new Russia and former USSR states, and they were relatively new to crime in the western world. "What about Marishov?"

"Nothing new on him, either," Jules said. "But that's no surprise. The guy's like a damned ghost. He might be anywhere."

"Yeah. Like here."

"Like here," Jules agreed.

Both men took a moment to digest that somber observation.

"We did use the prints off the cigarette pack you gave me to positively ID Ewing Bolt," Jules said. "He's Grigory Petrov, all right."

"Which means he's in the country illegally and we can pick him up and have him deported."

"If we would want to do such a thing. That'd be kinda like transplanting poison ivy instead of killing it."

"Doesn't Interpol have anything on Petrov?"

"Nothing that'd stick. Better to leave him right where he is for the time being, Donnie, where we can watch him and have a chance to nail him with hard evidence. But it isn't gonna be easy. He's risen high in the Russian mob, become a survivor because he's smart enough to cover himself."

"Maybe not this time," Donnie said.

"We hope." Up front, a blender began to whir. "You at a public phone, Donnie?"

Donnie figured the sound of the blender must have stirred Jules's appetite, like when a cat hears a can opener. He told Jules where he was, then gave him the number.

"A DQ, huh? You ever try one of their banana splits?"

"Never," Donnie said.

"You oughta."

"I'll do myself a favor one of these times."

"I'll find out about C. J. and call you right back," Jules said, before hanging up.

And he did call back, within five minutes.

"I've got you an alarm expert," Jules said, "but it isn't C. J. It's Sue Bristol. C. J. can't be pulled off the case he's on without jeopardizing it."

Donnie felt a worm of uneasiness stir in his stomach. "I don't like this, Jules. I want C. J."

"Why's it have to be C. J.?"

"Because we both know he's the best."

"Whitten was adamant about it, Donnie. He can't square it with the Bureau if he pulls C. J. And Bristol's said to be as good as they come at alarm bypass."

"Said to be, huh? Listen, Jules—"

"Politics, Donnie."

"Screw politics!"

"Sure. And get screwed back. You can trust Bristol, Donnie. Fact is, you got no choice."

"Less and less choice every day," Donnie said glumly.

He told Jules to set up the meeting with Sue Bristol, then went up front in DQ and ordered a large chocolate Blizzard and french fries.

Not a banana split, but still it was comfort food.

36

Sue Bristol met Donnie on the Esplanade for a stroll along the Riverwalk. On their left, on the other side of a continuous glass wall, were the sprawling shopping mall's restaurants and stores. On their right lay the river portage of barges, tugs, and oceangoing freighters. Donnie remembered that a few years ago one of the freighters had drifted off course and wiped out part of the mall, including the Riverwalk branch of Cafe du Monde.

It was difficult to imagine the Riverwalk as the scene of tragedy on this bright, warm morning. Sue, wearing a sleeveless white blouse, flowered skirt, and straw sandals, looked more like a prairie housewife than a crack FBI agent with alarm-bypass expertise.

She'd studied the diagram of Circe Donnie had given her, and she'd managed to copy the architect's and builder's renderings and blueprints from public records in Julep's city hall without attracting undue suspicion.

"The alarm system at Circe is sophisticated stuff," she told Donnie, gazing out at the sliding dark waters of the river.

"Can you handle it?"

"I can get you in and out," she said confidently. "But we have to deal with video as well as motion and pressure alarms."

"You mean there's somebody always watching TV monitors?"

"No. But there are videotapes."

"Then we take the tape when we leave," Donnie suggested.

"The signal's sent to a remote site, where the images are preserved on a forty-eight-hour loop."

"Which means we might get in and out, but there's no way to keep it a secret that someone's been there."

"That's about it. So why not let them know somebody's been there? Just an ordinary burglary."

"That'd work," Donnie said, "but I still don't like the idea that we might be on tape. Even with masks, they'd still get a permanent record of our general appearance, height, weight, maybe hair coloring and age. They'd know how many of us there were, how we behaved and moved. And if you forget one little thing, make one small mistake, and it's on tape, an expert can spend days looking until he finds it. I remember a case where a burglar was identified by a computer expert who noticed the label showing inside his collar when he had his head down."

"So they traced him through where he bought his clothes?"

"Easier than that," Donnie said. "The guy had his name written in laundry ink inside his collar so the cleaners wouldn't lose his shirts."

"Nifty."

"Scary."

"You'll have no worry here. And masks won't be necessary. I'll black out all the cameras. It will be obvious that the tape's been interrupted, but that's better than preserved masked images of us."

"Is there any way to place photos of the scene in front of the video cameras, fool the tape so there's no interruption?"

"Works in movies and mystery novels," Sue said, smiling. "It doesn't work so well in real life. There'd still be a second's interruption, and the different shadow and texture of a photo would be obvious. Trust me, Donnie. The best bet is to disable the cameras early on, give up on the idea nobody will know there's been a break-in, then move fast and sure and make the break-in seem like a simple anonymous burglary. Except . . ."

"What?"

"It's a skilled burglar who can get past that alarm system, then not screw up and set off bells and whistles once he does get inside."

"A bank B-and-E expert like Donnie Wells might have those skills," Donnie said.

"Just what I was thinking. You might raise suspicions and bring some heat down on yourself at Circe."

"We'll have to take the chance," Donnie said, knowing she was right and they were creating another chink in his armor. "You clear the way; then I'll do the rest. I'm taking Nordo in with me."

"Bad idea," Sue said. "And what makes you think he'll agree to go in?"

"He's supposed to be snooping around in the service of his uncle Vito. And he's a young stud always looking for new ways to almost get killed, so he'll jump at the chance."

Sue looked dubious. "This a guy thing?"

"Guy thing," Donnie confirmed. "When can we go in?" he asked, to forestall any argument.

"It can be done tonight, after the club closes, if that's what you want," Sue said.

"Tonight's fine."

"You go in through a window designated on the floor plan, then follow the course I give you. The video cameras will already have black spray paint on their lenses, so you won't have to concern yourself with them. Motion and pressure plate alarms will have been either marked with an X or deactivated. What time do we go?"

"We? All you're supposed to do is clear a path for us, then get well away from the place."

"No, that might not work. There's always the unexpected to deal with. I'll go in first, move ahead of you. You and Nordo follow me exactly and you'll be all right. We'll all get out okay."

Donnie was silent, brooding.

Sue smiled at him. "You don't like this? I should think it'd give you confidence. I wouldn't want to go if I thought there was a chance an alarm would sound or we'd be caught on tape. It'd jeopardize my own life, not to mention my career."

"I've got enough confidence already."

"You think I'm a fucking amateur?"

"It isn't that. Don't get your feelings hurt."

"You don't like not being in complete control? Is that it?"

"That's it," he said honestly.

"This has gotta be a team effort, Donnie. Circe's a casino. They plan on the best in the world trying to sneak in and break the bank after hours."

Donnie looked into her eyes. Mistake. "Are you as good as the best?" he asked.

"We're gonna sure as hell find out, Donnie. And the *we* includes me."

End of discussion. She had him. He knew it. Politics. More than politics.

"Nordo and I will pick you up in the lot at Other Rooms at three-thirty a.m. sharp," Donnie told her. "You park as close as you can to the highway sign. I'll be driving a rental car."

"You really sure you want to take Nordo? He's an unknown."

"Not as much an unknown as he was until recently. And I'll tell him exactly what to do. He'll listen."

"What makes you think so?"

"He's only dumb because he's young. But young or not, he'll know what'll happen to him if we get caught with our hands in that particular cookie jar." Donnie also figured that if Nordo was along he could at least keep an eye on him. And if they did come upon something worthwhile, Nordo as well as Donnie would make much needed points with Uncle Vito. All the while Sue was building up points with the Bureau and advancing her career prospects.

"I'm still not crazy about the Nordo idea," Sue said.

"And Nordo still goes with us. For various reasons. Politics among them. Bureau politics. Mafia politics. Goddamn bureaucracies!"

"You don't like politics?"

"Hate them. Hate bureaucracies."

"They're not so bad," Sue said, "once you learn how to get them to work for you."

Donnie thought she had a lot to learn.

"You with me?" Donnie asked Nordo, after briefing him on what was proposed for the early morning hours.

Nordo grinned. "Sure, I am."

Donnie had been confident of Nordo's willingness to participate, but he was a little surprised by the casualness of his answer. "This is gonna be dangerous, Nordo."

"That's, like, why I'm doing it, man." The grin widened, and he added, "Not the only reason."

Donnie didn't reply immediately, and Nordo stared at him.

"What're you thinking, man?"

"I'm thinking I don't often meet a cross between a sixties hippie, a character outta *West Side Story*, and a wanna-be NASCAR driver."

Nordo shrugged. "You'd have to know my family, how I was brought up."

Again Donnie was silent.

"Now what are you thinking?"

"I'm hoping you'll grow up soon enough to grow old."

"Cruel, man."

37

Sue went in first. In the hot, moonless night, Donnie stood next to Nordo in the shadow of the building and watched her penetrate Circe to duel with the sophisticated alarm system. The smell of the swamp on the faint breeze seemed to warn of predators.

"How come that window wasn't wired to set off an alarm when it was opened?" Nordo asked.

"It was," Donnie said. "She knows how to deal with alarms."

"Still not gonna tell me her name, huh? I'd like to get to know her better."

"That's what she doesn't want. She's a specialist who doesn't like to take unnecessary chances. She does a job, then moves on to the next one."

"Some life. So do *you* know her name?"

"Probably not."

"Where the fuck'd you get her, man?"

"She helped in half a dozen bank robberies in the East," Donnie said. "Some years back." Vague enough, he hoped.

"You, like, robbed banks?" Nordo asked. He seemed impressed.

"In another life, before prison," Donnie told him, trying not to lead the youth of the nation astray. *Crime doesn't pay, Nordo, but watch closely tonight and you'll learn about breaking and entering.*

Sue was dressed completely in black. Her slight figure seemed no more than a shadow unless she moved. Almost like an illusion, her dark, lithe form climbed through the opened window and was inside.

Fifteen minutes passed before she reappeared at the window and waved to them.

Also in black, Donnie and Nordo approached the window.

"I go in first," Donnie said. "Stay close behind me. Try to walk in my footprints. I'll be keying off our tour guide in black."

"I'll be like the fuckin' caboose, man."

"And don't talk unless it's necessary," Donnie added.

He climbed through the window before Nordo could answer, moved a few feet into the carpeted room, and listened as Nordo entered behind him. Donnie cringed when he heard one of Nordo's shoes scrape the window ledge.

Crouched low, Donnie switched on his penlight, rotating the lens to narrow the thin yellow beam. Ahead he saw Sue motion them forward. He moved carefully, staying low. Nordo seemed to be doing okay. He was breathing deeply but evenly behind Donnie, the only sound in the room. Unless Donnie's heartbeat was as loud as its pounding in his ears.

Sue led them to the hall, then along it to Ewing Bolt's office. The door was standing open. Donnie didn't figure Bolt had left it that way. Another of Sue's many skills had been put to use.

"This room completely safe to move around in?" Donnie asked.

"It is," Sue told him.

"What about video cameras?"

"Neutralized. Like the rest of the system along our route in and out. Just as we discussed." She sounded testy. Without waiting for Donnie to say anything more, she turned her back to him and led the way inside the office. She'd already closed the blinds, or found them that way. Now she switched on a desk lamp, knowing the light wouldn't show from outside. "I'm going to work on neutralizing the window alarm while you boys do your job."

"Why the window?"

"Don't you think we should go out the easiest and shortest possible way, now that we've located the office? Keeping in mind we're simple burglars with a talent for alarm bypass."

"Makes sense," Donnie said, wondering why he hadn't thought of it.

"Beauty and brains," Nordo said, smiling at her.

Sue looked at him as if he were a piece of furniture that didn't go with the decor.

Working at the edges, without opening the blinds, she got busy with the window wiring. "Circuitry's imbedded in the glass," she said. "Gonna be tricky."

"Can you do it?" Donnie asked.

She didn't bother answering. Maybe she hadn't even heard him.

"Do you know where the office safe is?" Donnie asked Nordo.

Nordo shook his head no.

"Good," Donnie said. "Look for it like a good burglar while I search for what we came for. It won't matter if you don't find it. It'll be locked anyway, and we don't have what we need to get into it even if we didn't mind making noise with drills or explosives."

Nordo didn't question Donnie before getting busy removing pictures from walls and tearing up carpet. Donnie liked that.

The file cabinet contained only the records and information anyone would expect. Everything seemed to be carefully compiled and standard business. The correspondence and personnel files revealed nothing useful.

Donnie went to the computer and plugged in a zip disk, then attempted to transfer information stored on Bolt's hard drive.

Nothing happened. Apparently the computer was programmed to resist such efforts.

Donnie decided any self-respecting burglar would steal a computer.

Not this computer. He couldn't lift it. It was bolted to the table, and the table was bolted to the floor.

For a moment Donnie toyed with the idea of prying the computer's case open, and simply stealing the hard drive.

But he decided against it. A possibly damaged disk drive would be of no use to the kind of hit-or-miss burglar that had supposedly made his way into Bolt's office. Anyway, what were the odds that Bolt would leave anything incriminating in the computer? Everyone had learned long ago that nothing was ever really deleted.

Donnie removed his useless zip disk, then turned his attention to Bolt's desk.

He was immediately disappointed. Bolt hadn't even bothered to lock the drawers. Which meant their contents would be innocent.

Or maybe that was what a burglar was meant to believe.

Donnie hoped.

But the drawers indeed yielded nothing useful. They might as well have been the desk drawers of a legitimate casino manager. Just like the files.

Donnie looked inside the desk's kneehole for a wastebasket and wasn't surprised to see that the basket had a paper shredder on it. He dragged the round metal basket out anyway, removed the shredded paper, and stuffed it in several envelopes, which he folded and jammed into his jacket pockets. Then he got some plain paper from the computer's printer tray and shredded it to replace what he'd removed from the wastebasket.

"Any progress?" Sue asked. She'd finished with the window alarm and was seated with her back against the wall, replacing delicate metal tools of some sort in a dark velvet pouch.

"Probably not," Donnie said.

"We can leave whenever you're ready," she told him.

Donnie turned to Nordo, who was examining the

woodwork to see if there was a break in it that suggested a hidden door. "Find the safe?"

"Does it look like I found it, man?" Nordo seemed disgusted. "Damned waste of time!"

"Not really. The important thing is that Bolt thinks someone searched for it. Remember, we're just innocent burglars—relatively speaking."

"Then I wouldn't mind walking outta here with some money," Nordo said. "Like, relatively speaking."

"Nordo, Nordo . . ."

A section of paneling suddenly yielded to Nordo's touch and swung inward. It was the concealed door Donnie had seen Drago use to enter the office.

Nordo jumped back a few steps. "Lookie here! Just like in one of those old cult movies!"

Donnie went to the open door and shone the flashlight beam inside. The door led only to a narrow hall that appeared to run along the side of the casino, into the hill.

"Not a safe," Donnie said. "Just a private way to come and go. In case important visitors who don't want to be seen pay Bolt a visit."

"What kinda visitors?" Nordo asked.

"The kind who own Circe," Donnie said, giving Nordo something to tell his uncle even if Vito already knew it. Cantanzano himself had probably used the private entrance long ago, before selling Circe to someone he knew was only a straw party concealing the identity of the real new owners.

"We've been in here awhile," Sue told them. "It'd be wise to leave."

"Why?" Nordo asked. "I thought you were the alarm-bypass babe who could do anything."

"There's always the possibility of hidden silent alarms that indicate when the system's been bypassed."

Previous misgivings crept into Donnie's mind. "Didn't you take that into account?"

"As much as possible," Sue told him. "What I'm telling you is there's never a way to be absolutely sure."

"Christ!" Donnie said. He pulled the door in the paneling closed.

Nordo was grinning, beginning to enjoy the precariousness of their position too much. High on danger. Donnie understood.

It was time to go, all right.

Donnie nodded to Sue, then switched off the desk lamp a second before she raised the blinds.

"I'll throw the window open and go out first," she said. "Follow fast, even if you don't hear an alarm."

"Why all of a sudden do you not sound so sure of yourself?" Nordo asked.

She smiled. "With alarms, especially complicated systems like this one, there are often secondary activators. So the deeper you go into a job and the longer you stay on the scene, the worse are the odds of success."

"Until finally the odds turn against you," Donnie said.

"Hey, cheer me up!" Nordo said.

"You oughta know the truth," Donnie told him.

"Have they?" Nordo asked. "I mean the odds. Have they turned against us?"

"Some time ago," Sue assured him. "Let's get the hell out of here."

She abruptly raised the window and scampered out into the night.

No alarm.

Donnie breathed easier.

He signaled for Nordo to go. Nordo dragged a shoe on the sill again. Second time. The local cops would probably see the markings and regard them as signatures a real pro wouldn't have left. Good. They weren't supposed to be real pros.

With a last look around to make sure Bolt's office was a proper mess, Donnie followed Nordo out the window.

This had worked, he was thinking, as he and Nordo moved quickly away from the building and began jogging across the flat, dark plain toward where they'd left the rental car parked near distant trees. They'd gotten in and out okay and maybe learned something.

"We did the deed, man!" Nordo said beside Donnie, his voice breaking as he ran.

Sue was off to the right and slightly ahead of them, part of the night and invisible.

The ground became more uneven, the grass and undergrowth denser, as they approached the trees. Donnie thought he glimpsed the dull glimmer of metal ahead between the trees, the car roof.

The glimmer disappeared.

Reappeared.

Something had moved across Donnie's line of vision, between him and the car.

Not right.

He halted, grabbed Nordo's shoulder and stopped his forward momentum, then yanked him back.

"Stay low and run to your left," Donnie told him. "Make your way out to the main highway, then go to where Harry Lomer's body was discovered in his car and wait for me to pick you up later."

"What's up?" Nordo asked. "Something wrong?"

"Maybe. Just get on the move."

"But how come, man? Like, what's the game?"

"The object is to live till morning," Donnie said.

"I'm in, then," Nordo said, and was gone.

Donnie headed off in the opposite direction, glad for the moonless night.

He didn't hear the shot until an instant after the bullet plucked at his jacket sleeve, almost like an impatient child tugging to get his attention.

He dropped to the ground and rolled into a shallow depression, where he lay perfectly still.

Trying not to breathe so loud, he assessed his situation. He would be almost invisible in the tall grass, and whoever had shot at him might think he'd been hit, maybe killed.

Donnie slowly reached around to the small of his back for his Walther PPK.

It wasn't there. It must have fallen from where it was tucked in his belt as he'd rolled.

He slowly stretched out an arm and explored the damp, grassy earth around him, groping for the compact blue-steel handgun.

No gun.

Donnie was unarmed.

Something moved in the night and he lay still again.

Heard the faintest of sounds.

His gaze fixed on a form that gradually became distinct from the darkness. The figure of a man, lean, wide-shouldered, wearing a broad-brimmed hat and carrying a rifle or shotgun at the ready. From Donnie's low angle of vision, he looked especially tall and ominous.

Donnie lay motionless, but within a few seconds he knew it wasn't going to help. The man with the gun was moving inexorably toward him with the instincts of a hunter.

There was nothing Donnie could do now but try as silently as possible to find his own gun in the grass. He inched out his left arm, running his hand through the rough grass, low to the ground, feeling with his fingertips, trying not to search where he'd felt before.

And the tip of his little finger touched something hard.

Cool and metallic.

The gun!

Not soon enough.

The tall man was standing almost directly over him, leveling a shotgun at him. Donnie couldn't make out his features in the night.

Through the darkness he could see and sense the man's smile, hear it in his words: "Say hello to the next world, motherfucker."

Donnie grabbed for the PPK, knowing what he was trying wasn't going to work, saying hello, saying good-bye, as he rolled to his left and prayed.

Knowing that even if he somehow avoided the shotgun blast, reached his gun in time, and brought it up and around, he never could shoot worth a damn with his left hand.

38

The man looming above Donnie with the shotgun suddenly grunted and turned to his left. The shotgun, now aimed away from Donnie, roared. The man's head jerked back so violently that his hat flew off, and he fell almost on top of Donnie. In the dim light Donnie could see blood like black oil on his face.

Donnie sat up in time to catch a glimpse of a dark, lithe figure moving swiftly away in the night. There was a slight irregularity to the shadowy form's motion, possibly a limp, but Donnie couldn't be sure.

He scooted back away from the dead body of the man who'd been about to kill him, then gained his feet but remained low in a crouch.

The man might not have been alone. Donnie knew he should take a cue from the slight figure dashing away in the dark.

Gripping the PPK in his right hand, he stayed low and sprinted for the jagged line of trees concealing the parked rental car.

He stayed so low as he ran that his tensed back muscles ached. Any second there might be another shotgun blast, this time aimed his way. Fear was like acid beneath his tongue, a claw in his gut, trying to draw him up in a ball and paralyze him. He couldn't let it. Couldn't give in to it.

He made the line of trees without incident, then had to slow and felt his ankles drag through dense underbrush as he fought his way to the parked car. This was like a nightmare where you tried to escape something terrifying while every action was as constrained as if you were running underwater.

And suddenly there was Nordo, leaning casually with his rump against a front fender of the rental car. He started, surprised, when Donnie broke into the clearing, then grinned in relief. "You okay, man?"

"Somehow," Donnie said, bent over with his hands on his knees as he caught his breath and regained the notion that he was going to live at least a little while longer. "Thought I told you to head for where they found Lomer in his car."

"This car was closer, man. Besides, I didn't have time to get any farther. So who fired the shot? Sounded like a goddamn cannon."

"A guard of some sort was about to shoot me when Sue took him out."

"Sue?"

"Our alarm specialist."

"So the lady saved your life."

"You bet she did."

Leaves rustled. Donnie and Nordo ducked low.

Sue emerged from the darkness and stepped into the clearing.

"You hit?" Donnie asked, straightening up and remembering the lithe figure's limp after the shotgun blast.

"No. I thought you might be."

"He didn't have time to get an accurate shot off before you nailed him. Thanks for what you did."

Sue frowned, puzzled.

Then something Nordo had said struck Donnie. Nordo was right: There had been only a single shot. The shotgun blast.

"You carrying a piece with a silencer?" Donnie asked Sue.

She shook her head no. "A twenty-five-caliber ankle gun. Revolver. Silencer wouldn't work on it."

"You didn't take out the guy who was about to finish me off with a shotgun?"

"Not me," Sue said. "No thanks necessary."

And Donnie understood. The night turned colder. Marishov!

There was no way to be sure, but it was likely that Marishov had found him and was here in Julep. Here in the darkness around Circe! The legendary Russian assassin was like a high-tech missile programmed to home in on its target.

Target Donnie.

"You sure you're, like, okay, man?" Nordo asked.

"Yeah. For now."

Donnie knew why Marishov had killed the man with the shotgun. The Russian had seen him as an interloper. It was *his* job, Marishov's, to assassinate Donnie. To fulfill the terms of his contract. No professional, not one with Marishov's perverse but deep sense of honor and obligation, would have stood by and let someone else kill his prey. It wasn't kindness or compassion that had prompted him to save Donnie's life. It was the pride and arrogance of a man who practiced killing as a specialty, as a calling that had consumed him. It was sportsmanship.

Marishov was simply saving Donnie for another day.

It was possible that Marishov was wounded, had caught some of the shotgun blast. But it wasn't a sure thing. With Marishov, nothing was sure.

"Time to get outta here," Donnie said. He was opening the door of the rental to climb in behind the steering wheel even as he spoke.

Nordo scrambled into the backseat. Donnie waited for Sue to hurry around the front of the car and throw herself in beside him before he twisted the ignition key.

The engine's growl was loud in the night, giving away their position.

Right now, Donnie didn't give a damn.

Within seconds their position was changing at sixty miles per hour.

Couldn't be too fast for Donnie.

39

Nothing about the break-in or the killing was mentioned the next day at Circe. Donnie noticed an unmarked work van pull away from around the side of the building a little after six that evening and drive off. He guessed whatever damage had been done to the alarm system or Bolt's office had been repaired.

Diners and gamblers came and went. Money came and went. Donnie and Nordo parked cars and minded their own business. Just your average night at work, though only hours earlier hearts had raced and one had been stopped forever.

After Donnie had parked a Cadillac and returned to the kiosk, Mitki, who'd been standing just outside the restaurant entrance smoking a cigar, wandered over to him and smiled. He was wearing wrinkled gray slacks and a charcoal black sport coat made out of some kind of nubby material; he and the sport coat needed a shave.

"One nice day, eh, buddy?" he growled, amiable as a gruff uncle. Not at all like Mitki.

"Just about like yesterday," Donnie answered, not buying into the act.

"Cooler, though," Mitki said. "Feels good."

"It's a few degrees hotter, according to the weather report."

"I don't pay any mind to those reports." Mitki puffed on his cigar. Actually blew a pretty good smoke ring.

"That kinda thinking'll get you rained on."

"Naw. Those TV weather clowns are fucked up. One on channel five's got a nice rack of tits, though, don't you think?"

"Never noticed."

"Warm front," Mitki said. "Take a closer look next time."

Donnie said he would.

Mitki smiled even broader, took a final puff on his cigar, and tossed it away into the grass. He nodded, agreeable as all get out, though there was a glint like cut diamond in his eye, and swaggered back into the club. Everything was so, so normal at Circe.

If you considered making small talk with a circling shark normal.

Donnie stood motionless, still smelling the lingering smoke from Mitki's cigar. He thought the inane, chummy conversation with Mitki was the most ominous one he'd had.

"Nothing," Donnie said the next morning to Jules Donavon, after briefing him on the reaction to the break-in and shooting death. "Situation normal at Circe."

They were sitting in the sun on a wooden bench on Decatur. There was a new, gold-painted statue of

Joan of Arc in the middle of the street. St. Joan was on horseback and ready to slay injustice. The statue gleamed in the morning sun like a freshly minted coin.

"They've got one of those gold statues of her in Paris, right downtown," Jules said, nodding toward the statue. "Some great restaurants in Paris."

Donnie wasn't here to talk about Paris and restaurants. "We break into the place, mess up the alarm system and toss the office, then kill a guy, and somehow they cover it all up, act as if nothing happened."

"That's no problem," Jules said, "if they don't want the police to catch whoever broke in. If they'd rather take care of the matter themselves. They're probably still trying to figure out exactly what happened and why. You think they suspect you or Nordo?"

"I don't know about Nordo," Donnie said, "but they suspect me. I could tell by the way Mitki talked to me yesterday. He never said anything the slightest bit out of line, but he managed to let me know I was in his sights."

"Question is, does Bolt suspect?"

"I'm not sure. I kind of doubt it. My impression is, his trusting me runs pretty deep."

"You have that effect on people," Jules said. "The ones who don't know you."

Donnie wasn't sure how to take that. "Speaking of people I don't know, what about Wells's old buddies, Gundi and Meyers? Got any kind of fix on them?"

"Not yet, but if they stick to their AAA travel

plans, we're almost sure to pick them up when they get into New Orleans and find a place to stay."

Almost sure, Donnie thought, knowing that was the best he could hope for.

"We'll know within fifteen minutes if they register at any of the hotels downtown or in the Quarter. They'll probably call and make reservations."

"These kinda guys might stay in a cheap motel outside the city limits," Donnie said.

"Might," Jules admitted.

"Meanwhile my cover gets thinner and thinner."

"If Bolt still trusts you," Jules said, "then let the rest of them suspect you all they want. For that matter, let Bolt suspect, as long as he doesn't suspect strongly enough to act on it." A breeze off the river kicked up, and Jules placed a hand on top of his beret to keep it from sailing off his head like a soft Frisbee. "It didn't take the Bureau techs long to piece together and decipher everything you brought that had been shredded in Bolt's wastebasket."

"Anything interesting?" Donnie wasn't optimistic, though he'd seen what the techs could do with shredded documents.

"Mostly not." The breeze died and Jules cautiously removed his hand from the beret. It stayed put. "But there is one document, a single sheet of paper with handwritten columns on it. There's a copy inside the newspaper."

Donnie casually picked up the morning *Times-Picayune* folded beside Jules on the bench. He opened it and pretended to read the news, actually reading a letter-size sheet of copy paper.

The techs had done a good job, bringing out the ink lettering, fading away the long vertical lines where the original had been shredded before dropping like dull tinsel into the wastebasket beneath Bolt's desk.

In the left column was a list of about twenty companies: Rand River Transport, Ohio Nuclear Power, Intercontinental Restaurants, Portland Lumber and Paper. . . . Donnie scanned down the list. He'd heard of none of the companies, though several sounded vaguely familiar.

The right-hand column contained figures, some of them up to seven numerals, unbroken by commas or decimal points.

"Doesn't mean much to me," Donnie said, without raising his head or averting his gaze from the paper. "But then, I never made a dime in the stock market."

"The notable thing about these companies," Jules said, sitting slouched with his legs straight out, his head thrown back now so the sun was on his face, "is that none of them exist. They're not registered in any state. Not listed on any of the exchanges. Not traded over the counter. None of the Bureau contacts in finance have ever heard of them."

"Hmm . . . So what are all the numbers opposite them?"

"I don't know. It's something worth finding out, doncha think?"

Donnie knew a rhetorical question when he heard one. "I'll look at this copy awhile longer, commit what I can to memory, then leave it in the newspaper. It wouldn't be smart for me to wander around with it, or have it hidden in the apartment."

"The individual company names and figures probably won't help you anyway," Jules said. He was silent for a few minutes, relaxing with his eyes closed to the warm sun.

When Donnie had refolded the newspaper with the list inside and set it back on the bench, Jules pulled back his legs and sat up straight. "You were careful enough to substitute some shredded paper in the wastebasket in Bolt's office," he said. "They won't think anything of value is missing."

"If the list *is* of value," Donnie said.

"It must mean something," Jules told him. "Everything means something."

"Tell me about it. That's what can drive me nuts. And it's starting to in this operation."

"Want a guardian angel from the Bureau?" Jules asked. "In case Marishov makes another move on you?"

"If the fleeing figure I saw *was* Marishov." Donnie himself knew he wanted only to doubt that it was Marishov. That way maybe he wouldn't wake up so often drenched in icy sweat. Other people dreamed of Death as a gaunt figure in a tattered cloak and hood, carrying a scythe. In Donnie's dreams Death was a fair-haired man slim as a teenage girl, deadly as a human-size scorpion, carrying an Uzi. Either apparition was terrifying, but Donnie's was real and often near.

"You think it was really Sue Bristol who shot that guy?"

Donnie thought that was an odd thing for Jules to ask. That the shadowy form he'd glimpsed was actually Sue despite her denials hadn't occurred to him. But it was an interesting thought. "You're the one who's always telling me not to doubt her."

"That's the word I get from on high. And probably it's the straight word."

"I don't think she had a silencer on her piece that night. Nowhere to hide it. She was wearing skintight black clothing. Said she had an ankle gun. A revolver."

"Must have been something to see," Jules said.

"A revolver?"

"Donnie, Donnie . . . You never answered my question about the guardian angel."

Donnie remembered an FBI agent named Bert Clover, guardian angel specialist. Remembered Clover dead in his car in New York when he was supposed to be guarding Donnie. "The last time a guardian angel tried to protect me from Marishov, he was killed."

"Is that a no?"

"It is. Only because I don't think it would help. And if whoever took out the guy with the shotgun was Marishov, there's a good chance he's wounded and will lie low for a while."

"Hell of a chance for you to take," Jules said.

"What the job entails. Weighing the odds, saying piss on them. Going ahead."

"Pithy way to look at it."

"I guess. Anything else you want to know? Or tell me?"

"Yeah. I saved the best for last. You were right.

Frank Allan's widow, Ida, identified Marla Grant's real estate glamour shot. She said Frank cropped it, scrawled 'Love forever' on it, and carried it in his wallet as part of his cover. She thinks he probably picked it up at a hotel in New Orleans where there was a real estate convention."

"Christ!" Donnie said. "Poor woman . . ."

"Ida Allan?"

"Marla Grant. They must have thought she was Allan's wife or girlfriend, tortured her for hours. She wouldn't have had any idea why she was chosen, who Frank Allan was, why her photo was in his wallet. Whatever she told them, they wouldn't have believed her, because it couldn't have been anywhere near the truth. They would have just started in on her again. Over and over."

"Hell of a situation," Jules said. "For everyone involved. Once she saw the photo, Ida Allan figured it all out right away, past, present, and future."

Donnie understood. "Agent's wife."

"We've leaked the story to the media. It'll be on the news tomorrow, how Marla Grant was killed by mistake, how Allan's widow stayed here in Julep after her husband's death."

"When will she be here?" Donnie asked.

"She's on her way now. The trap'll be set soon."

"Guard her well," Donnie said, thinking of Elana, what he must have put her through before their marriage finally disintegrated under the strain.

"Well as we can," Jules said, being honest with Donnie.

There was a limit to how well you could guard

bait. They both knew that was what Ida Allan had agreed to become, bait. The next Marla Grant. And there was no doubt in either man's mind that Ida Allan realized it.

Someone had wanted to know what her husband knew, and had tortured and killed him. They hadn't gotten what they wanted. Maybe Ida would.

Ida wanted revenge.

40

Before she arrived, Jules showed Donnie where Ida would be staying. It would be a good idea for Donnie to know her location and the layout of the house, which was a small bungalow on a quiet street in east Julep. The TV news reports and newspaper articles were going to give the impression that she and her husband had lived in Julep since Frank Allan had begun his undercover work at Circe, that she'd stayed on after his death and hadn't yet made up her mind what to do. "It's always wise to wait a year after death or divorce before making any major decisions," she'd be quoted as saying.

Donnie sized up the place when they parked in front of it: faded green clapboard siding, black shutters that had been painted recently, tan tile roof. The yard was large, with a long front lawn that was brown in spots and obviously needed watering. There was shrubbery up close to the house, and a few trees and bushes farther out in the yard. A long, stepping-stone walk that curved around a rotting tree stump led from the sidewalk to the house.

They got out of the car and went inside. The house

contained old furniture that was in good shape, a hodgepodge of styles. The air in the place was hot and stifling, the only sound that of a wasp buzzing frantically somewhere. As he and Jules walked around, Donnie caught sight of the frustrated, persistent insect probing futilely at the clear glass pane of a front window, trapped by an invisibility it didn't understand. Who did the wasp remind him of?

Exploring the house didn't take long. Donnie was surprised to find there was only one bedroom. The kitchen was large; every other room in the house was small. There didn't seem to be any central air—only window units.

Here in these cramped, hot quarters, Ida Allan would be tested, would play a game whose loss would mean her life. Donnie thought they were asking a lot of her.

When they'd locked the front door behind them and were back in the car, Jules drove around the block and parked down the street, where they still had a view of the house.

"What now?" Donnie asked.

Jules glanced at his watch, then out the windshield. "That."

They sat in the car and watched Ida Allan arrive. She was a slender woman wearing jeans and a sleeveless tan top. She walked gracefully and wearily and had a head of long, flaming-red hair. Flanked by two agents in suits, she trudged along the stepping-stone path to the house, pushing a rolling carry-on suitcase in front of her. The suitcase wouldn't make it over the stones without a lot of trouble, so one of the agents took it from her and carried it by the handle.

"She's got some guts," Donnie said.

"Hell of a woman," Jules agreed. "Agents' wives, they all oughta get medals."

One divorced agent to another, Donnie thought, knowing Jules was right. Sad knowledge. "You gonna plant this address in the media?"

"No, that might be too obvious. All we have to do is let it drop she's in Julep, and the Russians will locate her soon enough."

Donnie didn't have to ask if Ida would be well guarded. He knew the house would be watched around the clock, and by the best in the business.

Jules put the car in gear and pulled away from the curb. "Keep your eyes and ears open at Circe, Donnie. The more lead time we have before they try for her, the better things will go."

Especially for Ida Allan, Donnie thought.

He went back to his apartment, and there was Mrs. LaValierre getting her mail from the bank of brass boxes in the foyer.

"Ah hope you are enjoying your stay in Julep, Mr. Wells," she said with a sweet smile to go with the Southern glide in her voice.

"I'm settling in," he said.

"It certainly must be an improvement over your former quarters, if you don't mind my saying."

"I don't mind." He made a show of checking his own mailbox, expecting it to be empty and finding it so.

"My dear son whom I mentioned," Mrs. LaValierre said, "who was in your position, so to speak, when he returned home after his stay away, he kept receiving offers from credit-card companies. Why, he could have obtained more credit than any amount he ever wrongly appropriated."

"I've been getting those kinds of offers, too," Donnie said. He smiled. "They're tempting."

"Ah know you are surely joking."

"Mrs. LaValierre, how do you feel about Elvis?"

She frowned. "The live one? The Olympic ice skater?"

"Yes," Donnie said.

"Rather short, or so he appears on the television," said Mrs. LaValierre, gathering her mail and wrapping a rubber band around it.

Donnie went upstairs to his apartment and drank a cold Heineken, then tried to get some sleep before leaving for work. He made sure the apartment door was locked and braced with a chair. The blinds were closed.

There was no way to get in through the windows without making a great deal of noise. Donnie crumpled some newspaper and put it beneath the windows and around the bed anyway. He was a light sleeper and knew anyone moving the papers around or trying to walk through them would awaken him.

Stretched out on the bed fully dressed except for his shoes, his fingers laced behind his head, Donnie considered his dwindling time. His cover was beginning to slip. Ida Allan was in town and pressure was building. Rat was intent on revenge. Don Wells's old pals Gundi and Meyers might be in New Orleans, possibly even Julep. Vito Cantanzano had made it clear that Nordo's survival was closely linked to Donnie's. And Marishov might have been only slightly wounded, if at all, and could be planning another attempt on Donnie's life.

The one thing Donnie didn't worry about was Marishov telling Bolt the real identity of Donnie Wells. Marishov operated alone, knowing the safety of isolation. And its loneliness. He and Donnie understood each other and observed the rules of their game. It struck Donnie that, outside the Bureau, Marishov might be the person he trusted most.

That was what his life had come to.

And possibly his death.

He turned his mind to the list of nonexistent companies and their corresponding numbers that Jules had shown him. Donnie was sure he'd struck ore during the Circe break-in and delivered the goods. It was now primarily up to the Bureau techs and corporate specialists to discover the uses of these fictitious companies. But would they be able to do so? Shell corporations created for the purpose of money laundering wouldn't be anything new. Only these weren't even shell corporations. These companies simply didn't exist.

But had they ever existed?

Something to ask Jules, Donnie thought.

Even Ewing Bolt might not have all the information about the fictitious companies. But Donnie knew who would: Drago, the mysterious thief-in-law who ran Bolt while Bolt ran Circe.

Donnie wished he could simply corner the Russian, grab him, and shake the answers out of him, learn what he needed to know before the entire operation collapsed around him.

Closed his eyes wishing it.

Wished it as he fell asleep to dream of death in the midst of life, in the midst of locked doors and windows and crumpled newspaper.

41

Donnie had decided the safest place to hide a wire when it wasn't being worn was in the motor compartment of a refrigerator. A microrecorder could be concealed behind or beneath the coils, and the microphone and wires could be integrated with the wiring of the motor and compressor. After the addition of a little grease and dust, to the untrained eye the equipment appeared to be part of the unit even if someone did go to the trouble of moving the refrigerator and removing the back panel.

He retrieved the recorder and button microphone now and wiped them off with a paper towel, then moved the small apartment refrigerator back against the wall by the sink.

It was plenty risky, wearing a wire at this stage of the investigation, but it could also be particularly effective in amassing hard evidence and building a case. If they didn't know already, the Russians at Circe would soon learn they'd tortured and killed the wrong woman. The one who would have participated in any pillow talk with Frank Allan, his wife, was alive and still dangerous to them, and still within reach. They would go for her. And before they did, they might talk about it. Donnie wanted that talk to be taped.

Mitki had phoned that morning and instructed Donnie to wear work clothes and bring gloves. This could mean anything from Donnie doing odd jobs before parking cars, to Donnie helping to bury a body.

He'd slept late and hadn't eaten, and planned to grab a late lunch before driving out to work at Circe. Using broad, flesh-colored adhesive tape, he affixed the tiny recorder high on the inside of his right thigh, then ran the wire up beneath his clothes. The button mike replaced the second button on his shirt, matching the other off-white buttons closely enough to be unnoticeable. Donnie knew the tiny mike was so sensitive it would have caught the sound of his swallowing if he'd worn it as the top button. If he was required to change to his valet uniform later this afternoon, there was enough privacy in the employees' locker room at Circe that he could leave the wire on. He could go into one of the two stalls if necessary, and simply run the tiny mike up to the inside of a shirt pocket, after cutting or ripping the material from behind, and it would work adequately, if only at closer range.

He stopped at Chicken Vittles for lunch, but decided not to eat in the car. This wasn't the day to spill something on his clothes and have to change before going in to work. This wasn't the day to draw any more attention to himself than necessary. This wasn't the day to die.

There were half a dozen small Formica tables in Chicken Vittles, and four yellow plastic booths along a wall. Donnie stood at the counter and ordered the three-piece Chick of Arabee special, crispy. Before carrying his tray of food to one of the tables, he stopped at the condiment corner, got a soda straw, napkin, ketchup for his fries, and, sealed in a plastic pouch with the Chicken Vittles ax-and-fleeing-hen logo on it, a white plastic knife, fork, and spoon.

He settled uncomfortably into a plastic chair at the table and went through the process of readying for his meal. Lots of cellophane to be torn, paper to unwrap, lids to be removed, salt to be sprinkled, a roll to be buttered. It was kind of a task, eating at Chicken Vittles. Maybe they were trying to discourage customers from dining inside instead of being served in their cars.

Donnie had eaten the crispy fried and breaded breast and was about to take a bite of mashed potatoes with his plastic spoon, when he was surprised to see the door open and Mitki, Rat, and Nordo enter. Nordo had on jeans and a gray cotton shirt. Mitki and Rat were wearing suits and ties with their jogging shoes, like rich bankers with foot problems.

Mitki paused just inside the door and glanced around arrogantly, as if he owned Chicken Vittles and everybody in it. No one met his gaze. Cock of the walk, Donnie thought.

Mitki and Nordo came over and sat at the table with Donnie. Rat went to the counter and got in line behind a haggard obese woman trying to control three preschool kids.

Nordo looked scared and didn't say anything to Donnie. Mitki looked amused and stared hard enough into Donnie's eyes that Donnie thought he might need sunglasses to keep his corneas from being burned.

"You guys eat here often?" he asked, playing it light, easing his hand down as if to scratch his crotch but actually activating the microrecorder.

"We eat where we fuckin' please," Mitki said.

Donnie smiled. "Like the five-hundred-pound gorilla."

"Add us up," Mitki said, and motioned with his thumb toward Rat without changing expression, "we *are* the five-hundred-pound gorilla."

"What's going on?" Donnie asked Nordo.

Nordo gnawed his lower lip and remained silent. Not like him.

"We're gonna have a light lunch," Mitki answered. "Then we're gonna do a job for Mr. Bolt, a kinda test to make sure you and flip-head here can be trusted."

"Some woman," Nordo said. "We're gonna hurt some woman. I heard them talking about it."

"It don't matter what he heard," Mitki told Donnie, " 'cause he's gonna help put the hurt on the cunt. And today we find out for sure whether you two got the stomach, whether you're in or out."

"What's 'out' mean?" Nordo asked. "Like, fired?"

"Not exactly," Mitki said. "Means we terminate you in such a way that you can't collect unemployment benefits." He grinned. "Cold, but it's good business."

"What woman are we supposed to hurt?" Donnie asked.

"You'll learn soon enough," Mitki said.

"Something about the FBI," Nordo said.

"Shut the fuck up," Mitki told him softly.

Nordo shot a look at Donnie and sat back silently. Whatever exactly Nordo had overheard, it had shaken him. He was into something deeper than he'd anticipated.

Donnie said, "My guess would be the woman's the wife of that FBI agent whose body was found in the swamp."

Mitki suddenly looked interested, leaning forward over the table. "Why would you guess that?"

Donnie shrugged. "Only widow of a murdered FBI agent in town. And the story's been all over the paper and TV news."

"I didn't think the papers or TV mentioned the guy was murdered," Mitki said. "I read the body was too badly decomposed after all this time to determine exact cause of death."

Great, Donnie thought, knowing he'd made a mistake. He should have read and watched more of the news on the "recently" discovered body before talking about it. "I assumed it was murder," he said. Rushing on: "What I'm wondering is why we want to hurt his widow, and why it's gonna take four of us."

Mitki smiled. "Keep wondering, asshole."

But Donnie was sure of both answers: The mob at Circe wanted to learn what Ida Allan knew and whom she might have told. Then they would be finished with her. She would become a disposable liability. And two of her interrogators were going to be killed along with her.

Probably one would be killed before she was, in front of her, to unnerve her and break down any resistance she might still have. It was far too late for any test of loyalty to convince Bolt of Donnie's and Nordo's reliability. The sight of one of them getting his throat slit could by itself be enough incentive for Ida to give in to her panic and irrational, desperate hope that cooperation might just save her.

Donnie knew that everybody hoped right to the final second. Everybody thought there was some slight chance of survival, even if they were in the hands of goons like Mitki and Rat. Everybody clutched at every sliver of opportunity to live, sometimes even during the act of dying.

And everybody talked.

"What was her name?" Donnie asked, trying to keep Mitki talking. "I remember it from TV. Ida something . . ."

"Allan," Mitki said. "Ida Allan."

"The late Ida Allan," Donnie said.

"Not yet, but soon. Think a tough guy like you is up to the task?"

"Killing a woman? Sure." Donnie made it sound easy as a card trick he'd done before.

Nordo looked horrified, almost sick, and scared enough to throw up. "That ain't my idea of sport, man."

"Nordo don't think real men kill women," Mitki said.

"Real men, real women," Donnie said, "they kill whoever they have to. What you gotta learn, Nordo, is you do whatever you need to do in this life."

"Listen to your hero," Mitki said. "Better yet, watch how he behaves when we got Ida all in a nice, neat bundle. Either way he goes, it's gonna be interesting."

On one hand, Donnie was glad to hear Mitki talking more freely, actually dropping Ida's name so the button mike could pick it up. On the other hand, he knew it meant that in Mitki's mind it no longer made any difference what Donnie or Nordo knew, as long as neither of them left his company until the end of their lives.

Rat had finally been waited on and walked over to the table with a tray with three medium soft drinks on it. He shoved Donnie's three-piece Chick of Arabee special aside and set the tray with the drinks in the middle of the table. "Fuckin' kids!" he said, jamming a straw through the slit in the plastic lid on his drink. "One of 'em stomped right on my foot." He sucked on the straw and glared at the obese woman at a table with her wild kids. The woman and one of the kids, a dark-eyed little blond girl about six, glared back at him. Donnie would bet she was the stomper.

"We got no time to drink those," Mitki said, glancing at his watch.

Rat looked devastated. "I got a cherry Coke. You know how hard it is to find a place that makes fuckin' cherry Cokes?"

"You can come back sometime," Mitki told him, "drink one right after the other."

"I'll take it with me, dammit!"

"And spill it all over everything while we drive? Take a sip, and then leave it here, Rat."

"Most places don't even know what the fuck you're talkin' about, you order a cherry Coke."

"I'm going to the can while you guys argue about it," Donnie said, standing up and at the same time palming the tiny plastic pouch that the plastic flatware had been sealed in. Before anyone could shift mental gears and say anything, he was walking toward the rest rooms at the back of Chicken Vittles.

He had much of what he needed on tape, but he knew that even if the Russians didn't check to see if he was wired before killing him, they might find the wire on his corpse. Or when they were toying with him before killing him. And even if they didn't discover the tape, it would be of no help if his body was never found.

There was one other man in the rest room, a guy in jeans and a red polo shirt, standing at one of the urinals. Donnie went immediately into one of the metal stalls and shut and locked the door. He was glad to see the lock was the sturdy sliding-bolt type.

He could hear the urinal flush outside the stall as he lowered his pants and underwear and sat down.

The rest room's swinging door opened and closed. The guy leaving without washing his hands?

But the hand blower began to whir. So someone else must have entered the rest room.

Using the sound of the blower to cover any noise,

Donnie ripped the tape and a lot of hair from the inside of his thigh, then from his chest, where it fastened the wire to his body. He shoved the microrecorder, wire, and mike into the clear plastic flatware pouch, then folded it over and sealed it with the tape to make it as waterproof as possible. Then he pulled a pen from his shirt pocket and began writing on the tape, hoping the ink was waterproof or wouldn't run too much and be illegible.

The dryer stopped and the rest room door swished open and closed again. The guy with clean hands leaving.

"Speed it up in there," Mitki's voice said, echoing off the tiled walls and floor. Donnie could see the designer toes of his jogging shoes in the space beneath the metal stall door. They looked big as sports cars.

"Be just a minute," Donnie said. "Damned greasy chicken!" He made a lot of noise with the toilet paper roll, then stood up and pulled up his pants, fastened his belt.

As soon as he worked the chrome handle to flush the toilet, he removed the lid to the white porcelain tank, broke the float from its lever, and dropped the sealed plastic packet inside. After jamming wadded toilet paper down the overflow drain, he replaced the tank lid as silently as possible, then opened the stall door and stepped outside.

Mitki stared at him as Donnie pushed the soap dispenser button, then quickly ran water over his hands. He held them for a few seconds under the dryer, rubbing them together as instructed, before pushing the door open to leave the rest room.

"Your hands are still wet," Mitki said behind him.

Donnie didn't turn around. "I thought you were the one in the big fuckin' rush."

Rat and Nordo were already outside waiting. When Donnie and Mitki joined them, Mitki said, "You ride with Donnie, Rat. I'll follow in the van with Nordo."

Rat got in the passenger side of the Honda while Donnie got behind the steering wheel.

"Where to?" Donnie asked, starting the engine.

"Your place. When we get there, park down the street a little ways."

"*My* place?"

"Drive," Rat said.

Donnie knew what this meant. After leaving the Honda parked near his apartment, he and Rat were going with Mitki and Nordo in the van. His parked car would make it appear that he never went in to work today. There would be nothing to connect his death or disappearance with Circe.

Nothing might be exactly what he had to look forward to.

He thought about the toilet overflowing in Chicken Vittles's men's room. About how long it might take before someone noticed and told an employee. He wondered how long before the employee lifted the porcelain toilet tank lid to see what was wrong. How long it would be before someone noticed the plastic packet in the tank. How long before they would realize what it was, read the message, listen to the tape.

If ever.

42

There was little conversation in the van on the way to Circe. Mitki drove, with Nordo seated alongside him up front. Donnie and Rat were in the seats behind them. Donnie thought the van still smelled faintly of half-thawed chicken. That and his recently consumed meal at Chicken Vittles made him slightly nauseated. Or maybe it was the fear.

When they reached Circe, a man Donnie had never seen before was wearing an ill-fitting valet uniform and leaning casually against the shady side of the kiosk, ready to park early customers' cars. There were only a few cars in the lot, a couple of Cadillacs and a Mercedes convertible.

Mitki drove the van around the side of the building and parked near where the brick wall angled into the hill. He got out and went around the side of the van, stood watching while Nordo opened the door and climbed down. Rat got out on the left and stayed put with his arms crossed, unmoving and looking like an intransigent fireplug, until Donnie had gotten out and was standing near Mitki and Nordo. Donnie noticed the slight change of attitude in Mitki and Rat.

Now they were treating Donnie and Nordo more like captives than confederates.

A dark brown steel door was set against the bricks. There was no doorknob on it, only a round brass cusp for a dead-bolt keyhole. Mitki inserted and twisted a key, then pulled, and the door inched stiffly outward enough for him to grasp its edge with his left hand and pull it open all the way. This wasn't a door that saw a lot of coming and going.

Cool air drifted out at them as Mitki stood aside and motioned for Donnie and Nordo to enter. Donnie let Nordo go ahead, then followed, feeling Rat close on his heels.

Out of the brilliant sun, into dimness. They were in the auditorium where the fight between Nordo and Rat had taken place.

Mitki threw a wall switch. The ring had been disassembled, but the rectangular framework of lights that had bathed it in a pool of brightness was still suspended on its chains from the girders above. Now the glaring lights illuminated a simple wooden chair. It was in the center of an eight- or nine-foot-square sheet of thick plastic unfolded to lie flat on the floor. On the plastic alongside the chair were several rolls of gray duct tape, a large pair of scissors, pruning shears, and two plastic gallon containers of bottled water.

Rat began to giggle, a shrill, nasty sound. He suddenly let out a loud, rasping scream, then grinned and danced around like a rotund psychopath, wiggling his nose at Donnie. "Fuckin' place is absolutely soundproof," he said happily.

"Good thing," Donnie told him. "You're acting like a total asshole."

When Rat finally settled down, Mitki moved close to Donnie. "We gotta do a little security check here," he said. "You got any objections?"

"What kinda check?"

"We need to know if you're wearing a wire."

"Whaddya mean, wire?"

"You heard of wires," Mitki said. "They record things."

"Like CD-ROMs?"

"More like tape recorders, I'd say. Don't you wanna take off your shirt and reassure us? You nervous about your nipples or something?"

"Whether you cooperate or not," Rat said, sneering, "we're gonna have us a peek."

"So unbutton your shirt," Mitki told Donnie.

Donnie hesitated, letting them wonder. Then he unfastened the buttons on his shirt, revealing only bare flesh.

Mitki nodded, then patted Donnie down to make sure nothing was concealed beneath his pants legs. He would have found the microrecorder if it had still been taped to the inside of Donnie's thigh. He didn't stoop low enough to find the ankle gun, but he did remove the PPK tucked into Donnie's belt at the small of his back. "So you're carrying," he said.

"Aren't you?" Donnie asked.

"Am now." Mitki slipped the gun into his suit-coat pocket. "Now you," he said to Nordo.

"Why would I wanna tape anything?" Nordo asked.

"It's not so much you taping that we wouldn't

like," Mitki said. "It's more the idea you might be wearing something that'll transmit to another location, let somebody else know what's going on here."

"Like who?"

"Oh, maybe the police."

"You don't trust me?"

"Your word is our bond, kid," Mitki said. He and Rat grinned at each other. And at that moment Donnie thought he knew the reason for Lily's death, and for Frank Allan's and Marla Grant's.

"Are you nuts, man? You, like, think I'm a spy?"

"I think you're too dumb to be a spy. This is just routine."

Nordo unbuttoned his shirt and submitted to Mitki's pat-down. No wire. Donnie was relieved. It wasn't impossible that Cantanzano had instructed his nephew to wear one.

Mitki nodded to Rat while Donnie and Nordo were rebuttoning their shirts. Rat walked over to a phone mounted on a supporting post and made a call, talking for only a few seconds. Then he sauntered back over and stood with Mitki, silently regarding Donnie and Nordo.

It made Nordo nervous enough to stalk a few feet this way and that, then prop his fists on his hips and shake his head. His eyes were narrowed and he looked a little like he had when he'd begun fighting Rat for real in the ring. He was handling the pressure by getting mad. Sometimes useful, but right now a dangerous way to cope. "I don't wanna hurt no woman I don't even know, man! I mean that."

"Oh," Rat said, "he means it."

"You rather be hurt yourself?" Mitki asked.

"I'd rather he was," Rat said.

"Who'd hurt me, you little rodent?"

Uh-oh, Donnie thought; Nordo had his balls back, all right.

Rat's face grew red but he didn't move. "I'd hurt the holy fuck outta you. And for a long time."

"Why don't you eat a rat-poison Popsicle, man?"

"Both of you shut the fuck up," Mitki said almost absently. He was obviously waiting for something, expecting it at any moment.

A door in the far wall opened and Len came in. Then a large man Donnie didn't know, wearing a black sweatsuit. Then Drago and Ewing Bolt.

Drago was wearing a silky suit that despite its dark color reflected so much light when he moved that, outside the pool of illumination around the chair, it was still the brightest thing in the dim auditorium. He said nothing and didn't have to in order to establish himself as the dominant figure in the group. Alpha thug. Bolt calmly looked at the chair and the tools of the torture trade, the plastic sheet protecting the floor from stains.

"Everything prepared?" he asked.

Mitki said, "Yes, sir."

Bolt said nothing to Donnie or Nordo. Didn't even look at them. Bad sign.

Drago turned and nodded to someone on the other side of the still-open door.

A man even larger than the first entered the room.

He was wearing a black tracksuit exactly like the first man's. In his right hand was a huge Glock .357 handgun, the kind that can blow a man's arm off. His left hand gripped the upper arm of a woman with her wrists tied behind her back, her face half-concealed by errant locks of long, flaming red hair. Her visible eye was swollen. She'd been struck there or had been crying.

The second man moved like a strutting black cat as he led the woman directly toward the center of the room. His grip was tight enough on her arm that she walked along with him docilely, her head bowed. What had she already endured before arriving here?

Bolt was smiling as he observed the proceedings. "Our girl comes late to the party," he said to no one in particular, "but she's here."

"Had to kill her other date, though," the large man holding her said.

Donnie felt rage and fear take hold in him. The FBI agent guarding Ida Allan must be dead. Despite all the precautions, the bait had been stolen from the trap.

"Are you sure the room is sealed tight for sound?" Drago asked, looking around.

"No sound can escape, Mr. Drago," Bolt assured him. Then he looked at Mitki and Rat. "I don't care how long it takes—get everything from her."

"Few minutes from now," Rat said, "we won't be able to shut her up."

Bolt and Drago exchanged glances. "Call my office," Bolt said to Mitki, "and let me know when you're finished. The chopper's waiting."

The woman shivered at the word *chopper*, probably misunderstanding it. But maybe not.

Donnie figured they were planning on a short helicopter flight over water and an anonymous burial at sea this time, to play it safe. With weights in the thick plastic sheet to sink and hold its grisly load deep and forever far from land. And he knew Ida wouldn't be alone in her weighted plastic shroud. It would be a triple burial, and without much of a service as a send-off.

As Drago and Bolt walked away toward the door, Rat and Mitki removed their sport coats and draped them over the backs of some nearby chairs, then rolled up the sleeves of their pristine white dress shirts.

"We'll stay and watch," the large man holding Ida's right arm said, and shoved her into the chair. The other sweatsuited man clamped his big hand around her left arm.

Donnie glanced at Nordo, hoping he understood the game. Nordo still looked angry and scared. Still more angry, though, Donnie thought.

"Stay still, bitch!" one of the men holding Ida said. They'd untied her wrists and were trying to get her arms fastened to the chair with duct tape. "Easier on you if you fuckin' cooperate!" She made a gasping, sobbing sound and continued struggling, squirming desperately.

"Might as well be a good girl and get it over with," Rat said. "Ain't no reason this has to hurt more'n a few minutes." His sadistic, rodent grin belied his words. He was the rat that carried the plague, worse than death itself.

The woman in the chair began to squirm violently, and the large man grabbed her by the hair to yank her head back.

The hair came off in his hand.

He stood astonished, staring at the blond woman in the chair.

Sue Bristol used the opportunity of his surprise to elbow him in the crotch. In almost the same motion, she hacked at the throat of the other man, who backed away choking.

Donnie wasn't wasting time. He bent low and yanked the .25 free from where it was taped to his ankle, got off a shot at the big man before he could regain his breath and composure and lift the Glock more than six inches from where he'd dropped it on the floor.

Timing was everything in life. The man was still looking to the side and down at the Glock when the soft-point bullet struck him in the temple and spread and tumbled inside his skull, dropping him lifeless to the floor.

Sue stooped and grabbed his belt, trying to roll him to the side so she could get to the Glock he'd fallen on.

Something plowed hard into Donnie, taking him off his feet.

Mitki.

The big Russian had dropped to his hands and knees after the collision. Now he was scrambling to his feet, yanking a knife from his back pocket. Donnie instinctively raised the .25 to try to stop him or slow him down.

And realized the gun was no longer in his hand. He'd dropped it without realizing it when Mitki threw a lineman's block into him.

In the corner of his vision Donnie saw that Sue was still wrestling the inert, bulky form of the dead man aside so she could get to the Glock. Donnie's own gun had slid across the floor and was ten feet away—behind Mitki.

"I'll take care of this other fucker," Rat said behind Donnie.

"Don't shoot the woman," Mitki said, thinking ahead.

Gunshots roared, and Rat staggered past Donnie, toward Mitki. His arms were stretched out before him as if seeking someone to hold on to, but his eyes were already glazing over and blood gushed from his mouth and chest.

"There's your rat poison, man."

Nordo was standing with Donnie's PPK that Mitki had confiscated and slipped into his suit-coat pocket.

Even as Rat fell, Mitki was hurling himself at Donnie with the knife. Whatever else was going to happen, the determined Russian was making sure Donnie died.

Donnie was still on the floor, sitting with one leg straight out in front of him, the other buckled beneath him. He knew there was no way he could avoid the knife attack or successfully defend himself.

Death, always close, was finally going to have its way with him.

More gunfire, deafening. Mitki stopped in midair, stood stupefied, then danced in a tight circle in rhythm to the shots.

Donnie knew more power than that of the PPK had stopped Mitki. Sue had finally gotten to the brutally powerful Glock. She and Nordo had Mitki in a cross fire and held him there until he dropped.

Donnie struggled awkwardly to his feet and took in where they were.

The big Russian he'd shot lay dead. Mitki and Rat were dead. Len stood petrified with shock and fear against a wall. The Russian whose throat Sue had hacked was lying on his back, gasping and clutching his throat.

"His larynx is crushed," Sue said. "He'll be dead soon or in shock."

The suddenly shifted balance of power finally fell on Len. His eyes widened; then he came unglued from the wall and made a run for the door to the club's interior.

He was quick, actually reaching for the knob, when Nordo shot him in the back.

Breeding finally coming out, Donnie thought, just as Uncle Vito predicted.

Len turned around and stared in disbelief at Nordo.

Nordo shot him again.

This time the bullet nicked Len's shoulder and seemed only to infuriate him. He spun around and got a grip on the doorknob. He took another shot in the back but managed to stagger out. The door swung closed behind him.

"Shit'll hit the fan now," Nordo said.

Donnie knew he had to act fast. He couldn't let Drago or Bolt slip away.

He dashed to the door Len had used and opened it, starting out into the hall. Plaster and wood chips flew, and something stung the corner of Donnie's left eye. He backed away as automatic-rifle fire raked the walls and punched holes in the door as it swung shut.

He retreated, almost tripping over the body of the big Russian he'd shot. "Get to cover!" Stooping quickly to recover his .25, he followed his own advice.

Sue had shoved Nordo almost off his feet, and the two of them were huddled behind some stacked metal folding chairs. It wasn't the best cover in the almost bare auditorium, but it was something.

Donnie had just joined them when the lights in the sealed room winked out, leaving them in darkness.

Then there was a brief shaft of light as the door flew open and several men barreled inside, hitting the floor and rolling, immediately getting off shots meant for cover and diversion rather than to hit anyone.

The yellow shaft of light narrowed to a slender finger on the floor that revealed nothing, then disappeared.

There was quiet.

"This might be fun," Sue whispered. She didn't sound at all as if she meant it.

"Who the fuck *are* you?" Nordo asked her.

"Not who they thought," Sue said.

"You don't have to know the players," Donnie told him, "to know whose side you're on."

"That's for sure, man."

There were slight sounds in the dark—what might have been the door opening and closing again. Donnie knew the Russians had darkened the hall and were moving more reinforcements into the room. More than enough firepower.

"Don Wells," said Bolt's voice over the speaker system. "Or whoever you are. This thing is over." He sounded in control, even bored. Well, he had a right. He was in the gambling business and could figure odds. "In a few seconds the lights will come back on, and you'll see that you're surrounded and without hope. You'll have the choice between a bloodbath that will surely result in your deaths. Or we can talk. Everything can be negotiated. Talking's always better than dying."

"He'll kill us as soon as we're disarmed," Sue said.

"Sure," Donnie told her. "But better later than sooner."

The lights came on abruptly, glaring, causing Donnie to squint. Through narrowed eyes he could see at least ten men with automatic weapons, standing spread out around the room.

Every gun seemed to be trained on him.

Crouched exposed and clutching his small-caliber ankle gun, Donnie knew how right Bolt was.

They were without hope.

With nothing to risk that wasn't lost already.

His breath was shallow and loud. His stomach was

ice. His chest was so tight he could barely breathe. When he swallowed, it made a sound like muffled breaking glass.

The gamble at Circe was lost.

His finger tensed on the trigger.

43

The sound of an explosion barely made it into the auditorium.

Donnie knew it had to have been extraordinarily loud to be heard at all where they were standing. And he knew what it probably was.

The men facing him shifted position. A few stole uneasy glances at one another.

One of them, toward the back, kept his AK47 leveled at Donnie as he moved sideways to the door and carefully eased it open a few inches.

Immediately sounds of gunfire and shouting penetrated the auditorium.

The door suddenly burst inward, hurling the man who'd opened it back on his heels. Instinctively the men facing Donnie, Sue, and Nordo turned toward the sound and action.

It was a mistake almost any amount of training couldn't prevent. Two of the men fell before any of the others got off a shot.

Donnie knew for sure then that the explosion had been a flash-bang grenade, used by a SWAT team to paralyze opponents with surprise and noise before mounting an attack. He hunkered lower and opened fire with his pistol, dropping another of the remaining men before him, then heard Sue open up behind him with the Glock.

A second flash-bang grenade exploded inside the auditorium, deafening Donnie for a second with noise so loud and sharp it instantly became pain. Most of the smoke from the grenade drifted toward the high ceiling, but the diversionary device did its job, momentarily freezing everyone, as black-suited SWAT team members with bulky flak jackets swarmed through the open door, firing as they came, staying low and moving to either side.

Donnie hugged the floor, sighted carefully with his handgun, and brought down another of the confused assailants before him who didn't know which way to fire. In the tumult of noise and action, it soon became almost impossible to tell friend from foe. The only differences in the dark-clothed men were the bulk of the flak jackets, and the bright orange *FBI* lettered on the backs of the SWAT team.

In the noise, the blood, and the stench of gunpowder, another difference soon became evident.

Some of the dark-clothed figures began dropping their weapons and raising their hands above their heads.

Donnie sat up and glanced behind him. Nordo was on his hands and knees, looking around alertly. He seemed okay. On his left, Sue stood holding the heavy Glock aimed with both arms extended, eyes dancing side to side. Donnie thought she might be smiling slightly.

He got to his feet and moved away as the firing ceased and the SWAT team members began shouting instructions to their prisoners. It looked like only three or four of Bolt's men had survived the attack.

Donnie stepped over bodies and edged out of the door.

In the hall, a lanky SWAT team member blocked his way.

"I'm Donnie Wells—Brasco," Donnie said. "Special Agent Joe Pistone. Come with me!"

"You ain't proved diddly shit to me, pal." The man started to level his automatic rifle at Donnie. "If you were FBI you'd be flashing ID. Now get down on the floor and—"

Donnie couldn't take time to explain that working UC you didn't carry FBI identification, or that you'd been conditioned to use a name not your own automatically. He clipped him hard on the point of the chin, just so, with the heel of his hand so the man's head jerked backward, momentarily blacking him out. He caught the man as he fell and eased him downward, relieving him of his automatic rifle as he slid to the floor. Then he removed the man's flak jacket and slipped it on, quickly fastening the Velcro straps.

There was a lot of noise coming from the restaurant. Donnie made his way along the corridor that separated it from the casino, then down another, narrower hall to a door that he figured would be the concealed one he'd seen Drago use to enter Ewing Bolt's office.

He didn't bother trying the knob to see if the door

was locked. He kicked it open and charged into the office, feeling the door slap him on the shoulder as it rebounded off the wall.

Bolt was hunched over in his desk chair, the waste-basket with the shredder on top between his legs. He swiveled his head toward Donnie, astounded at being interrupted as the documents he was destroying were pulled from his grasp by the shredder.

Drago had removed his suit coat and was standing on a chair in the center of the office. He got over his surprise in a hurry and his right hand darted toward a gun in a small belt holster. Donnie shot the chair out from under him and he fell hard to the floor. He scooted back against a wall and raised his hands.

Donnie leveled the automatic rifle at Bolt and he sat back. He couldn't help glancing toward the ceiling.

Donnie followed his glance and saw why Drago had been standing on a chair. The light fixture was swiveled to the side. There was the office safe, set in the ceiling, and Drago hadn't yet finished the task of emptying it and handing down incriminating evidence for Bolt to shred.

"I'm saving you both some effort," Donnie said. "The shredder doesn't do anything but create work for the FBI lab."

Two burly, dark-uniformed SWAT team members entered the office. Then came a couple of suits. One of the suits was Jules Donavon.

Within seconds the SWAT guys had Drago and Bolt disarmed and handcuffed. Drago looked detached and bored. Bolt was smiling, already practicing his courtroom charm. Both men acknowledged that their rights had been read to them, then retreated into the silence that would be broken only by their attorneys.

"You hit anywhere?" Jules asked Donnie.

"Not that I know of," Donnie said, suddenly realizing that he might be. With the high of the action and adrenaline pumping, it sometimes took a while to know you'd been shot. He went through a cautious inventory, moving his limbs slightly to make sure he'd come through uninjured.

"Not like you," Jules said, joking now that he knew Donnie was okay. "Usually you at least need stitches."

"Sue and Nordo?"

"Sue took a slug in the right thigh."

"It wasn't enough to knock her down."

"Figures."

"Sure does."

"We'll all laugh about it someday when we're working for her," Jules said.

Donnie could see it.

The SWAT guys were leading Drago and Bolt out of the office. Bolt glanced at Donnie, curious. He obviously wanted to say something, ask Donnie some questions, but he maintained his silence. Donnie noticed that the club manager's sleek gray hair wasn't even mussed.

"C'mon," Jules said to Donnie. "Something I wanna show you."

Donnie followed him out to the parking lot. There were a lot of vehicles parked at angles, some of them with their doors hanging open. Donnie and Jules walked past the police cruisers, unmarkeds, and a SWAT van, to a plain black Ford Taurus.

Jules opened the car's trunk and held up a wad of bloody white towels.

"From the Lazy Bones Motel," he said. "The maid found them after a man registered as Adam Martin left without checking out. Desk clerk described him as young, slender, blond hair. He paid cash, and the address and license plate he wrote on his registration card don't exist."

"Marishov," Donnie said.

Jules felt around in the trunk and held up something else: a sealed plastic bag containing a tiny round object. "Shotgun shell pellet," he said. "Marishov took a hit. A serious one, judging by the amount of blood on the towels and in the motel room. He's probably too hurt to dog you for a while. Maybe he'll even die. We've got area hospitals alerted to tell us if anybody matching his description comes in with a gunshot wound."

"If he was well enough to treat himself and drive away," Donnie said, "he'll probably fade from sight and heal okay. Or find treatment someplace where they won't ask questions."

"Probably," Jules agreed. "But you can breathe easier for a while."

"For a while. Thanks, Jules."

They were returning from the car when Donnie noticed a stone-faced cop leading a handcuffed Nordo to a state patrol cruiser. Nordo had some problems with the law, not the least of which was helping to transport a dead body and fake a homicide, but Donnie figured that with Uncle Vito supplying the attorneys, he would walk.

Then he saw that behind Nordo two more troopers were leading Army and Frankie the Lounger.

"What the hell are they doing here?" Donnie asked Jules, who shrugged.

He repeated the question to the trooper who had Nordo.

"They were found hiding in the restaurant kitchen," the trooper said. "And they were armed."

Donnie looked hard at Nordo. "What's this about, Nordo?"

"Chickens, man."

Donnie pretended not to hear.

"Okay," Nordo said, "diamonds. The diamonds in the chickens."

Donnie understood now. Frankie and Army had assumed Nordo was accompanying Mitki and Rat willingly and had used the after-hours visit when Circe's alarm system would be down to make a try at the smuggled diamonds still on the premises. They'd been awaiting the opportunity, and with Nordo's knowledge and cooperation.

"Your uncle Vito know about this?" Donnie asked.

"Sorta. Well, I dunno. Like, it was more Frankie's idea."

"But you went along with it."

"Sorta."

"Damn it, Nordo!"

Nordo looked a little worried. "You think I can get outta this without jail time, man?"

"Long as you didn't swallow any diamonds."

"That being so, you think maybe I could become something worthwhile in this life?" The trooper cupped his hand over the top of Nordo's head and guided him into the backseat of the cruiser.

"I don't see why not," Donnie said, but he could think of a galaxy of obstacles.

"Like you, you think? Like an FBI agent?"

"You scare me, Nordo."

"Finally," Nordo said, just before the cruiser door slammed shut, locking him in.

44

Jules, having feasted for weeks on New Orleans cuisine, was unable to eat more than a few bites the next afternoon at Chicken Vittles. Donnie, sitting across from him in the booth, had spent the morning giving statements and depositions, and would spend the next few days in Julep or at the New Orleans Bureau field office, helping to brief prosecutors and prepare for official charges and future court action. Following the usual procedure, he would lie low until his direct testimony or more depositions were required. As for now, he was still learning about Circe.

"The shredded documents you gave us provided the key," Jules said, shoving aside his barely touched Chick of Arabee special. Then he confirmed in detail what Donnie had figured out when Mitki and Rat were searching to see if he or Nordo might be wearing a wire. *Your word is our bond, kid.* "Corporate bonds in the names of the nonexistent companies were sold in eastern Europe and some of the developing Russian breakaway states. Circe's casino not only laundered the money made from selling the phony bonds, but gambling profits were used to make interest payments to the bondholders, who continued to think they held legitimate bonds."

"And why wouldn't they think that?" Donnie said. "That's how and why Ponzi scams work."

"If a bondholder did try to sell a bond and was told there was no such company, the bond issuer would feign confusion. If the amount was small, the Russian mob would simply buy back the phony bond as if the company really existed and the bond were legitimate. If the amount was large, the bondholder would be dealt with the Russian way. But the fact is, the rate was so generous that hardly anyone tried to sell their bonds once they started collecting the interest."

"Not a bad investment, when you stop to think about it," Donnie said.

"The phony-bond scam seems to have been Circe's primary purpose, though they were also into more conventional ways to fleece the system. Taking on odd jobs like the smuggled diamond shipment. An occasional drug deal. Evidence from the documents Drago and Bolt were shredding when you interrupted them is still being developed."

So much for the riddle of Circe. So far. "What about Wells's old buddies?"

"Gundi and Meyers?" Jules smiled. "They made the mistake of arriving in New Orleans in a stolen car. They're in holdover cells now in St. Charles Parish. When they found out Wells died in prison, they were shocked, though it'd be an exaggeration to say they were grieving. I think they wanted to link up with him again to do some more bank jobs."

"Hell of a world," Donnie said.

"Hell of," Jules agreed. "And your friend Nordo will probably walk out into it free, now that his uncle's attorneys have finally convinced him to shut up. Clean as he is, and with that kind of legal representation, he'll make probation at the worst."

"He's not a bad kid, but he started making his deals with the devil."

"You seem to have been a good influence on him, Donnie. He admires you. Wants to be just like you. Whaddya think'll happen to him?"

"He'll either make a helluva criminal or a helluva FBI agent."

Jules nodded, fitted his beret on his head, and scooted out of the booth. Standing alongside Donnie, he glanced at his reflection in a mirror and adjusted the beret. Shot himself a jaunty grin.

"You can get rid of that thing now," Donnie told him.

"I dunno, Donnie. I've kinda gotten used to it."

"You can get used to anything, especially if it's on your head, where you can't see it."

A couple of skinny teenage girls entered Chicken Vittles to order carryout. When they glanced at Jules and giggled, he ignored them. "I'm driving back to New Orleans," he said. "What are you going to do now? I mean, after you're done with the prosecutors here?"

"Going back to be with Grace," Donnie said. "I'll

wait for the call to help fill in blanks as the case develops."

He imagined being with Grace Perez in her beach cottage on the Florida coast, in her arms. His shadow lover in his shadow of a real life. She'd lost her husband in a hurricane just before Donnie met her. She was the kind of woman who never really got over grieving. Donnie figured maybe she thought of him as a shadow lover, too. He'd learned it could be that way. Two of the half-dead, living out the remnants of existence together. They afforded each other peace, and something like happiness, during their intermittent times that were over too quickly. Made for each other.

"Tell Grace hello for me," Jules said.

"Sure." But Donnie wouldn't When he was with Grace he tried not to think about his alternate world— the one where he was always somebody other than himself, where Jules was his only lifeline to reality. He was jealous and possessive of that time. One of the things he feared most was losing his haven on the beach, his shelter from the thing he'd created and that rode him.

And there was always Marishov, who might be wounded now, might even be dead. But Donnie couldn't think of him as dead, and wouldn't be able to until he actually saw and touched the fabled Russian hit man's lifeless body. The world beyond Grace's cottage had become unimaginable without containing the threat and the force that Marishov had become. Always Donnie had to travel blue highways, not going directly to a destination, sometimes doubling back, watching his own trail like a cunning tiger doomed to be an eventual trophy.

He ate another crispy leg of a chicken that had fallen victim to the system. Then he deposited what was left of the two fast-food meals in a trash receptacle near the door and walked outside into the brilliant sunlight.

Two days later, he packed his scuffed leather suitcase and left for Florida.

He traveled a roundabout way.